THE CHIMNEY SWEEPER

THE CHIMNEY SWEEPER

a murder novel

John Peyton Cooke

THE MYSTERIOUS PRESS

Published by Warner Books

A Time Warner Company

First published in a slightly different form in
Great Britain in 1994 by Headline Book Publishing.

"Shine On You Crazy Diamond," lyrics by Roger Waters, © 1974 Pink Floyd Music
Publishers Limited. Reprinted by permission.

 Mysterious Press books are published by Warner Books, Inc.,
1271 Avenue of the Americas, New York, NY 10020.

 A Time Warner Company

The Mysterious Press name and logo are registered trademarks of Warner Books, Inc.

Printed in the United States of America

First U.S. printing: May 1995

10 9 8 7 6 5 4 3 2 1

Library of Congress Cataloging-in-Publication Data

Cooke, John Peyton
    The chimney sweeper / John Peyton Cooke.
        p.   cm.
    ISBN 0-89296-523-1 (hardcover)
    I. Title.
PS3558.O5565C48   1995
813'.54—dc20   94-43058
                                                                       CIP

This book is for
Allyn Watson
and for
Keng
"worth waiting for"

In the manner of thrusting the corpse up
the chimney, you will admit that there
was something *excessively outré* . . .

—POE, "The Murders in the Rue Morgue"

THE CHIMNEY SWEEPER

One

1

When I stepped off the bus in Isthmus City late that night, I wasn't carrying so much as a backpack. All I had to my name was an extralarge sweatshirt and a pair of too-tight blue jeans (without underwear or socks), a mud-caked pair of 14-eye Doc Martens, a battered paperback copy of *The Stand,* an empty plastic sixty-four–ounce 7-Eleven Big Gulp cup with cover and straw, forty-two cents in change, and a stolen .38 revolver that had four live rounds in a six-chambered cylinder.

I held the fat Stephen King book in one hand, the cup in the other, as I entered the bus station from the garage area. The others carried in their bags and rounded up their small children. Some were greeted by friends who awaited them inside. Nobody was waiting for me; no one knew me in Isthmus City. Anyone else anywhere else who might have once been kin didn't have the foggiest idea whether I was alive or dead or what—and I wasn't all that eager for them to find out.

It was late, and most of the orange fiberglass chairs in the lounge sat empty. The lone security guard stood at the ticket agent's window, talking with a curly-haired, mousy-looking woman who stood behind the counter while he stuffed his face with a Twinkie. His big beer gut hung over his utility belt, which I happened to notice contained a nine-millimeter semiautomatic pistol in blued steel. His stance was late-night–cop casual—he was leaning against the counter propped up on one leg, the other crossing at his shin. Crumbs clung to his gray mustache.

My eyes squinted against the fluorescent light, which, after the long night ride in a darkened bus, was harsh enough to give me an instant headache. While the other passengers had slept during the trip, I'd been leaning my head against the Plexiglas window, focusing on the shadowed prairie and farmland, feeling every jolt and vibration as we cruised down I-94.

The grip of my gun was hidden beneath my untucked sweatshirt. If anything was showing, it would be the long, skinny barrel that stuck straight down my crotch, behind the buttoned fly of my jeans. The gun's cold nose was tangled up in my pubic hair, tugging on it as I walked. My dick had fallen down along the left leg of my jeans, half-erect from the constant stroking of the worn-out denim—or perhaps from the caress of the gun's muzzle against my pubes.

The security guard, the last of his snack gone, was licking his fingers and glancing around. He caught my eye for a split second before his gaze landed on my crotch. He was looking not at my precariously concealed weapon but at the distinct outline presented by my dangling dick.

I thought, *Goddamned queer cop.*

My headache suddenly came on with a vengeance. I'd been eight hours without a cigarette—and that had been a Carlton, for Christ's sake, bummed off a bum at the Minneapolis bus depot. But now, with only forty-two cents to my name, even such a no-taste cigarette sounded good.

I could lift up my shirt and pull out the gun, aim at the security guard, and fire before he knew what hit him. The fat fuck would get it in the gut, and the blood would fly everywhere. Then I could stick the gun into the face of the curly-haired ticket gal and demand some cash. The security guard would be lying on the floor, staining it with a steady stream of bodily fluids. I could steal his nine-millimeter, too, and go out brandishing pistols in each hand, the wad of money shoved down my pants—like I was some kind of Old West outlaw robbing a frontier bank—Jesse James or something.

"What do you want, kid?" the security guard asked. The patch on his shoulder read BADGER SECURITY. He was a rental—not a Greyhound employee—and just there for his paycheck. *Easy pickins.*

"Huh?" I took a few steps forward.

"Why you hanging around?"

"I just got off the goddamned bus," I snapped. "There a law against that?"

"Nope." He pulled a crooked smile and winked at me—or maybe it was a nervous tic. "No law against it. Thought you had a question or something."

His girl behind the Plexiglas was busy counting the money in the till and paid us no mind.

"Actually," I said, taking another couple of steps closer, "I was wondering if I could bum a smoke."

"Sure, kid." The security guard fished into the breast pocket of his shirt, behind his badge, which was reflecting the fluorescent light right up into my eyes. He tapped a cig out of his pack and handed it over. "Need a light?"

"Yes, sir," I said.

The cig turned out to be a Parliament Light, whatever the

hell that was. The security guard held the flame of his disposable up to its tip until it was cooking.

I inhaled; even the smoke from this piece-of-crap cigarette felt good in my lungs. But it was simply filling a void. I needed something real, pumped full of tar and nicotine. I'd once tasted a Yak cigarette from China or India or Nepal or somewhere, and I longed for something like that—something rich and disgusting, like sucking on a chunk of road tar.

"Thanks," I said anyway, and grinned closed-mouthed.

The security guard dismissed me with a wave of his hand and went back to his girlfriend.

He wasn't looking at your dick, stupid. You're just paranoid about the gun.

But the rent-a-cop was right—what was I doing hanging around? What the hell was I waiting for?

I hadn't had a thing to eat since the frozen burrito Jeff Abbott had fed me the night before. I went over to the row of vending machines to try and find something I could afford—but pop and candy bars were past my budget. Packs of gum were offered at forty cents, but of my forty-two, seven were pennies and worthless. I didn't want to go up to the security guard's little fiancée and ask her to exchange them, so I looked for whatever I might be able to scrounge with my quarter and dime. This turned out to be a half-pint carton of chocolate milk.

I downed it; it froze my throat. I threw it away in an overstuffed trash bin, and my hand came away sticky with pop or something.

I hadn't wanted to use the toilet on the bus and now had to go to the bathroom. I went through the door marked MEN. A peek inside showed me I had the place to myself. I scarfed down the last of the cigarette, tossed the spent butt on the linoleum, and ground it beneath my boot heel.

In the mirror, I was a sorry sight. I felt sticky and gross; I'd gone days without bathing or shaving. I pulled my shirt off over my head. My chest hair was wet with perspiration. I raised my arms and could smell the musky odor of my pits, which I'd always thought kind of sexy.

Bet that cop caught a whiff of me, too.

The gun's grip protruded from my jeans, all too obvious to anyone who might come strolling in—but I was willing to take my chances. I stood back from the mirror and quick-drew the gun on my reflection, yanking out a matted nest of pubic hair in the process.

I stared down the barrel of the gun my reflected self was aiming back at me. My torso was naked and sweat drenched. My semihard dick could be made out through my jeans. The arm holding the gun was muscled and lean, the face holding a grim smirk. My dark hair shot out in a wild mane—too long for my taste (but then I hadn't wanted to waste any money on a haircut, and the only guy back in the Minne-apple who'd offered to do it for free was a Nazi skinhead with his own electric shears, to whom I'd said thanks but no thanks). My waist was narrow, abs nicely ripped.

This is why the queers go for me, I thought—*this badboy look.*

I returned the gun to its home in my crotch and turned on the cold water. I washed the sticky gook off my fingers. I doused my hair until it all lay back from my forehead. I splashed my face, chest, and armpits. I put the smelly sweat-shirt back on. I entered one of the stalls and slid the lock into place. I hung the gun up on the coathook by its trigger guard. I set the Big Gulp cup and the Stephen King book down on the grimy, wet floor. Sliding my pants down around my ankles, I finally felt free after those hours of hell on the bus. My cock began to relax, shrinking a little as I sat on the cold porcelain seat.

Good boy.

The walls of the stall were covered with the usual perverted scribblings: SHOW HARD FOR BJ, 10-8-88 and WILL SUCK YOUNG BOYCOCK, 2-10-90, 1–4 PM, LAST STALL, TAP FOOT and TIGHT HOLE CRAVES MONSTER DICKS, 555-2140. It was rare to see someone actually leave their phone number like that. Unless it was someone's idea of a joke, it was an invitation to danger. Old queens were often preyed on by enterprising young hustlers.

I took a mental note of the number.

The surrounding graffiti offered an opposing view: DIE, FAGS! and KILL QUEERS and ISTHMUS CITY—FAIRYLAND OF THE DAIRYLAND.

I chuckled at that.

The writings on the walls bore out what I'd been told by Jeff Abbott, the skinhead back in Minneapolis whose coveted boots I was now wearing: there were a lot of queers in Isthmus City.

I opened up *The Stand* and read a few more pages while I finished taking my crap.

I heard the door open and the approach of footsteps. I couldn't see who it was but figured from what sounded like the jangle of a utility belt that it was my Twinkie-loving old chum.

This was just what I didn't need, sitting here on the pot. Lock or no, the security guard could yank open the stall and harass me some more. Then the gun would come crashing down, and I'd end up spending my first night in town at the county jail.

The guard went over to the urinals. I could hear a trickle of pee while he whistled the tune to Rod Stewart's "Some

Guys Have All the Luck." He went on for some time, repeating the chorus over and over in a nightmarish, never-ending loop.

It was annoying. I wanted to yell at him to cut it out but held my tongue.

I heard him go over to the sinks and wash up. Then he paused in front of me. I could sense him bending over to look under my stall door. He came closer, until I could see the glossy tips of his black patent-leather shoes.

He rapped harshly on the door; the gun on the coathook clattered against the metal.

"You OK in there?" he asked, jiggling the handle.

"Hey!" I snapped back.

Keep this up, buster, and you're gonna be bacon on a meathook.

"Everything coming out all right?" At this, he laughed. He jarred the flimsy latch to where it nearly came loose.

"What are you, some kind of pervert?"

"Sorry, kid," he said, and stopped. "We had a young lad slit his wrists right here on the john once."

"Don't lay it on me, man."

The security guard swore under his breath, then left. I heard the door swing shut.

"Pig," I muttered to myself. If the stall door had sprung open and he'd come in, I would have leapt off the toilet and throttled the son-of-a-bitch.

I put myself back together. I washed out the Big Gulp cup in the sink and filled it with cold water. I checked my shirt in the mirror and made sure the gun handle was well hidden.

Out in the lounge, I ignored the apologetic wave from the security guard. His woman was blowing her nose. I exited through the glass entry doors and out into the starry night.

Fucking queer cop, I thought. *Bet he wrote that himself about craving monster dicks.*

2

I found myself on a park bench, reading *The Stand* by streetlight. Across the street stood a row of Victorian homes with dark windows. No one was around.

Beside me were the sculpted figures of what were supposed to be two women also seated on the bench. The hand of one was resting on the thigh of the other. Standing nearby and cemented into the sidewalk were the figures of two men "cruising" each other. Each of the four appeared gray in the dim light and looked made of papier-mâché. But when I touched one of the women, I found her hard as stone.

Anyone sees me sitting here, they'll think I'm a queer, I thought.

Jeff Abbott had bragged to me of having once struck the gay-liberation sculpture with red paint and been arrested by the Isthmus City police. If so, the statue had since been cleaned up.

I grew restless and got up, closing my book. I had no idea what time it was. The chocolate milk must have cleared my kidneys, because I had to take a piss.

I stood between the two male figures, like I was conferring with them over what to do next. They looked like they were sizing me up. I unbuttoned my fly and felt around the muzzle of the gun for my dick. I pulled it out and pissed on the men's legs, snickering. Water sports, this was called. Some queers went for it in a big way.

I buttoned up my fly and grabbed my Big Gulp cup from where it lay on the park bench between the thighs of one of the dykes. I looked around but again saw no one. The town was totally dead.

I walked back to Williams Street, which I'd crossed on my way to the park. Somewhere along here, within blocks of the bus station, stood an abandoned house Jeff the skinhead had said was a crack den. It would be a good place to crash, if I could find it. But for the moment, I wanted to keep walking around. I had to make some money somehow. I'd lost some muscle mass since leaving Denver. I hadn't been getting enough to eat, and my body had begun consuming itself.

I went up Wisconsin Avenue, heading for the courthouse that stood fully illuminated by floodlights in the town square. Along the way, I considered going into the Amoco station and shoplifting something to eat—but if I was caught, the gun would get me into deeper trouble; the risk was too great.

I walked around the square for a while. Jeff Abbott had said this was a place where queers cruised each other, but so far I'd seen no one driving around but cops, who eyed me suspiciously as I ambled along, like I was a queer myself. I was beginning to wonder if Isthmus City really had any action after all, or if Jeff Abbott had been full of so much shit.

A moment later, a midsize pickup pulled up to a stoplight and the driver rolled down his window.

"Hey, you know where's the nearest motel?" The driver and sole occupant was a blue-collar–looking dude with dirty shoulder-length hair and a wispy mustache. Country music blared from his radio.

I pegged him as a farm queer who'd grown tired of sheep.

I placed my hands in my pockets, thumbs out, shoulders slumped, and approached. I could go for my gun in a flash if I had to. You never could tell with these farm queers—I'd once seen a personal ad in a queer magazine where this guy wanted to be hooked up to an automated milking machine. Maybe this guy was looking for a motel, and maybe he wasn't.

"I don't know, man," I said, and shrugged.

"You sure?"

"Sure, I'm sure." I was cautious. It was possible he was genuinely asking for directions, not trying to cruise me.

"Can you tell me how to find the Super Eight, then?"

"Nope. I'm not from around here."

"Neither am I," said the driver, on a hopeful note.

"Oh, yeah?" I said.

Yeah, bud, you're from up north, the woods—inbreeding country. My thumb stroked the butt of my gun.

I could whip out the .38 and stick it in his face. I could ask for money, but this guy didn't exactly look like he had a bankroll hidden in his shorts. I could pop one right between his eyes, point-blank. Placing the muzzle up against his skull would deaden the sound as surely as a silencer.

"I know what you really want."

"What's that?" he asked, playing stupid.

"My dick."

The driver gasped. With the streetlights shining down from above, my gaunt face would have been mostly in shadow, with hollows below my brow and cheekbones. I probably looked diseased or something.

"Forget it!" The driver gunned the engine and tore off through the blinking red, after-hours streetlight.

I laughed out loud; the guy was either a good judge of character or stupid as shit.

But I wouldn't have drawn the gun, anyway. Too many cops had been driving around for me to pull off something like that. The square was a shit-poor location after all.

Fairyland of the Dairyland. I smiled at the thought.

I headed east on Madison Street—supposedly the red-light district in this burg. I wanted to see what the whores looked like here. And although I had no idea whether any johns cruised for young studs along Madison as well, I was sure determined to find out.

3

I saw only one whore along the way—and a pretty unglamorous one at that. She was standing at the corner of Madison and Jefferson and had pale white flabby skin, dirty blond hair, a polyester top stretched over hefty breasts, and tight jeans that revealed folds of cellulite at her hips. Her makeup was brightly overdone. She stood directly in my path.

"Wanna party?" Her speech was slurred, and she gave off a strong odor of whiskey.

I tried to ignore her and pass by.

"White trash!" she called after me.

"Fuck you," I said over my shoulder.

"Goddamned gay maggot! You just goin' off to suck yo' boyfrien's cock!"

Fucking bitch, I thought, but kept on walking. The whore was screaming loud enough for the whole damned neighborhood to hear, probably waking people up.

"You think I need you?" she said. "You go to hell, cock-sucker! I don't need no nelly eatin' my pussy!"

I stopped short, turned around at the opposite side of Jefferson Street, and headed back in her direction. My thumb stroked the butt of my gun.

"You better shut up."

"Oh, yeah? Who's gonna make me? You? *Ha!* You just

can't wait to get home so yo' boyfrien' can slip his big dick up yo' tight white ass."

She sounded black but looked like a fat little Dutch girl, all blond and rosy cheeked—the face of a baby doll.

I decided against drawing the gun. If this was indeed a well-known red-light district, the police probably did routine surveillance and might be watching. Worse still, she could be a cop herself trying to entrap johns. If she was, it was awfully convincing—but cops could be sneaky.

"Shut your fucking face," I said.

"What, you change yo' mind? Want a taste of my honey?"

"I want you to shut the fuck up."

"Oh, yeah? Child, I wouldn't party with you if you was the last man on earth. You probably got them AIDS runnin' around inside—lettin' yo' man fuck you like you was his ho. I bet you into some crazy fag shit."

I dropped my Big Gulp cup and, without even thinking, whipped the gun out of my pants and placed the muzzle against her forehead.

"Shit, man." She seemed hardly surprised.

"I told you to shut up." I looked around quickly. No cops. I was in the clear.

"I . . . I'm sorry." Her voice dropped to a whisper. "I didn't mean nothin'. Don't kill me."

"You think I'm a queer?" I said, cocking the pistol.

"Please," she said.

"Just shut up."

I pulled the trigger, but the hammer fell against one of the two empty chambers; nothing happened.

The whore's scream evaporated in a sigh before she collapsed in a dead faint on the sidewalk.

"Jesus fuck!" I said.

I was quaking like an aspen. I slid the gun back into my

pants and ran down Madison Street, back toward the bus station.

My heart was racing. I couldn't believe it. I'd wanted to kill her. If the gun hadn't come up empty, she'd have been dead. I'd thought I'd kept it ready to fire in case I had to defend myself against some queer. But somehow while I was walking around, the chamber must have revolved against my belly and reshuffled the live rounds.

I could hear nothing but my own heavy breathing and hurried footsteps. The Doc Martens were clumsy for running, but I wanted to get far away from the whore. She might come to and send someone after me.

I was a block away from the station when a subcompact car approached with its bright headlights on—too small for a cop car. It crept to a snail's pace as it neared.

I stopped short and slowed to a walk. I told myself to act casual, pay no attention.

"Hey, baby," said an effeminate voice, "want a ride?"

Fuck off, I thought. I'd just almost killed somebody and wanted to be left alone.

The car ran up into the driveway of a vacant parking lot, cutting off my path. I stopped in my tracks, still breathing hard.

The driver looked like a woman, but from the obvious wig and masculine features, I could tell it was a transvestite.

"Out of my way," I said.

The transvestite emerged from the tiny car. His wig was a well-coiffed brunette bouffant with small flip curls at either ear. He wore two large golden earrings and a gold choker. His eyebrows were penciled in above eyeshadowed lids. His cheeks were rouged, lips done up a glossy red. His dress was a slim, sleeveless one-piece that zipped up the front but was left open to reveal some cleavage. He had a womanly figure with modest-sized breasts, a narrow waist, and full hips—though his shoulders were broad without any obvious padding. He kept his knees together as he emerged from the cramped car; the dress went down to just above the knee. He wore sheer panty hose and platform shoes. For a guy, he had decent legs.

Looking closer at the tight dress, I could make out a bulge at his crotch.

"What cat dragged you out?" the transvestite asked, stepping closer.

"Get away from me," I warned.

"Why, you uppity piece of trade!"

Trade—that was a big queer word. "What makes you think I'm trade?"

"You?" He laughed like I was being a perfectly silly goose. "Look at you! You're the rough trade poster boy." He was rubbing his crotch through the fabric of his dress.

"Stay away from me."

"That's no way to treat a lady."

"You're no lady."

"We'll see."

"Anyway, you'll get nothing from me."

"Every piece has its price."

"I'm no queer."

"Girlfriend, I've heard *that* before!" He stood close enough, I could smell his breath.

"I'm not looking for service."

"Oh, you don't get it." The transvestite chuckled. "I want you to suck me."

"No way."

"I bet you know how to sing for your supper."

"You go to hell."

"I'll bet you fifty dollars."

14

The transvestite flashed me some paper money, but the light was dim and I couldn't make out much before he removed it from view.

"Leave me alone." I started to step around the car.

But he placed a powerful hand on my shoulder. His biceps flexed as he squeezed tighter. His sleeveless dress showed off well-muscled arms. This wasn't your usual frail, doelike transvestite; this was a boxer in a dress. I was suddenly frightened, and wondered, *Who is this guy?*

"I don't think you understand, honey." He spoke low, up close. I smelled gin. "I'm offering you *dineros*. Fifty—hell, a hundred—whatever you like, rough boy. Except I want to see your head up my skirt. I want to feel your tongue licking my shaft. I want to fuck your face till you're choking on my cock. You think you're not a queer—well, baby, I'm going to turn you into one."

He grabbed my hand and pressed it against his crotch. I felt a hard, huge cock underneath the tight fabric.

"Nice?"

I said nothing. Yeah, I'd sucked cock before—I'd had to, just like he said, so I wouldn't starve. But I could never take one so big. I *would* choke on it. The fucking thing would probably kill me. And I *wasn't* a queer.

But I could use the money, so I just stood there, passive, not sure if I could afford to run. My stomach was growling. I had to eat.

The transvestite grabbed me by the shoulder roughly and led me into the empty, darkened parking lot, out of reach of the streetlights. The headlights of his car shone against the wall of one building, but he led me away, into the shadows against the warehouse across from it. There were three cars parked across the street—a Ford Maverick, a Jeep, and a

BMW—but I didn't see anyone inside or out walking the street.

"Get down on your knees," the transvestite ordered.

I obeyed; I wasn't going anywhere.

The transvestite pulled up his dress. I was overwhelmed by an incredible sense of déjà vu, as if I'd been through all this before and was doomed to repeat it. I felt exposed and vulnerable, like we were being watched—but I shrugged it off; I couldn't see anybody around.

"Suck it," the transvestite said, though it sounded distant, like he was talking to himself. "I want to feel your mouth on my cock."

He slapped my cheek several times with his hard-on, while I sat with my mouth hanging open.

I winced at the sting and went for my gun. The transvestite didn't see. He grabbed my hair and yanked back my head.

"Come on, baby, suck it!"

I placed the gun's cold muzzle against his smooth, clean-shaven scrotum.

He gasped. His dick began to shrivel.

"One more word and I'll blow your balls off." I stood up. "Now you get on your knees."

"Y-yes, sir."

"Not a sound," I reminded him.

"P-please . . . "

"Shut up!"

The transvestite's mascara began to run, his eyes tearing up. I grabbed him by his wig and held his face at crotch level.

"Now close your eyes," I ordered. "And open wide like you're going to suck me."

Shaking, the transvestite complied, shadowed eyelids firmly shut, glossy red lips widening to reveal the tongue.

I placed the barrel in his mouth.

He closed his lips around it. The barrel glistened with saliva. He opened his eyes and looked up at me through long, thick lashes.

I took a deep breath.

The gun went off twice—two shots through the back of his brain, two bright flashes but little noise—less than that of a car backfiring.

The transvestite fell against the brick wall of the Mertz Paint warehouse, his skirt up around his hips, exposing his shaved cock and balls.

Suddenly disgusted, I threw the gun several yards away. I didn't want to be caught with it on me.

I hadn't noticed that the transvestite had further unzipped the top of his dress, exposing his womanly breasts. I stared down at them now and couldn't believe my eyes, for rather than false padding or rubber prostheses, they were real—firm boobs with large, pink, erect nipples.

I stood there for a moment, confused, and wondered what exactly it was that I'd just killed.

Two

1

I had to get out of there.

I snatched up the money still clutched in the corpse's fingers, thinking it was a fifty. It turned out to be a two-dollar bill, like the one my Grandma Aylesworth had given me when I was a kid. I stuck it in my pocket and cursed my bad luck. I needed a smoke.

I took one last look at the transvestite and thought: *A three-dollar bill, that's what you are.*

The motor was still running in the transvestite's subcompact. I got in and found the driver's seat still warm. I tossed *The Stand* beside me on the passenger seat, where it landed atop a pile of cassette tapes by Erasure, Pet Shop Boys, and RuPaul. I backed out of the parking lot. The headlights swept over the prone body lying in the pool of blood. I turned away, but the headlights quickly veered off to show the street ahead, and the image of the corpse faded into the pitch-blackness of the warehouse wall.

No one had heard the shots. No one had come running. The streets were deserted. The bus station stood a mere block away, but the Greyhound sign was out and the station dark; the last bus of the night must have come and gone.

I sped off down a side street until I hit Williams. I searched up and down, looking for the abandoned house Jeff Abbott had told me about. I imagined a large Victorian with steep, shingled gables, circular attic windows, and ginger-bread decorations, done up in gray and surrounded by a wrought-iron fence. The furniture within would be draped with dusty sheets, the rooms filled with cobwebs. The house would be haunted, too.

But what I found instead was a two-story white clap-board, windows boarded over with plywood panels. Both the siding and the panels were covered in indecipherable spray-painted gang graffiti.

With the car engine off, I found myself in a world of quiet. Through the rolled-down window, I heard a far-off train blowing its horn. Many blocks distant, a dog barked once, briefly. Crickets rubbed their legs together.

I found among the cassette tapes a box of Virginia Slims with two cigarettes inside. *You've come a long way, baby,* I thought, and stuck one in my mouth. I lit it with the car lighter. When it was finished, I tossed it out the window. Then I lit the other one, rolled up the window, grabbed my book, got out of the car, and locked the door. I took a good look around the neighborhood before heading up the front lawn. No one was about, all the houses along the street dark and quiet. It had to be about three in the morning.

Jeff Abbott had never told me how to get into the house, and I found the front door boarded shut. I tried prying it loose, but it held firm. The boarded windows were similarly secure. I went around back and found concrete steps going down to a basement doorway that was padlocked shut.

When I tugged the lock, it fell open in my hand; it had been hanging there just for show.

Once inside, I closed the door firmly and was in total darkness, save for the glowing tip of my cigarette. I hoped no one else was there with me. I took small steps and began feeling my way around the cellar. The soles of my Doc Martens scraped the gritty floor.

A skittering noise made me halt for a moment and turn in its direction—probably a mouse. But when I turned back around, my nose slammed flat against a cold stone wall.

"Shit!" I said, clutching my nose and grabbing the wall for balance. I kicked over a metal pail.

Following the wall, I stumbled upon a narrow staircase and took it up, bumping my head on the low ceiling. The old boards creaked beneath my weight. I stepped on an aluminum can that went clattering down the steps to the basement floor. I felt ahead of me, expecting to meet a door but finding instead a turn in the stairs—the doorway on the right was fixed shut with a hook latch. A faint blue light showed through a crack at its base.

I unhooked the latch and found myself in the kitchen. Enough light crept in to make shapes such as the sink and the old refrigerator visible. The light was coming from the living room; the plywood panels covering most of each window failed to reach the upper few inches, and moonlight filtered into the dust-filled room from on high.

There was no furniture whatsoever. The wood floor was littered with crushed cans and broken bottles, paper wrappings from fast-food joints (one with a petrified half-hamburger still inside), empty plastic baggies, charred and broken tubes of glass, cigarette butts, used matchbooks, spent condoms, and disposed-of disposable lighters. The cigarette I'd been smoking came to its end. I snuffed it out on the floor, adding one more butt to the pile.

I picked up one of the lighters and flicked it, only to discover that it still worked. I set fire to one of the fast-food wrappers and tossed the flaming ball into the fireplace. I watched the ball uncurl as the flames engulfed it. But rather than being sucked up the chimney, the smoke billowed up into the room.

I looked closer and found the flue closed; it was an ancient square thing like a submarine hatch, with a large lever locking it shut. When I slid the lever back, the flue fell open and clanged against the brick. Soot fell out of the chimney, onto my arms and up into my face. I spat it out and sneezed a few times.

It was at that moment I realized I had to go back, get the body, and hide it. I couldn't leave it there to be discovered. I'd been seen by at least three people. The security guard might say I'd acted suspiciously. The driver of the pickup truck might say I'd threatened him. The whore might report my having drawn the gun on her and pulling the trigger; she might identify the gun the cops recovered at the scene as the one I'd stuck in her face. The security guard might be able to describe me well enough for a police sketch artist to come up with a reasonable likeness. If the guard recalled what bus I'd come in on, that might lead the cops to sniffing around the Minneapple. Out of that they might find a way to track me to the farmhouse and then back to Denver and Tom Latimer. The police sketch would be confirmed by the whore's description. Basically, if the police found the body, they'd be able to rack up a substantial case against me based on circumstantial evidence, and even if they had difficulty learning my identity, I couldn't escape them forever. The sketch might be shown nationally on one of those TV shows like

Raymond Burr's Mysterious Disappearances, along with a 1-800 number, and some housewife glimpsing me at a grocery store down in Texas would phone in a tip that would lead to my arrest. Once they got me in custody and matched my fingerprints against those found on the gun, I would be had.

Using the disposable lighter to light my way, I went down the back stairs and out the back door of the basement. I threw the nonworking padlock back on the latch just as I'd found it. I ran across the street to the car and pulled out of the parking space as soon as the engine was running.

My only hope was that no one had yet come across the body. If luck really was a lady, I still had time to fix everything.

2

The scene was just as I'd left it. I backed the car up to where the body lay, turned off the ignition, and shut off the headlights. All was quiet except for the sound of my boots on the asphalt as I got out of the car. Here there were no crickets, no barking dogs.

My eyes stung from no sleep. My stomach was growling, hands shaking. The brief taste of nicotine had me craving more. My feet had blisters from the ill-fitting boots.

Let's get this over with and get the hell out of town.

I was standing in the parking lot of the Mertz Paint warehouse. This stretch of Madison Street was industrial. Not far away stood what looked like some kind of electrical power plant with several tall smokestacks. I couldn't see any homes for several blocks in either direction. Everything here was shut down for the night—no prying eyes to disrupt my work, unless a car should come rambling along.

"Motherfuck," I said, looking at the body.

Blood had trickled out of the mouth and both nostrils. The bouffant wig had fallen askew. Pieces of brain matter lay in the pool of blood beneath the head.

I was wearing no gloves; this was going to be messy work.

I unlatched the back hatch, revealing the small space behind the front seats, the rear seat folded down. The transvestite had used this as a waste bin. It was filled with cans of diet soda, used tissues, issues of *Vogue*. I cleared a spot by dumping the garbage out into the parking lot. The cans clattered as they fell, echoing off the warehouse wall.

I took a precautionary look around but saw no one. I noticed then that the Maverick and the BMW were still parked across the street but that the Jeep was gone. I worried that someone might have come along and seen the body. But the police weren't here yet; if I could get the body out of here in a hurry, they would never find it.

I squatted down and placed one arm beneath the transvestite's knees, the other at the small of his back. Hefting the body was no easy task. I dumped him clumsily into the cramped space in the back of the car. The wig and platform shoes fell off. More blood oozed out of the skull.

"Jee-sus!" I said, and tucked in a dangling arm. I grabbed the fallen wig and shoes and tossed them in back.

Someone's going to find me driving around with a dead body, I thought.

I found three small chunks of bloody brain tissue lying around, one shard of bone, and one small piece of scalp. These I picked up by hand and also tossed into the car. But I wouldn't be able to do anything about the blood on the asphalt. With luck, it would dry, and whoever ran across it would think it the remnants of a spilled can of Mertz Paint.

I wiped my bloody hands on an unsullied portion of the

transvestite's dress, yet they remained red-stained, as if I'd been fingerpainting. I slammed the hatch and locked it shut.

The one thing left to do was find the gun; I'd thrown it away without thinking. I rummaged through the glove compartment and under the seats looking for a flashlight but couldn't find one. I went out into the parking lot and searched everywhere for the revolver. It seemed like I'd simply stumble across it, yet the longer I searched the more baffled I became. Had someone come upon the scene already and taken the gun? Had they noticed the body and phoned the police? Could the cops be on their way? I sped up my search, but it was hard to make out much in the darkness. Whenever I saw something, it would turn out to be a broken beer bottle or a length of pipe.

The gun was nowhere. I would have to cut my losses.

I heard a car approaching and ran for cover behind the subcompact. Headlights came around the side of the building. They passed beneath the car, illuminating my boots for a moment before vanishing. The car kept on going without so much as slowing down—and it wasn't a Jeep or a police car.

I figured they didn't see a thing. There was nothing to see, anyway, except a car sitting empty in a parking lot.

Despite this, my heart was racing. I gave up looking for the gun. I had more important things to do. The dead body lying in the car was like a ticking time bomb that I had to get rid of before it blew up in my face. And as long as the police didn't have a body, a found gun was simply a found gun. They would run a fingerprint check and find no match; I'd never been arrested as an adult, so my fingerprints wouldn't be on file anywhere—I knew that much. If they could determine the gun was stolen (which it was), they would try to contact its rightful owner; if no one came forward to claim it, it would be destroyed. Without a crime to attach to the gun, it would serve no purpose. I could afford to leave it.

I drove the car back to the abandoned house. The weight in back shifted whenever I struck a pothole. I pulled the car up the driveway to the back of the house and parked it behind the back stairwell. None of the nearby houses had any lights on.

I went down first and opened the back door. I retrieved the body from the car, hefting it just as before. The body had stiffened up slightly and felt cold to the touch. The way down the back stairs was narrow, and I ended up scraping my knuckles against the cement wall trying to fit both of us through the tight space.

I knelt down and dumped the body on the basement floor, then closed the door behind me. It remained pitch-black in the cellar, yet I had a fair idea of where the staircase lay.

I grabbed the transvestite by his ankles and dragged him across the floor. He was leaving a trail of blood, but I could do nothing about that. The only people who would come to this house wouldn't notice or even give a damn if they did.

I backed into the same wall into which I'd bumped my nose earlier. I found the staircase and went up backward, pulling the body up by its legs bit by bit.

At the top of the stairs, I opened the door to the kitchen and dragged the body across the linoleum, into the living room. In the dim light, I could make out the dark trail left by the transvestite's head. I stopped before the fireplace and released my grip, allowing his legs to fall to the floor.

The transvestite's pale, firm breasts stared up at me.

I was breathing heavily and had to sit down and rest. I wasn't sure I was up to the task. I was a mess, my clothes speckled with blood, arms bloodstained up to my elbows. My boots had left bloody prints across the dusty floor.

I removed boots, sweatshirt, and jeans, and stood naked in the filtered moonlight. It felt like my whole body could breathe again.

The flue remained open, just as I'd left it.

I dragged the corpse feet-first toward the fireplace. I remembered having once helped my uncle carry a heavy sleeper-sofa up three flights of stairs and figured this couldn't be any more difficult.

First, I searched the transvestite's dress for any wallet or identification cards but found nothing. It was probably all in a purse or some such thing in the car. I removed the golden earrings and the choker and put them with my own pile of clothes. I pulled the dress down over his crotch and zipped it up over his tits.

I wondered why the guy had chosen that moment to accost me, why he'd been so aggressive. If I hadn't had the gun, I never would have killed him. Such things had happened before—when I'd been powerless to defend myself and been forced to do what someone else wanted. I would have ended up sucking the transvestite's cock and might have felt like killing him, but I would have taken the money and run. It was a fluke in the first place that I'd even been carrying a gun. Until I'd stolen it back at the Minnesota farmhouse, I'd never before even held one in my hands.

"You dumb fuck," I told the corpse as I inched it farther into the fireplace.

By now, the transvestite's panty hose were filled with runs. The shoes remained outside in the car. I put his feet up into the chimney and bent his knees so that the legs would straighten out. I had to crawl inside the fireplace with the body to stuff it up. I grabbed hold of the dress at the hips and used it to help pull the body up. His knees bent and I had to straighten out the legs again. I hefted the body up a few inches, then shifted my position and grabbed hold of his shoulders. I shoved the body against the far wall of the fireplace; his hips cleared the flue.

I had to hold it there for a moment to catch my breath. The corpse's arms were dangling down on either side of me. I wanted them going up with the rest of the body. I crept down lower and rested the corpse on my shoulders, trying to free my hands so I could grab his arms and pull them inside. But I couldn't do a thing with them. I scooted up and, throwing my weight behind it, pushed the body up. I met with some resistance as the corpse hit a narrowing of the chimney. I put my shoulders into it until I was squatting within the fireplace and shoving the body up.

I had to stop and rest again—crouched like Atlas holding up the world. The corpse's arms dangled down in front of my face. I was going to break my back.

As I pressed up again, I heard snapping noises; relaxing for a moment, I noticed the body was firmly jammed up into the chimney, hips apparently caught tight. Holding the body up with one hand in case it slipped, I folded its arms inside and tucked in its head. I grabbed the handle of the flue and slammed it closed, latching it securely into place. I was alone in the room now, the corpse quite effectively hidden.

Blood dripped into the fireplace from the hinge of the flue. Nothing I could do about that.

I collapsed onto the floor and lay there resting for probably half an hour, my naked body covered in blood, sweat, soot, whatever. After a while, I caught myself nearly dozing and rose to my feet. My body ached all over, and I couldn't go anywhere looking the way I did.

I lucked out and found a bathroom upstairs, with a working shower. When I turned on the water, the pipe groaned and the showerhead spat out rust-colored gook, but once I allowed it to run for a while, it came out clear. The water was cold, but I liked it. I climbed into the shower and scraped myself clean, scrubbing my skin with my fingernails.

3

Driving north on the interstate, I panicked about the boots. They had left their mark in blood back at the house on Williams Street. If the body was discovered and I was found wearing the boots, they could use that to convict me.

I pulled over onto the shoulder. The subcompact shook as an eighteen-wheeler zoomed by. At this time of morning, before the sun had come up, few drivers were on the highway except for commercial truckers.

Hurriedly, I untied the lacings and yanked them out, then took off the boots and placed them on the seat beside me, along with my book and the transvestite's dance music tapes. (I'd been listening, in fact, to the Erasure tape; it was pretty good.) The transvestite had left Virginia Slims cigarette butts on the floor with pink lipstick traces on the ends of the filters.

Once back on the highway and doing sixty-five, I unrolled the window and tossed one of the boots out onto the grassy median. About ten miles later, I got rid of the other.

I was at once sickened by what I'd done and overcome with euphoria. It seemed like a bad dream—my being accosted by the transvestite, his staring up at me with the gun in his mouth, the splatter of blood out the back of his head as the gun went off.

Hey, baby, want a ride?

I'd come to Isthmus City thinking I might be able to

scam off some queers but had ended up killing some kind of hermaphrodite.

Old Tom Latimer back in Denver had once shown me a porn movie starring people like that: guys with tits, chicks with dicks. One scene had a supposedly straight couple in a threesome with a transsexual. The guy ended up in a sandwich, porking his girlfriend while the transsexual fucked him. It looked like a guy and two girls, only one of the girls had this huge dick that was plunging in and out of the guy's ass, and the guy was getting off on it.

Stealing that gun from the farmhouse had been my first mistake. Since then, I'd hardly stopped thinking about using it on someone. Holding a loaded gun in your hand is one of the most nerve-racking things on earth; the fucker is begging to be used.

I'd stolen some money from the farmer as well, and with it I'd planned the trip to Isthmus City. Before leaving Minneapolis, I'd added Jeff Abbott's boots to my inventory. While I was on the bus, the gun had been a constant presence hidden in my jeans. I could have killed the security guard, the pickup driver, the whore—but chance had thrown the transvestite my way. By then, I'd been left no choice. The gun had gone off in my hand—as if it had made the decision itself.

But now, with it gone, I no longer felt like killing anybody—like the whole world had slipped off my shoulders.

Over the loud Erasure music, I heard the whine of a siren. I saw flashing lights and looked in my rearview mirror. Coming up fast on my tail was a pair of highway patrol cars, red and blue lights spinning on top.

Here it is, I thought, *I'm fucked.*

I'd thought driving the car would be safe enough, since the only person who knew it had been stolen was now dead and stuffed up a chimney. I slowed down and pulled over to the shoulder.

The first patrol car approached without diminishing speed, then swerved suddenly around me and sped past on my left. The second one followed suit, taking the outside lane. They vanished over the next hill.

My heart was racing. Although I was relieved they'd been chasing someone else, the encounter had scared the shit out of me. I laughed nervously—that I could have killed someone and been driving a stolen car, and yet the police were after some speeder or making an emergency blood run. For all I knew, one of the taillights could have been busted; I could have been pulled over on that alone. The first thing a cop would do would be to give the car a once-over with his flashlight through the windows, just in case there happened to be any kilos of cocaine lying around. The cop would discover that I had no license—or any identification for that matter—and that I was driving a car registered to someone else that had fresh bloodstains in back. The fact that I had no ID was reason enough for them to bring me in. . . .

I took a moment to compose my thoughts, wishing the transvestite had had the courtesy to buy an extra pack of Virginia Slims. I found his purse on the floor but no wallet, ID, or any more cigarettes. I took his choker and earrings out of my pants pocket and put them in the purse along with his makeup, assorted tissues, and, oddly, a tampon.

I had to find a place to ditch the car.

I got going again and, after allowing a few large trucks to pass, reemerged onto the right lane. Another mile and I came upon an exit, which I took. Atop an overpass, I met a junction with a farm road and turned onto it, then followed it for half a mile before spying a dirt road that led off toward a distant farmhouse. I turned off and drove the car up the road a bit, then doused the headlights and turned off into a field that lay fallow. I shut off the ignition and left the keys dangling.

I grabbed *The Stand* from the seat beside me, and then on second thought ejected the Erasure tape from the deck and slipped that in the back pocket of my jeans. I left the car without locking up.

The night was humid and barely cool. The sky was beginning to lighten up with the approach of dawn. Dark clouds hung still in the sky, surrounded by a blue field of stars that were starting to burn out.

My feet were bare and blistered. I crossed the field until I met the farm road, then followed that back to the interstate. At the overpass, I took a moment to decide which way. I could head north, back to Minneapolis—or south to Milwaukee or Chicago or even back to Isthmus City. But then I figured Minneapolis would be a bad idea because of Jeff Abbott—so I headed down the on-ramp that merged into the southbound lanes. My final destination would depend on where the driver was headed.

All of a sudden, I felt like I'd just awakened from a nightmare feeling refreshed and totally alive. No longer could anyone connect me to the crime, were they ever to discover that one had even taken place. At best, the transvestite, whoever he was, would be listed as a missing person, and when the car was discovered they might assume the worst, yet without a body or witnesses they had no murder.

And I wasn't about to confess.

I was practically back where I started—although slightly worse for wear without boots, Big Gulp cup, or gun—in my blood-spattered sweatshirt and jeans, with a two-dollar bill and seven pennies in my front pocket, an Erasure tape in my back, holding the Stephen King book in one hand, and thumbing for a lift with the other.

4

At dawn, bugs were chirping in the fields. The sun rose beyond a bank of trees and seemed to hover there in a veil of pink mist. I heard the sound of a tractor starting up in a distant field and the occasional *whoosh* of a passing car on the highway. My feet were rubbed raw from walking the rough pavement. I'd been ambling in a sideways, ass-backward fashion, keeping my eye on the sparse traffic behind me so that I wouldn't miss an opportunity to attract some driver's attention. I probably didn't stand a chance. I was bedraggled—some might say scary looking—suffering from lack of sleep, with my long hair and ratty clothes. No one could have possibly mistaken me for a "nice" boy, and even those few who might want to pick up a hitchhiker would likely have a second thought when they saw me.

Yet soon, an eighteen-wheeler was blowing its horn as it overshot my location, before stopping along the shoulder many yards ahead. The horn blew again: *Hurry up*.

I ran despite the sharp pain in my feet.

The rig stood still, its engine idling with a heavy rumble. The passenger door swung out for me before I'd reached the cab. I leapt up onto the ladder and climbed in, tossing *The Stand* onto the seat before I sat down.

"Thanks." My voice was raspy. I no longer sounded like me. I closed the flimsy door perhaps too hard.

The driver was unshaven with a bushy, untrimmed mustache. His arms were bulky from both muscle and flab, and his sizable paunch hung over jeans that were too tight and probably didn't quite reach high enough in back to cover his ass crack. He wore a green John Deere cap on his head, out of which straggled his brown hair, long and wispy; underneath that cap, he was probably bald as ol' Ben Franklin.

"What's your name, kid?" he asked.

"Jesse. What's yours?"

"Don't matter. Where you goin'?"

"Where are *you* going?" I asked back.

"Pittsburgh," said the driver. His laugh was a snort. "But don't think I'm takin' you there."

"Chicago's fine, then."

"Chicago, eh?" The driver slapped my thigh so hard it stung. "We'll see."

Another queer, I thought. *Just my luck.*

With a loud, hydraulic hiss, the beast came to life and rumbled forward. Several upshifts later, we were cruising at full speed along the highway. I relaxed in my high seat, glancing down at the shoulder just outside my window and at the careening reflector posts. I began to nod off, resting my head against the window like I'd done on the bus.

"Jesse, you look bushed. Why don't you hop on in back? There's a bed back there, you can stretch y'self out." The driver hitched his thumb back over his shoulder. His sideways grin showed off a set of yellow choppers speckled with flecks of tobacco.

I mumbled my thanks and turned to climb over the back of the seat, into the shell in back. As I was halfway through, the driver swatted my butt as if to help me inside; it stung smartly, like the slap on my thigh. But I was so exhausted that I had no will to fight back and so said nothing but simply crawled onto the bed and shut the curtains. Within minutes, I was out cold, sleeping facedown on a pillow that smelled cloyingly of the truck driver's sweat.

I slept but had no dreams. . . .

5

I awoke crushed beneath a vast weight, clammy palms on my back. My hands were behind me, and someone was sitting on them. I couldn't have slept long. I was lying on a bed but for the moment couldn't remember how I'd got there. Then I smelled the truck driver much more strongly than before and realized what was happening to me.

The rig had been brought to a stop somewhere. The engine was idling. We were at a standstill.

Without a word, the truck driver stuck the knotted end of a pair of socks into my mouth and tied them harshly behind my neck, stretching my lips back in a rictus grin. The bulky knot depressed my tongue and kept my jaw uncomfortably open. A pair of handcuffs were slapped onto my wrists and locked painfully tight so that it hurt even to try to move my hands. The weight of him on top of me eased somewhat as he reached underneath to unbutton my jeans in a single strong ripping motion and then yanked the denim down over my ass, to my knees.

I growled from behind the sock gag as the driver's sweaty hands groped at my flesh from my chest down to my naked flanks. My smelly sweatshirt was pulled up around my shoulders, leaving most of my back bare. I struggled under his weight, but I was going nowhere. The driver grabbed a handful of hair and yanked my head back like he was holding onto a horse's mane.

"Jesse-boy," he whispered, "you're gonna *love* this."

"Mmph!" I said. *Get off of me, you queer!*

His hands found my buttocks and, gripping them firmly, pried them apart.

"Oh, yes," he said—a gruff, smoker's voice. "Nice li'l beaver you got there, boy. Purty li'l thang."

The driver stuck a spit-slicked finger up my hole.

"Tighter'n my bitch's twat."

"Mmph!" I tried to rock out from under him but could hardly move. I tried to relax my butt so it would be less painful. The next thing I felt wasn't a finger.

I bit down hard on the gag. The cloth had absorbed whatever moisture had been left in my mouth. My tongue and the roof of my mouth were dry, and I could no longer even swallow. I felt like I was going to choke.

The man's fat belly slapped against my ass. With each thrust he went all the way in. It wasn't until he pulled my hips up off the bed and reached underneath to grab my dick that I realized I was hard myself.

"I said you was gonna love this!" he said. He had me up on my knees now, my face pressed against the pillow, my weight resting on my shoulders, my ass up in the air like a perfect whore.

No, I thought. *No, goddamnit!*

I was ashamed and humiliated.

You think you're not a queer—well, baby, I'm gonna turn you into one.

The man shoved me back down upon the bed.

"Fuckin' faggot!" he said. "You got off on that!"

He punched my ass hard, and I let out a muffled cry of pain. The truck driver pummeled me with both fists and then began beating my thighs. Tears sprang to my eyes, and my jaw muscles tightened against the pain. He grabbed me roughly by the shoulders and turned me around so that I was sitting up and leaning against the wall of the cab shell. He

36

yanked my jeans down to my ankles and sat on my legs. My cock had grown terrifically soft.

"You thought you could get a free fuck, huh, faggot?"

I tried pleading with him with my eyes, but he landed a firm fist in my stomach, knocking the wind out of me. I doubled over, gasping. The driver left me alone while I struggled to breathe, but when at last I was able to fill my lungs, he yanked my by the hair against the wall once more and punched me in the ribs.

"Fuckin' sissy cry-baby!" he said, and landed another punch to my gut. "Pansy-assed little *fuck!*"

I'd firmed up my stomach muscles as best I could; it was all I could do to protect myself. He had planted all of his two-hundred-plus pounds on my legs, and I felt that if he moved, my legs might break. The truck driver was using me as a human punching bag, slamming into my gut, my chest, my shoulders and biceps.

I took it in the face a couple of times; the sock gag probably kept me from biting off my tongue. Salty, warm blood trickled into my mouth. One of my eyes swelled shut. The other I simply kept closed; I didn't really want to see any more of this.

Finally, he seemed to have had enough and simply stopped.

I attempted to catch my breath, but with the gag in my mouth and mucus filling my nose, it was difficult. I leaned against the wall for support, breathing uneasily and feeling like I was going to pass out.

The truck driver got off me and climbed back into the cab. The engine roared to life. The hydraulic brakes hissed. Suddenly, we were moving again, the huge tires humming along the interstate.

I was much too sore to move so remained where I was,

aching and bleeding, half-naked, bound and gagged, my vision obscured by tears and a gross swelling around my eyes. I heard loud country music and the occasional hoot of laughter from the cab. But I was so worn out from the beating that the vibrations of the cab lulled me to sleep.

6

I lay in a grassy ditch. The sun was much higher in the sky and had warmed, maybe burned, my skin.

I rose to my feet with difficulty, not realizing how much pain I was in. My ribs were sore, but I didn't think they were broken. I was dressed in my blood-spattered jeans and sweatshirt, but with bloody socks on my feet—presumably the socks the driver had used to gag me with. My jaw was sore from the gag and from being struck in the face. My eye remained swollen shut. I could hardly stand upright from the pain in my stomach, so I remained slightly hunched over as I tried to walk.

I scanned the tall grass where I had been dumped but found no trace of my Stephen King book. It was probably still sitting on the front seat of the cab—a memento for the truck driver and his latest rape.

I'd thrown the gun away too soon. I should have hung on to it long enough to drill a few holes through the truck driver's greasy skull.

I didn't know where I was, but I could see an interstate overpass in the distance. Turning around, I found myself directly in back of a twenty-four–hour truck stop with a filling station and a café that said on its sign BEST DAMNED COFFEE IN ISTHMUS CITY.

So I was back.

A couple of eighteen-wheelers were parked in back of the truck stop, but the parking lot was largely empty. I racked my brain trying to remember what my assailant's rig had looked like but thought that neither of these trucks bore any resemblance. It was the height of morning, so most trucks were likely out on the road already. The guy who had picked me up was probably past Chicago by now—if he was even going that direction.

I walked gingerly across the warm asphalt, toward the café, where I spotted an empty phone booth standing along the shadowed side. I went inside the booth and closed the door. I dug into my front pocket and pulled out the seven pennies and the two-dollar bill. Neither would be of any use. I could go inside the café and get change for the two, but I didn't want anyone to see me like this; they might call the cops, and cops weren't exactly my kind of people.

I picked up the receiver and listened to the dial tone. I thought about calling my ma down in Texas. I could call her collect and tell her what I'd done—tell her about stealing the gun, the money, and the boots, and about the transvestite and the chimney and how I'd run from it all. I hadn't talked to her in a couple years. She was probably wondering where I was, if I was even alive; she was sure to accept the call. I could confess to her and maybe everything would be all right. But I knew what she would say—that I should go to the cops and tell them everything.

No—I couldn't call her. I was awfully scared but would rather stay that way than turn myself in.

Another telephone number popped into my head out of nowhere. This one was local. I remembered it number for number. I'd still have to call collect—and it might not be accepted—but it was worth a try.

"Wisconsin Bell, how may I help you?" asked the operator

in a high-pitched, effeminate man's voice. He sounded like the transvestite.

Hey, baby, want a ride?

"Yeah." My voice was dusty and my tongue felt thick. "I'd like to place a collect call—555-2140."

"Your name?"

I thought for a moment. The man might take a collect call from anybody, in which case I could use my own name. But perhaps I should use a more common one.

"John," I said. Everyone knew someone named John.

The phone rang four times before it was answered.

"Hello?" came the voice—sleepy, slightly annoyed.

"I have a collect call from John. Will you accept the charges?"

"Uh, yes," said the man, and cleared his throat.

I heard a *click* as the operator disengaged.

"Hello?" I said.

"Hello, who is this?" asked the voice. I couldn't make out his age.

"You still got a craving for monster dicks?" I asked.

What my Grandma Aylesworth would have called a pregnant pause hung in the air before the man acknowledged, "Uh, yes."

"Well, I got one."

"Are you at the bus station?"

"No." I described the truck stop to him. "Listen, I'm in a bit of trouble."

"You boys usually are," said the voice, with a sigh. "You want me to come and get you?"

"Yes," I said, and added, "please."

Three

1

"You're in dutch now, Jesse James Colson!"

From my hiding place underneath the trailer home, I watch her small bare feet come down the cinderblock steps, followed by the smaller, hairy feet of our dog, Gene.

"Come on, Gene Colson," she says excitedly, trying to whip up the dog. "Go get that boy! Wher-r-re's Jesse? Where is he, huh? Go on, go get him! Find my Jesse!"

I've always thought it weird that not only has Ma chosen to name the dog after my runaway pa but also that she persists in using the last name of Colson whenever she addresses the mutt. She herself has long since reverted to her maiden name of Margaret Aylesworth and likes to be addressed as "Miss," if you please. Meanwhile, I'm stuck with the hated last name of Colson—hated because my pa, the real Gene Colson, vanished off the face of the earth when I was like about four years old.

The dog Gene Colson, on the other hand, is an eight-year-old Heinz 57 splotched with longish yellow, white, and brown hair, with a rust-colored patch over one eye. He is friendly and doesn't deserve the abuse he gets at the hands of my ma.

Gene immediately comes scurrying under the trailer, having easily sniffed me out lying there in the dirt. Gene's tongue washes my face until I'm all slimy with saliva. The dog's wagging tail dislodges dust and spiderwebs from underneath the trailer.

"Go away, Gene!" I whisper, pushing the dog away. "Shoo!" My voice cracks, too loud by far.

Already I see my ma crouched down and looking straight at me, holding back her hair to keep it from falling in the dirt—but it's too dark in the shadow of the trailer for her to see much of anything.

"Jesse, you come on out now, hon. It ain't safe." Ma always says that—as if the trailer's in danger of toppling off its cinderblock foundation any minute. We've lived there all my life, and it hasn't yet fallen or even been struck by a tornado. We've got old tires on the roof to try and keep it from blowing away in a storm, but still the trailer seems pretty sturdy and I don't ever feel like it's going to come tumbling down on my head. Under the trailer has always been my most convenient hiding place.

I come out on the other side of the trailer home, Gene playfully biting at my bare heels. My clothes are dirty; when I try to wipe my wet face with my shirtsleeve, the dirt simply sticks to the liberal coating of dog spit and streaks my face with mud.

My ma comes around from the other side brandishing a rolled-up newspaper. Her trim figure is dressed in jeans and a flowery print top. Her auburn hair tumbles down past her shoulders, pulled back from her forehead and held by a white terry-cloth headband. She'd be beautiful up there in the warm light of late afternoon if it weren't for the hard expression on her face—the firm set of her lips, the manic gleam in her eyes, the cords pulling taut on her neck.

"Look at you!" she says through clenched teeth.

I try to shrink away from her, but she's too fast for me, grabbing my wrist with a firm grip and swatting my bottom with the newspaper. I try to squirm away, but she won't let go. She drags me around to the front of the house, sits on the front steps, and throws me over her knee—this in full view of the whole neighborhood.

"You little sneak thief!" she yells. She tosses aside the newspaper and begins smacking me with her hand. "Where's that ten dollars?"

"What ten dollars?" I say. I've got the crisp bill right in the front pocket of my jeans.

Gene jumps up and down excitedly, barking and wagging his tail.

"Mama's ten dollars. The ten you *stole* from me."

"I didn't steal nothin'!" I say. She smacks my butt with her open palm, and I shout, *"Yee-ow!"*

"You keep your hands out of your mama's purse, mister!"

The neighbor ladies are coming out of their trailers tentatively, sneaking a peek at what's going on. They're all around the same age as my ma, but what children they've got are a lot younger than me. In the entire trailer court, I've got no other kids my own age to play with. They're all either babies or little snot-nosed runts fresh out of their diapers.

"Ow! Ma, stop!" Slung over her knees, I've got a good view of the neighbor ladies standing there gawking. "You can't do this! I'm too old!"

"Never too old to be spanked," Ma says. "You're a lousy thief and a liar like Gene Colson!"

The dog barks.

"Not you," says Ma to the dog. Then she calls out to the

neighbor ladies, her closest friends: "Come on out, girls! I want you to see what happens to a little sneak thief when he goes and gets himself caught! I caught him swiping money from my purse."

"Ma, stop! Ow!" My butt is really getting sore.

But she won't stop. The neighbor ladies are gathering in a small circle out in the gravel cul-de-sac and gabbing among themselves. Gene is barking nonstop.

I can't stand it. I kick and struggle and try to get away. If I could escape, I'd simply keep on running and never look back—I'd go off and find my pa. But my ma's grip on me is too strong and she won't release me. The more I struggle, the harder she spanks. I'm shrieking now, and the neighbor ladies are egging Ma on.

"That-a-way, Margie! You show him!"

"Whup him good!"

"Give him what he deserves!"

My butt is raw even though Ma's spanking me through my jeans. Suddenly I feel this warm wetness in my crotch and realize I'm peeing my pants.

"Oh, my God!" says Ma, and pushes me off. "Ick!"

I fall to the ground, watching helpless as the dark stain spreads from my crotch down the leg of my faded jeans. I try to cut off the flow, but my bladder must be overfull and now it's letting loose. I stand up quickly to get off my sore butt.

Gene is jumping up and down, barking. He hasn't joined in on so much excitement in a long time.

"Just look at you!" says Ma, raising her voice higher. "You sure ain't too old to be spanked. You're wetting your pants like a little baby."

The neighbor ladies are laughing, some patting their own babies held over their shoulders.

"I'm not a baby!" I protest.

"Jesse James, you get out of those clothes before you step one foot in that house. You are a pile of filth from head to toe. And you give your mama back her money."

I fish in my front pockets and pull out the newly soggy ten-dollar bill. I hand it to her and say, "Here."

"Oh!" Ma shrieks, holding it by the tips of her fingers and crinkling up her nose. "Oh, my Lord! Jesse, you get out of those duds this instant!"

"But—" I look over my shoulder at Ma's friends, who are still watching and whispering into each other's ears.

"Now, young man," says Ma.

I stand there dumbfounded.

"Your mama has spoken!"

I remove my T-shirt and use it to wipe the slime from my face. I hesitate before unbuttoning my jeans.

"Didn't you hear a word I said?" She sighs in exasperation. "Go on. Don't mind the girls. Believe me, Jesse, you've got nothing they'd want to see."

The neighbor ladies let out a whoop.

I undo the button and unzip the zipper, then pull down my pants, keeping my back turned from the neighbor ladies. I keep my legs together, bending over and pulling the damp denim all the way down to my ankles.

"You do that just like a girl," says Ma.

I feel the blood rise to my face. I step out of my jeans and leave them on the ground. I'm down to my plain white briefs, now stained yellow and clinging wetly to my skin. I try to get past her and up the steps without having to take them off too, but she blocks me.

"You peed your panties, now take them off."

"But—" I protest yet again.

"Oh, for goodness sakes!"

45

With that, she reaches out and yanks down my briefs with both hands, leaving me stark naked.

I try to cover myself, but Ma bats my hands away. As she stands up, holding my dirty clothes bundled in her arms, she looks down at my crotch and sees what has recently begun happening to me.

"Since when did you start growing those little curly hairs?" she asks, in a lilting tone of voice that seems much more gentle and concerned. Distracted momentarily, she then comes back to herself and says, "Now you run along inside and draw yourself a nice hot bath."

I burst into tears and bound up the few steps into the trailer, my brain still echoing with her cruel voice and the laughter of the neighbor ladies.

"Come on, Gene Colson," I hear her say. "We'd best go in and fumigate these clothes."

Gene barks and comes skittering inside, his untrimmed claws clicking on the linoleum.

I close and lock the bathroom door. I turn on the bathwater full blast to keep my ma from hearing me cry. Gene scratches at the door and whines. I see his front claws trying to dig under. As the steam rises up from the tub, I look down at the hairs that have sprouted from my crotch in the last few weeks and wonder what exactly is wrong with me. . . .

2

By the time I'm fifteen, I've long since come to grips with my pubic hair. I jack off at least three times a day and am privately proud of the size of my cock. I've got five issues of *Penthouse* my uncle has given me hidden under my mattress, and I'm particularly turned on by the "Forum" section, in which *real people* recount their wildest sexual adventures. The length of the cocks described is always given in exact inches—usually at least twelve; this prompts me frequently to measure my own erect dick to see if it's grown any past what I've found to be its normal ten. I keep a box of tissues handy on the lamp table so I can clean up messes in a hurry, and I'll often forgo homework in favor of stroking myself.

I've gone through a growth spurt that has given me not only more height but broader shoulders and bigger muscles as well. The previous year as a freshman, I'd been tapped by the gymnastics coach to join the team; the daily workouts before school have built up my body—arms and chest in particular—and left me with a narrow waist with nicely hardened abdominal muscles.

This alteration of my physique has prompted my ma to alter my clothes, as well.

"They just don't fit you right," she says one day when, at her request, I'm modeling a new pair of jeans she's brought home.

"What do you mean?" I'm standing in front of the TV, blocking her view of *Donahue.* She's sitting across from me on the couch, one highly glossed red fingernail hanging between her teeth. "They feel fine to me," I say.

Ma uncrosses her legs and rises to her feet. "Jesse, darling, don't you see? Take off your shirt, I'll show you."

Grudgingly, I comply. The room is cold, and goosebumps come out all over my already-hairy chest. I notice with embarrassment that my nipples are hard.

Ma sticks her fingers in the waistband of the pants and tugs up on them. "This is much too high, too loose. They're snug at the hips but not at the waist. Store-bought jeans just ain't tailored for your physique, sugar-bear." She snaps the

47

elastic of my shorts, and my abs tighten up. She grabs her measuring tape and wraps it around my waistline. Her fingernails scratch my stomach; I wince. "I'm just going to have to take them in."

From that point on, every new pair of my pants goes through an alteration process in which the waist is lowered a few inches so they ride just above my ass in back and hang way below my belly-button in front. One day I see a photo of Jim Morrison my ma's got lying around and realize she's making my pants look just like his, even though mine aren't black leather. After this procedure, the pants actually do fit quite well and only serve to highlight my build. They make me seem longer in the torso and reveal my tapered waist to good effect. My growing muscles in the shoulders and chest stand out more visibly. I, myself, am suddenly impressed with the way I look and begin to carry myself differently, with a real swagger to my gait. Ma no longer buys me plain white jockey shorts, because they're too high-waisted, but instead gives me colorful, skimpy bikini briefs that won't ever show above the waist of my jeans. Like a lot of kids in Texas, I've worn cowboy boots since I was a kid and continue to do so. My usual shirt now is a T-shirt or muscle T or, in the summer, a tank top to show off my shoulders and pecs.

The girls in my sophomore class tend to laugh at me, but that's OK because I think they're silly, too. They don't know anything, and they look nothing at all like my favorite "pets" in the pages of *Penthouse*. I've got no desire to date any of them. They're nothing more than girls, when what I want is a real woman.

I think that I find her in the person of my English teacher, Miss Jensen. It's said that a guy can get an easy *A* in her class simply by wearing tight jeans, sitting in the front row, leaning back, and spreading his legs. I try to sit in front as often as possible, and the way my ma's fixed my jeans, I've always got a visible bulge in my crotch—spread legs or no—even without being hard. I always give Miss Jensen direct eye contact, trying to drill through her brain with my laser-beam eyes. Sometimes when she's talking to the class and everyone around me has fallen asleep, I'll reach into my jeans to readjust my dick. If she notices this rapid movement, I'll look up and flash my winningest grin. My first clue that she's starting to pay attention is when she begins sending me out on errands with a hall pass to deliver messages to other teachers or fetch a book she wants from the school library. She always chooses me so she can follow my ass out the door with her eyes.

Sometimes, when I'm in bed late at night jacking off, I like to fantasize about Miss Jensen keeping me after school, closing all the blinds and locking the door. I'd be sitting right on the corner of her desk, my cowboy boots planted firmly on the floor. On her knees, she would reach for my zipper with her red-lacquered nails and pull it down slowly over my bulge. My fly would spread open as she unzips me, thrust apart by the growing mass in my crotch. Her fingers would reach in and pull down the waistband of my bikinis to reveal my cock, which would spring to full erection as she opened her mouth to engulf it. She would leave lipstick traces at the base of my cock. Her sucking would feel like a special high-powered Hoover attachment. Then when I came, she would drink my full load and not spill a drop— and then she would thank me for it.

This fantasy never fails to turn me on—and I've got others about Miss Jensen. I like to imagine her in the poses favored by the *Penthouse* models, with her legs apart to show off her twat. I like to imagine me sticking my cock in there, seeing if she can take it. . . .

"Jesse, you're not paying attention."

"Huh?"

Sometimes my fantasies pop into my head in the middle of class, in a sense right under her nose. A moment ago she was naked and sweaty and begging for my cock. Now she's standing over me fully clothed, wielding a ruler. During my daydream, my cock has grown half-erect within the cramped confines of my jeans. I notice her eyes dart down to the tight mound in my crotch as I shift my legs further apart. "Um, sorry, Miss Jensen."

Miss Jensen smiles down at me and withdraws the threatening ruler. "We were talking about *All Quiet on the Western Front*. We're on chapter five."

"What page is that?" I ask.

"You haven't even bothered to read it yet, have you, Jesse?"

"No, ma'am," I say brightly.

I hear snickers from the class.

"Any of it."

"No, ma'am." I glance down at the paperback on my desk, its spine still uncreased, it's pages unbowed. It's a fresh copy, newly marked with the school's official PROPERTY OF stamp, with the unit number 76 scrawled in permanent ink below. "You mean this book right here?"

Miss Jensen sighs audibly. My classmates suppress giggles and sit in rapt attention. It's the first exciting thing that's happened all day.

"Mr. Colson," Miss Jensen says, "if someone told you that you could ace my class simply by wearing tight pants and stuffing a balled-up sock down their front, I'm afraid you were grossly misled."

My classmates laugh at me. My face turns bright red and I start feeling itchy under the collar, pinpricks all over my skin. Miss Jensen stares down at me, looking smug.

I push my books onto the floor and get up and leave the classroom, slamming the door behind me just as Miss Jensen is saying, "Jesse, wait!"

I'm the only one in the halls. I stop to get my jeans jacket from my locker, then walk out the nearest exit. I walk down the street to the bowling alley and spend all afternoon plugging quarters into a pinball machine, but it tilts on me all the time because I keep thrusting my hips to try and make the ball go where I want. The manager asks me to stop being so rough on it.

This is the first time in my life that I ever feel like killing anybody.

Four

1

A year after I killed the transvestite, the house on Williams seemed not to have changed much, other than some new graffiti. I went by every now and then to take a look—but only from outside. It was true, then, what they said—that a killer always returns to the scene of his crime—although, technically, this wasn't it, and I'd never once gone back to the lot in back of the Mertz Paint warehouse. Checking out the house on Williams was something I'd allowed myself every couple of months just to see if everything was still A-OK, but even then, I seldom took more than a glance over my shoulder.

I'd long since reached the conclusion that it wasn't abandoned after all but that some small-time investor had bought it with the intention of tearing it down and constructing condos, and the bottom had fallen out of the market or he'd absconded to Mexico with his partners' funds or something, and the house had simply sat there in real-estate limbo. By night, it was creepy, drawn up in the shadows, its lawn overgrown with weeds; but by day, it looked ridiculous—such a ramshackle old place. The red-brick chimney loomed tall over the bowed roof, and I often thought what a bitch it would be to sweep.

It's not uncommon for a chimney sweeper to find a dead cat in a chimney, not to mention a squirrel or a rat. Most homeowners never bother calling in a chimney sweeper, anyway, unless there's something clogging their flue altogether. No one notices they need a cleaning until smoke starts billowing up in their living room. Even then, few realize that chimney sweepers still exist outside of *Mary Poppins* until they open up their yellow pages and find one listed, right under their forefinger. Then they call to have him do the dirty work, and that's how the dead cats are found.

I was sure that if any human remains had been uncovered at the house on Williams, the story would have been on the front page of the *Isthmus City Sentinel,* which I read religiously every day for that very reason—although sometimes I wondered if the police hadn't already made the discovery and simply kept quiet so they could try and smoke me out.

2

Down on the dance floor, queerboys bumped and ground. It was the height of summer, and everyone had dressed down. Most wore shorts and tank tops, though these were of seemingly endless variety. Tanned flesh flashed under the colored lights; those on the dance floor both had it and flaunted it—gym-toned bodies cooked to perfection in the sun, with chiseled faces to match and hair gelled just so.

"What can I get you?" I asked a blond queerboy, sweaty and worn out from dancing, who had taken refuge on an open barstool. I had to practically scream above the pounding music before I could be heard by my customer.

"Bud Light?"

"You got it."

I went across to the beer chest and leaned over perhaps more than was necessary. This showed off my butt, which was clad—barely—in a tight pair of blue Spandex short-shorts that showed off my crack in back and my bulge up front. Atop I wore a loose-fitting Wisconsin State University tank top. The getup was all a tease, designed to earn big tips, and it worked. Tending bar at this joint could be lucrative on a busy night.

"Here you go." I opened the can and served it on a small napkin for the blond guy, who smiled appreciatively back at me.

"What's your name?"

"Jesse."

"You're kidding! Like Jesse James?"

"That's my name, don't wear it out."

"No way."

"Way!" I used the popular rejoinder. "Jesse James Colson. That's me."

"A real outlaw."

"Yeah."

"On the lam."

"That's right."

"Funny," said the blond guy. "And me a cop."

"No shit. Listen, I gotta help someone else a moment."

The bar experienced a sudden flurry of drink buying. I became occupied for the next ten minutes mixing cocktails, popping tabs on beers, showing off my ass, and generally keeping the queerboys entertained. But I kept sneaking glances at this one who claimed to be a cop. He was still sipping at his beer, and every time I looked his way he was staring at either my butt or my crotch.

"What, you undercover or something?" I asked, replacing the queer cop's empty can with a fresh one.

"Off duty is all. Want to see my ID?"

"Sure," I said.

He whipped out a trifold wallet from the back pocket of his shorts and pulled from it the official ID card issued him by the Isthmus City Police Department, which I grabbed and examined closely. First of all, the photo matched—a smooth-faced, tan, friendly queer with a full head of blow-dried, sun-bleached hair parted neatly at the side, and dark eyebrows. The name on the card read WILHELM T. GUNTHER, and it went on to give his home address. I committed it to memory and handed back the card.

"Officer Gunther?" I queried.

"Just plain Will." The cop laughed good-naturedly and pulled some bills out of his wallet to pay for the second beer.

I refused the cash. "Naw—on the house."

"Your boss let you do that?" asked Will Gunther.

"Why not? He's my partner."

"Business partner?"

"Domestic partner." I threw the cop a challenging look. I'd picked up on the lingo the queers were using. Domestic partner, my ass. The guy I was with called me his "midnight cowboy."

"Oh." Will's face fell in disappointment. "You mean that old fatty? Oh, excuse me, I'm sorry."

I shrugged. "Why? He *is* fat. But it's a good gig."

"A good gig?" This clearly went over Will's head.

"Sure. How do you think I got this job?"

With that, I had to go tend to some customers, besides which I'd fallen behind in the constant cleaning that was incumbent upon me. I had spills to wipe up, glasses to clean, empty cans to toss into the recycling bin—even tips lying around to be picked up. I couldn't afford to chat all night with this pretty-boy cop who wanted to suck my cock.

When I'd first come to Isthmus City a year ago, I would have been considerably less comfortable talking with a cop in such a manner. The very fact of the cop's sitting there would have bothered me to no end, and I would have wondered what ulterior motive he might have in coming to hang out with and talk to me, besides wanting my ass. But I realized this cop was simply and truly queer—lonely and looking to pick up some hot stud—and irresistibly drawn to me, which wasn't surprising when you stopped to think about it.

Will Gunther struck me as a rookie; not every cop was bold enough to come to a queer bar and announce himself to the barkeep—who, if he were anyone other than yours truly, would have been sure to spread the news around. In fact, not only was Will Gunther undeniably green as a cop but he was grossly naïve. It was goddamned stupid to flash your ID around like that and not expect the lookee to use it to some advantage or other.

"Jesse James!" called Will. "How's about another?"

"You got it." I pulled out a crisp, cold Bud Light and set it before him, grabbing the empty he'd duly crushed as evidence of his manhood. "You a rookie?"

"Just graduated the academy," said Will. "Last month."

"Never would have guessed. They all know you're a queer?"

"Ugh! I hate that word, I'm sorry."

"Guess I'm too PC for you."

I'd always used the word *queer*, long before gays my age had claimed it as their own. Where I'd grown up, a queer was a queer. Now when I said it, people thought I was hip.

"Whatever. They all know you're gay?"

"Of course. I've always been out of the closet."

"They give you any shit?"

Will shook his head, laughing. "No, listen, if anything it was a big help. I'm a white male—" He belched. "Excuse me—obviously—but I'm not that well educated and the competition is pretty fierce. Being gay gave me an 'in'—at least in this state. They couldn't have *not* hired me, if you know what I mean. I would have filed suit. It was cake."

"Cake, huh? Well, Will, here's to you," I said, clinking Will's can with the crushed empty I still held. My cock was stirring in my shorts as I thought about his lips curling around it. Will sipped his beer, and I tossed the spent one into the recycling bin.

"So you live with him?" asked Will, none too subtle. "What's his name . . . Saul, no, Simon something, Simon Scalia?"

"Scales," I said. "Simon Scales."

"That's it."

"Yeah, I live with him. He's got a nice house."

"I was here once on a call and met him. This is my beat, downtown here—David Three."

"Like Adam Twelve."

"Right."

"Oh, I've seen you." I recalled a young cop accompanying an older one on a call a month earlier when a fight had erupted on the dance floor. The older cop had asked all the questions, his blond charge mostly standing around gawking at the scenery. "So you had to come check us out on your off-time?"

"Yeah," said Will. "I'm not exactly what you'd call a social butterfly, and this past year I haven't had any time to go out and have fun. Mostly I've been hanging around with my lesbian cop friends. Now with academy over, maybe I can start dating someone."

"Like me?" I asked huskily, leaning closer across the bar—within striking distance. Playing along with him was getting me hot; I was obsessed with the idea of getting this cop to chow down on my bratwurst. The thumping music seemed to fade into the background. I had him in the palm of my hand.

"I'd like to get to know you," Will said.

"You like my butt, Will Gunther? Is that what you want?"

"Sure, you've got a great ass. But you seem nice, too."

"Give me your phone number. I'll call you."

Will pulled a business card out of his wallet that had the official logo of Isthmus City on it (a representation of two lakes with a thin strip of land in between), Will's name, and his affiliation with the Isthmus City Police Department, along with his phone number at work. I gave him a pen, with which Will neatly printed his home phone number on the back of the card. I planted a chaste kiss on his cheek—I knew this would get him going. Will leaned across the bartop and slipped his business card down my Spandex shorts, lodging it alongside my dick.

"Razor stubble," said Will, surprised.

"Simon likes it that way." I shrugged, nonchalant. Some queers were kinky, and the more I played along, the better I made out.

"Oh, I get it." Will smiled knowingly. "Simon says, Jesse does."

"Something like that."

"Listen, I don't want you to lose your job," Will said. "Does he get jealous?"

"Don't worry." I spoke absently, wiping the inside of the highball glass. "Simon's just an old queen, and what he doesn't know won't hurt him."

"That sounds awfully mercenary." Will raised a questioning eyebrow.

"That's the kind of world we live in," I said. "Or did your ma never tell you that?"

3

"What's cooking?" Simon called from somewhere upstairs.

"Pasta carbonara," I yelled back over my shoulder. The kitchen bar opened up onto the living area, with its spiral staircase, vaulted ceiling, giant ferns, and soft leather sofa and chair ensemble.

I tossed the fresh pasta from Marconi's into the kettle of boiling water on the back burner, while on the front one the chopped bacon in butter had turned properly translucent. I added some milk and red wine vinegar to the sauce.

"What did you say?" Simon was perched on the upper landing of the staircase, leaning against the banister, his terry-cloth bathrobe barely tied in place, exposing gray hairy cleavage down to his navel. It was typical of him to ask a question and not bother to listen to my answer, then ask me to repeat it.

I hated him.

"Pasta carbonara," I shouted.

"Are you trying to kill me?" Simon said lightly.

"Go get dressed, Simon. Five minutes."

"Oh, dear." Simon disappeared down the hall.

I stirred my sauce and allowed it to cook down a little. In a few minutes, I tossed the cooked pasta together with the butter-bacon sauce, poured in a raw beaten egg, and added grated romano cheese and freshly cracked pepper from

Simon's brass Turkish grinder that was endorsed by Jeff Smith, TV's "Frugal Gourmet." Along with the main course, I would serve a red-leaf salad, an Italian red wine, and a fresh baguette from The Ovens of Normandy.

I was wearing my customary apron and, underneath, a pair of white Calvin Klein boxer briefs, just the way Simon wanted me. The apron was narrow at my chest so that my naked pecs poked out on either side; Simon liked to dress me in things that exposed my nipples.

By the time it was ready, Simon was bounding down the stairs, his white shoulder-length hair blown dry and flowing behind. He wore black square-rimmed designer glasses he'd picked up somewhere in SoHo in New York City, an open-neck polo shirt clinging to his sagging pectorals and ample belly. He had a silly grin on his face.

"Oh, how proletarian of you!" Simon said as he sat down to eat. He tucked his napkin into his open collar, staring with pleasure down at the pile of fresh rotelle pasta on his plate, smothered in a creamy, pale yellow sauce with flecks of pepper, cheese, and bacon. "My cholesterol will go through the *roof!*"

"But the red wine will clean up your blood," I added. I hung up my apron and sat down. "It's all give and take."

"Mostly take." Simon stuffed a red lettuce leaf into his mouth with a fork. I'd used a new bottled fat-free dressing from the store; I wasn't trying to kill anybody. If I really gave a shit, I would have resented the remark.

"Can I take the night off?" I asked, out of the blue.

Simon paused, still chewing. He washed down the bite with a sip of wine. "What for?"

"There's a movie at the Lyceum I wanted to catch, and tonight's the last night. I haven't had a chance to go, and now it's almost gone. Please?"

"Only if Timmy can cover for you," Simon said, digging into the rotelle swimming in greasy carbonara sauce. He was staring at my chest.

"I'll go call him." I got up from the table and went upstairs to use the bedroom phone in private. I called Timmy Matheson, a bartender Simon employed part-time and who had not been scheduled for tonight, and Timmy said he'd be happy to fill in and earn some extra bucks. It was settled, then, and I hung up. Then I dialed the home phone number Will Gunther had given me.

"Yeah?" came the voice.

"Will? Jesse. We're on for tonight. What time do you want me?"

"Hey!" said Will. "All right!"

Yeah, I thought. *I'm going to give you just what you want.*

4

"So when did you met Simon Scales?" Will asked, emerging from his kitchen and handing me an open bottle of Leinenkugel.

"Thanks," I said, and took a sip. "Last year. I'd just got into town and was kind of down on my luck. Simon took me in. He does that for people. I guess I owe him something. He taught me bartending and helped me get my license, taught me how to cook for him, then set me up at his club. I'm not paying rent or nothing. I provide him company. He lets me put my earnings from the bar away into an escrow account. He's real savvy with that stuff. I don't know a thing about finances."

Will sat down next to me, resting his arm along the back of the sofa, putting his feet up on the coffee table. We main-

62

tained an intense eye contact, even while knocking back our beers like a couple of good ol' boys. Will seemed pretty normal for a queer.

"What is he, sort of a daddy type?" Will queried.

"I guess."

"That turn you on? Older guys? Daddies?"

"No, not really. But it's a good gig."

"You said that before, when I met you. What, you give him sex, and he gives you whatever you want?"

"What the hell is this?" I stared him down, smirking.

"Sorry." Will looked away, at his beer. He swiveled his wrist and sloshed around the bottle before taking a gulp.

"No, actually, I don't mind telling you, if you want to know. He's got money and could buy anyone he wants, but he likes keeping me around. He's got a playroom in his basement."

"Playroom?"

"More like a dungeon."

"Sounds kinky."

"It is. Simon's a real pervert, into bondage and leather. You wouldn't believe half the shit he likes to do to me."

"And you do this just for his money?"

"No way, man," I said. "I work. I earn my money bartending. I do the other shit to keep the old guy happy, OK? If I didn't, he'd get tired of me and I'd be out on my ass. I'd rather go along than go hungry on the street."

"You always dress like this?" Will tugged at the left shoulder strap of my tank top, lightly brushing the tanned skin stretched taut across my pectoral muscle. I was also wearing a tight pair of stonewashed Girbaud jeans cut into knee-length shorts and turned up into cuffs, as well as a broad black leather belt with a plain silver buckle.

"I like everything tight," I admitted, smiling to show off

my teeth. "It turns me on. I'm always half-hard just walking down the street, thinking of everybody staring at my body. They say, 'Look at that fucking queer! What a slut!' I say screw 'em. I guess I get off on it. I catch queers eyeing me all the time, never my face, always my crotch. I guess I'm a fucking tease."

"You should become a police officer."

I laughed; I didn't quite follow Will's logic. "You just want to get into my pants."

"I'm serious."

"So am I." My hand fell automatically down into my lap, and I began stroking my dick through the denim. I wanted him to suck me bad.

"No, really," said Will, his voice rising with excitement. He seemed taken with his sudden inspiration. "Do you want to be a bartender all your life? Simon's kept boy?"

That's exactly what I was—kept boy, midnight cowboy, sex slave—any way you sliced it, I was a hustler, a whore, no better than that fat blond bitch I'd nearly killed my first night in Isthmus City.

"Get out of here," I said. "They'd never take me."

"Sure they would. Being gay makes you a shoo-in."

I held my tongue and held back my anger. I couldn't blow my cover, or my top. I'd wondered a lot in the last year if the transvestite's prophecy had come true—had he turned me into a queer? Or had it happened when I was raped by the truck driver? Was I even really a queer at all? I used to know for sure but didn't anymore. I'd always let guys suck my dick, hadn't I? I'd sucked dick myself, and fucked other guys, and been fucked . . . how could I think that I wasn't a queer? All these years of selling myself had really fucked me up. I didn't know which way was up. I didn't know what the hell I was anymore—whether I was still scamming queers or had been scammed myself.

"They can't turn you down," Will added.

"I wouldn't sue them if they did, anyway."

"They don't know that. Look, they're hiring now for the next class. I'll bring you an application from the chief's office. They pay a full salary during academy, more on graduation. It's not as tough as you might think. Some of my coworkers aren't all that bright, if you want to know the truth—but they know their police work. You'd make a great cop, believe me."

"Why?" I wanted to know. Will was off his fucking rocker.

Will shrugged. "You'd look awesome in uniform, for one thing. You've got that Tom of Finland kind of body—big chest and shoulders, tight round butt. I bet you've got a big cock."

"And?" I was getting hard just thinking about it. I'd known all along—all he wanted was my cock. Flattery could get you my dick shoved down your throat. "What else?"

"And I could use the company."

Will leaned over and kissed me, forcing in his tongue, which I accepted passively, though I tensed up a little. I set my Leinenkugel down on the coffee table and pulled Will down on top of me, thinking, *Yeah, I can handle this.*

"Hey, Officer Colson," he whispered in my ear. "What do you think of that?"

I directed his hand down to my zipper.

5

It was a few weeks later that I told Simon I'd passed my physical exam.

Simon was stretched out on the leather sofa leafing through the pages of *Architectural Digest*. "Of course you did. You're a healthy boy."

"Just one more hurdle to go." I sat down in a chair and sighed in relief. "The background check."

"You'll do fine," Simon said. "Did you see these pictures of Madonna's penthouse?"

"That's an old issue," I said. "You're not going to tell them anything, are you?"

Simon shoved his glasses back up on his nose and peered at me over the top of the magazine. "About what? I'll tell them you're a hard worker at the bar and do a great job taking care of me at home. What else is there to tell?"

"How you picked me up." I was twiddling my thumbs nervously. Simon could speak volumes under the right circumstances, and I was more than a little worried that during an interview with a shrewd detective, he might tell more than he ought.

"You think I'm going to admit I put my own phone number on the wall of a bus station tearoom?" Simon sat up and put the magazine aside, slipped his bare feet into suede moccasins, took a cigarette out of a lacquered Russian box on the coffee table, and lit it with his table lighter. "I've got a business reputation to protect, honey."

"I know. I just don't want you to say anything."

"Believe me, Jesse, I'm not about to tell them that I drove out to the truck stop and brought home a washed-out drifter who looked like a ripped-up rag doll. I know how foolish it would look to them. They wouldn't understand."

"You're an angel of mercy, Simon," I said. Sometimes I really wanted to cause him some serious harm. "I don't mean to sound ungrateful. I just don't want them to learn anything that could jeopardize my chances."

Simon stood up and stretched, reaching his arms up toward the cathedral ceiling and flexing his fingers. "I'm not about to do anything to screw this up."

"Not consciously," I said.

"Oh, give me a little credit!" Simon reached out and ruffled my hair. "It's exciting, one my boys becoming a cop."

Simon Scales had been doing this since 1971, taking in street trash and turning them into productive members of society—ever since starting up his disco, Major Tom's Rocketship, which had since been renamed Glitz and was now long overdue for another name change. He had shown me photos—some naked—of the guys that had come before me, as well as letters and Christmas cards he still received from his "boys," all of whom had benefited from his benevolence in some fashion and continued to acknowledge their debt. One owned his own nightclub in Atlanta, another had become a successful Chicago businessman, and another more recently had become a steward on United Airlines. In his own way, Simon was quite the philanthropist, helping his boys put away their earnings or even helping out with small loans that were always paid off, in time. During the year I'd been with him, Simon had forced me to watch *Boys Town* several times. "I'm Spencer Tracy," he would say, "and you're Mickey Rooney."

"So what are you going to tell them?" I asked. I didn't want him telling anybody that he picked the clothes I was to wear for the day, or that he kept my body shaved, or that he had an S&M "playroom" that was hidden behind a bookcase in the basement.

"I'll say that I met you at a friend's party shortly after you moved to Isthmus City—"

"Whose party?" *Details, Simon—details.*

"Oh, I don't know." Simon wiggled his fingers. "Brian Bellman's. It was May, right? Brian always throws his garden party around then."

"OK, so how did I move in?"

"I told you I had all this room in my house and you could move in temporarily until you found a place."

"And?"

"And the rest is *her*story." Simon shrugged. "What else can I say? You moved in and you stayed, and I hired you at the club. You've been a loyal employee, and a real . . . *asset,* so to speak."

"Don't tell them that."

"You do attract business in those getups I bought you. I never knew a boy quite as . . . *up front* as you."

"Cut it out." I was terse.

"You rake in tips like nobody's business."

"You can't tell them that. You've got to control yourself. When they talk to you, just give them the facts."

"The *false* facts," Simon corrected, tidying up the coffee table and stacking the magazines in a neat pile.

"Exactly. The agreed-upon story. Mine's got to gel with yours, understand? Any discrepancies and I'll never pass. You tell it just like you told me, OK? Only no embellishments."

"No baroque detail."

"That's right."

"No recounting how I truss you up in my playroom."

"That goes without saying," I said. I couldn't wait to get the hell away from him and for him to keep his greasy mitts off me. If I made the cut and became a cop, I'd be pulling in my own salary without having to put out for anyone or having to degrade myself.

"I'll tell them you don't drink, you do smoke but you're trying to cut down, and that you always wear your rubbers."

"Simon," I warned. "You're making me nervous here."

"Oh, all right, all right! I can't help myself. But I promise I'll be good with the nice detective. I do have a business persona, you know. Without it, Tommy Thompson would never invite me to his parties in Madison. I *am* capable of holding my tongue. I'll do you proud. You couldn't get a better recommendation than what you'll get from me. I've got the magic touch. Electricity *flows* through my veins."

Simon scuffed his slippers on the carpet on his way over to where I was sitting. When he touched my face, his fingertip gave off a small electrostatic shock.

"See?" Simon said, and kissed me on the lips the way my ma used to.

My muscles tensed up. I wanted to hit him.

Or something.

6

I went into Glitz early that afternoon, before anyone else was scheduled to come in. I needed time to do some cleaning up, but I also had a phone call to make from Simon's office phone—the one with the WATS line.

"Hello?" came the woman's voice on the other end.

"Ma?"

"Jesse," she stated. A great pause hung across the thousand miles of phone line. "Jesse, is that really you?"

"Yeah, Ma, it's me."

"You . . . oh, my God . . . I'd convinced myself you were dead."

"Ma—"

"How could you leave me like this, not knowing what had become of you?"

"That's why I'm calling."

"Years, it's been years, I don't know how long, I hardly remember anymore," she said as if talking to herself.

"Ma, I need a favor."

"A favor? You dare to—"

"Ma, it's important."

"You ask for a favor after what you've done to me? You're just like Gene Colson—"

"Ma—"

"Running out on me like that. Must be in your blood. You're no different from that snake."

"Ma, if you don't shut up I'm gonna hang up on you."

"Jesse, don't."

"I'm serious, Ma. I thought you'd be happy to hear from me, but I guess I was wrong."

"Well . . . well, of *course* I am, honey. I . . . I missed you something *awful.*" Suddenly she sounded like a little girl.

"Yeah, sure." I rolled my eyes. "I bet you did."

"I'm sorry, Jesse James. Don't hang up."

"Don't call me that," I said through gritted teeth.

"What?" Ma said innocently. She knew very well how it bugged me.

"That Jesse James shit. That's like naming your kid Adolf Hitler. Jesse James was a cold-blooded killer."

"It was your father who named you! Go blame him—if you can find him." I thought I heard her laugh a little.

"Ma, don't get hysterical."

"I'm not hysterical!"

"Come on, Ma, just settle down."

"I don't have any money, you know."

"I'm not looking for money. I'm doing all right, really."

"Then what the hell do you want from me?"

"I've been working as a bartender. But I'm trying to become a policeman—"

"You, a cop?" She laughed. "My little badboy?"

"Shut up, Ma, I'm serious. It's a real opportunity and I don't want you to blow it for me, OK?"

"They must be desperate. Where are you, Detroit?"

"No, Ma. Isthmus City. That's in Wisconsin. I passed their test. I impressed them in my interview. I just passed my physical today. The only thing is, they have to conduct this background check. I gave them your name. They're going to be trying to contact you."

"I don't want to talk to nobody."

"Come on, Ma. Don't let me down—"

"I don't owe you a blessed thing. I did my part. I raised you. You left. I washed my hands."

"Ma, if you don't talk to them and help me get this job I'll never speak to you again, you got that?"

"Go ahead, Jesse. I'm a survivor. If you never called me again, it would be no big deal. You just go on, then, pretend your mama doesn't even exist!"

"Stop it," I said. She'd always driven me up the wall.

"What, you want me to tell them you were a lovely boy, easy to raise, never a bit of trouble?"

"Yeah, why not?"

"I know you, Jesse James Colson." Her laugh was deep and throaty. "You're pulling a fast one on them, and I don't want any part of it."

"Fine. Forget it. Forget I even called. I'm hanging up."

"Wait!" she screamed.

"You don't need me, right? You're such a goddamned survivor!"

"Don't hang up, baby, I need you."

"You know why I ran away?"

She said nothing.

I let her hang there for a moment. "To get away from you, that's why."

"Honey, don't—" Now she was crying into the phone, or pretending to.

"That's right, and you know it. I had to get the hell away from you before I killed myself."

"Jesse, wait, you can't—"

But I'd given up on her. The call was going nowhere and it would only be a waste of Simon's money. I slammed the cheap phone down in its cradle, causing it to chirp once, briefly, as if it were a bird and I'd killed it.

Goddamnit, I really *hated* her.

Five

1

I'm lying on the couch in Simon's vast living room. All the lights are off, yet the vast space is illuminated by the blue moonlight coming in through the front picture windows. The ferns begin to rustle as if a window has been left open. The pages of the magazines on the coffee table turn by themselves, as though caught by a draft.

I see all this despite my eyes being closed. Somehow I'm unable to open them but at the same time able to see. I cannot move. My limbs would never respond even if I wished them to. My arms lie folded, locked together. My legs are crossed, frozen in place. The leather upholstery is cold against my skin, my own body heat even unable to warm it up. Every few seconds I shiver uncontrollably. I feel none of the drafts affecting the ferns and the magazines; I'm simply chilled to the bone.

The fireplace is spotlessly clean. My closed eyes remain fixed upon the spot, waiting for something to appear. In a moment, something does. Moonlit fingers with clawlike fingernails reach down from the chimney and curl themselves around the bricks beneath the mantel. A pair of knobby elbows appear, and a hairless head hanging upside down. Its face is charred, features unrecognizable.

I want to get up and leave but cannot budge or even avert my

73

gaze. The figure rights itself, climbing out of the chimney and into the cramped space of the fireplace, naked and hairless from head to toe, glowing a dim and shadowed blue, except for its burned face, which is the gray-black of soot. It pushes aside the fireplace screen, unfolding its limbs like a praying mantis. It stands up and climbs down from the flagstones. The figure is gaunt, without muscle, skin stretched taut over its bones. Its once-feminine breasts are withered and sagging, with dark blue nipples splayed on either side. Its uncut cock is shriveled, its balls wrinkled up.

It steps gracefully across the small distance until it stands before me. I know that if I can only open my eyes, I can make it go away. The figure climbs on top of the couch and straddles my face, dangling its cock above my mouth. The cock grows within its sheath. The ancient foreskin parts to reveal the barrel of what I somehow know to be a .38 caliber revolver. The loose skin stretches back from the silvery barrel, which grows until the mouth of the gun nudges my lips apart and plunges down my throat. My teeth clamp down on the cold steel tube. I look up at the figure's skull-like face. Charred flesh clings to it in paper-thin layers that are peeling away, caught in the breeze from the open window. Its glassy eyeballs seem ready to drop from their too-wide sockets. I want to beg for mercy. I know that if only I can open my eyes, I'll be safe.

The figure reaches down with its blue fingers and, using its sharp fingernails, pries my eyelids open. In a flash of recognition, I understand that the figure is actually my ma come back for me.

Then the gun fires and I wake up in a cold sweat.

2

"A murder is like a marriage," Det. Harvey Bender told me with a perfectly straight face.

Before my class was issued our uniforms and let loose on

the street, I spent a couple of shifts riding along with Detective Bender, whose specialty was "person crimes"—including homicides, of which Isthmus City generally had three or four in the space of a year. I'd been able to count on the fingers of both hands the known murders subsequent to my coming to town, with room for one or two more, depending on how one chose to count a murder/suicide:

There had been a drug deal gone bad, in which the prospective buyer had slit the throats of the two dealers in the front seat of their Le Sabre.

A man had shot his wife and then himself in front of their four-year-old son.

A card shop owner on the Strand Street mall downtown had been shot in the head in a botched robbery attempt.

A sixteen-year-old had been shot during an argument outside John D. Hockstetter Memorial High School.

A mental outpatient who routinely invited homeless people to stay overnight in his apartment had been found stabbed to death—not, as it turned out, by one of his guests, but by an irate neighbor.

The latest had been an Isthmus City cab driver shot in the back of the head in another botched robbery attempt—this one with a juvenile culprit who'd used his father's nine-millimeter semiautomatic, which happened to have been loaded with hollow-point bullets; the victim had been buried in a closed coffin because Detective Bender hadn't managed to recover much of his head at the crime scene.

Bender had been either the primary or secondary investigative officer in each of these cases, all of which had been closed, half of them successfully prosecuted, the others still pending in court. In each instance, they'd had ample evidence to charge their suspect, who had always been apprehended within forty-eight hours of his committing the murder. Bender had a great track record, no doubt about it, but few of his cases had ever been more than routinely challenging—or so he confessed to me during a bright April twilight while we were cruising down Wisconsin Avenue toward the courthouse square at what was easily forty-five miles an hour in a twenty-five zone.

It was nearly two years since I'd killed the transvestite. They still hadn't found the body, and I still didn't know who he was. I think a part of me actually wanted them to find him.

Bender cut an imposing figure even while sitting behind the wheel of his unmarked Crown Vic. He was a tall, burly man with thinning, gray hair and a full beard, wearing a plaid short-sleeve shirt and grungy blue jeans and carrying a stainless steel snub-nosed Smith & Wesson .38 Special in a shoulder holster that he slung on his right. Chicken scratches creased the corners of each eye, and the lines across his forehead had become deep troughs; I pegged him in his late forties. His nose was rosy, probably from burst capillaries, which might have meant he was an alcoholic. The reddish-purple tip of a disfiguring scar poked out from under his beard, hugging his right cheek bone; he probably wore the beard to cover up the worst of it.

"Want a cigarette?" Detective Bender reached across with his left as if for his gun, but instead pulled a pack of Pall Malls from his right breast pocket. Suddenly steering with his knees, he tapped the pack until a few cigarettes poked out their heads, then pulled one free with his lips. He proffered the pack to me, and I grabbed a cigarette and allowed Bender to light it with the car lighter.

"Thanks," I said.

The detective took a long drag and then let loose a thick cloud of smoke through his nostrils. The open driver's window sucked out the smoke. I noticed a notepad affixed to the small corner of dashboard to the left of the steering column, presumably for Bender to scribble notes on while prowling around in his nondescript cruiser.

"All city vehicles are supposed to be smoke free," he said, "but I don't give a goddamn."

"I'm trying to cut down," I said, exhaling smoke. "I can take it or leave it."

"When I started, over in Patrol, you could smoke any-where—at your desk, in your vehicle, wherever. We used to have inspections before briefing, like it was the fucking military. Shoes had to be polished, buttons shined. Had to wear ties, for Christ's sake. Weren't any women, either—not a one. Now everything's different, and a damned sight better."

"Must have been before I was born."

"When was that?"

"Seventy-one."

Bender chuckled. "That's when I completed my tour of duty."

"Is that how you picked up that scar?" I asked.

"What scar?"

I figured Bender was pulling my wang but didn't pursue it further. My uncle had served in Vietnam and had never wanted to talk about it.

"Now what was I saying?" Bender asked while we made the one-way circuit around the La Follette County Court-house. The setting sun glinted off the windows of the old sandstone building. Bender squinted his eyes against the bright light as he turned the corner; I hoped he could see through the sunlight and haze, because I sure couldn't.

I remembered precisely what he had been saying. "You were giving me some bullshit about murder being like a marriage."

"It's no bullshit, Colson," he said, all seriousness. "Believe me, I've seen enough of both. I've been put through thirty-six homicides and three wives. The murders I figured out."

"I still don't get you," I said warily. This was the first I'd ever discussed murder theory with anybody. "A murder's just a simple act of violence."

We'd stopped at a traffic light. Bender turned to me and pulled a crooked smile. "There's nothing simple about it. The victim's name is always going to be linked up with the killer's, just as surely as if they'd been married by a priest. Once it's done, they can never be separated. Think of Oswald and JFK. Or Ruby and Oswald, for that matter. James Earl Ray and Martin Luther King. Charles Manson and Sharon Tate. Mark Chapman and John Lennon."

"Who's John Lennon?"

"Colson, I hope you don't turn out to be a shit."

"Just kidding," I assured him, flashing my badboy grin.

Ever since that night, I'd debated whether hiding the body was such a good idea. I'd been lucky not to get caught with the thing in the back of the car, lucky that no crackhead had come into the house while I was there. I'd had no connection to the transvestite; if I'd let them find the body, maybe I wouldn't still be worrying about it. If I'd have fled right away, I probably would never have met up with the trucker, and I never would have come back to Isthmus City.

All I know for sure is that I'd hit rock bottom and was unable to see my way out. The transvestite was at the wrong time, in the wrong place. All I ever gained was an unlucky two-dollar bill—which I still kept around my apartment somewhere—and a nightmare that wasn't likely to end anytime soon. . . .

An alert tone sounded over the radio. Bender reached across with his left and turned up the volume.

"City and listening units," came the dispatcher's voice. "Report of multiple shots fired, fifteen sixteen Maugham Terrace. Possible injured party in second-floor hallway. Fire Rescue en route. Charlie Four?"

"Charlie Four, copy," came a female officer's voice over the channel, siren already in the background. According to the second-detail schedule I'd been given, Charlie Four was Lydia Kurtz. I liked Kurtz; she was all right.

Bender gunned the squad and started flicking toggle switches on his console, turning on his siren and the magnetic revolving light that was currently resting on the dashboard next to his coffee mug.

"Get that thing on the roof, will you?"

I did as he asked. We were already passing cars left and right down Gilson Street. Units near the scene were reporting in over the radio in an orderly but hurried fashion. Everyone knew this was at least an attempted homicide. Bender was the highest-ranking person-crimes detective on duty, so this case would be his baby and he wanted to get there fast. I was along for the ride, my life decidedly in his hands. I wasn't sure he even saw the cars he was swerving around in his mad rush to get to the housing projects at Maugham Terrace.

Bender keyed his mike. "Twelve sixty-two," he said, reporting in with his call number. "I'm at—"

"Five hundred block of Gilson," I told him.

"Five hundred Gilson."

The dispatcher came back on. "Possible suspects fled in a brown-over-beige late-model four-door, possibly a Pontiac or Buick, last seen southbound on Kipling, partial plate James Mary Ida, possibly an eight or a nine."

"David Three, copy, I'm northbound at nine hundred

Kipling," came a male officer's voice. It was Will Gunther's. "No sign yet."

The dispatcher then came on and advised all units involved to switch over to a tactical channel. Steering with one hand, Bender reached over with the other and pressed the tac channel button without taking his eyes off the road.

A couple minutes later, Officer Kurtz's voice came back, huffing and puffing: "Charlie Four. . . . We're in the hallway . . . outside apartment two-B."

"Copy, Charlie Four," said Dispatch. "What's the status of the victim?"

"We've got a pulseless nonbreather here," she said. "Request a supervisor and an SI."

"Copy, Charlie Four."

Bender floored the accelerator and went through a red light at Tompkins. "Well, kid," he said, "sounds like some lucky couple just got themselves hitched."

3

The secret background check had proved amazingly smooth. Since the only arrests I'd ever had were as a juvenile, they weren't likely to have turned up any of those incidents unless they got them from my ma. She must have played along and kept her mouth shut, after all—but then that maternal instinct is pretty strong, and what reason would she have to sabotage the only real chance I'd ever had at a life?

They'd seen me as underprivileged and deserving of extra consideration. Plus, from the beginning, they'd thought I was a queer because Will Gunther had spread the word around somehow—and in Wisconsin, this was something of a trump card, since queers were protected by a statewide law.

After being accepted into the academy, I'd moved into my own apartment and started "seeing" Will. Word about that got around the department as well, which only served to confirm the rumors the chief's office had heard about me. But apparently, their investigation hadn't turned up a damned thing against me, probably because ever since running away from home, I'd stuck pretty much to myself. The only person aside from Simon who had ever employed me for long—Tom Latimer back in Denver—was dead, so they couldn't ask him a thing.

I'd done well in the academy, and once it was over, I was going to be an honest-to-God cop. My ma would be proud of me—and I was grateful for whatever help she might have provided—but I prayed that she wouldn't come up to Isthmus City and look me up now that she knew I hadn't ended up as carrion along the roadside somewhere.

4

We entered the hallway. Bender had his service weapon drawn, yet the only person we encountered aside from uniformed patrol officers was a black kid lying facedown, limbs sprawled, a dark, syrupy stain still spreading across the carpet from the hole in his head.

"Jesus," said Bender, halting before the body and replacing his gun in its shoulder holster.

One of the victim's legs lay halfway within the open doorway to apartment 2-B. Bender reached down and checked for a pulse, though the victim looked positively dead to me.

"Apartment's clear," announced Lydia Kurtz, her voice as gruff as a marine's. Following her out of the apartment was her backup, Jodi Sommers. The radio on Kurtz's utility belt squawked, the tac channel filled with the chatter of the multiple units out searching for suspects.

The hallway was so narrow, they had no choice but to disturb the crime scene in the process of securing the area. I noticed blood on Bender's fingers from having checked for the victim's pulse. He should have put on a latex glove before coming into contact with it, but it was too late now.

The victim was a light-complected black teenager. His face, though covered in blood, was intact; the right side of his head had been blown off, leaving the ear dangling at the lobe. At least two additional shots had struck his back, as evidenced by gaping holes and blood in the insignia area of his black L.A. Raiders jacket and a separate distinct pool of blood on the carpet that had oozed out from his midsection.

"Hey, Bender!" barked Kurtz from within the apartment. "Come here, have a look."

Officer Sommers stood and guarded the scene in the hall while Bender stepped through the doorway. I followed but tried to remain out of the way.

The apartment was a mess, and the destruction appeared recent. Holes had been punched all over the drywall, which itself was marked up with graffiti. The torn carpet was littered with empty bottles and cans, encrusted spaghetti and dried tomato sauce, dirty clothing, broken glass, and a few busted children's toys. The sickly sweet smell of garbage, along with the odor of urine, permeated the air. In plain view on the laminate counter in the kitchen were several empty plastic baggies containing small white flecks of what I'd learned during academy training was likely cocaine base, or crack. One of the burners on the gas stove had been left on, turned up high and glowing with bright blue flame.

"Check it out, Harve," said Kurtz, showing him the open door to the apartment. "No lock—no doorknob, even."

"Yeah, the landlord's a real fuck," muttered Bender. Then he turned to me: "We'll leave everything where it is until a special investigator can get here to take photographs and do evidence collection."

"Help him! Do something!" came a woman's angry voice from outside in the hallway. "Why don't you people do something?"

Bender and Kurtz hustled out into the hall to assist Sommers, who was physically restraining a young black female, preventing her from entering the crime scene. The woman wore a bright pink tank top and baggy blue jeans. Her collar-length hair was straightened, curled on the ends.

I tried to stay clear of the fracas.

"Ma'am," said Sommers, "calm down. There's nothing we can do for him now. Just go back to your apartment and stay there until we get a chance to talk to you."

"That's my brother!" said the woman. "You can't just let him lie there bleedin' to death!"

"You want to tell us his name?" asked Sommers.

"Bitch, I ain't tellin' you shit till you get a ambulance."

"Taneesha," said Bender, stepping between her and Sommers. "Let's go back to your apartment, all right?"

"I ain't goin' nowhere till I know what you gonna do 'bout Tyree!"

"Come on, Taneesha. Let's go inside." Bender grabbed her gently by the arm and led her back into her apartment, number 2-F, across the hall. She offered no resistance.

"Tyree didn't do nothin', Detective. He don't deserve this."

Bender was obviously known here and must have known some of the residents from past professional contact.

"Taneesha," said Bender in a gentle tone. "I don't think Tyree's going to make it."

"You think I don't know that?" she snapped. "You think I'm stupid?"

"Are you the one called nine one one?" Bender asked her.

"Maybe it was me, maybe it was Latricia."

I closed the apartment door behind us and noted a number of other people present. An older, obese woman was being comforted by a girl who looked like Taneesha's sister. Running pell-mell around the apartment were four children ranging from two to five years of age. Talking animatedly among themselves were some black youths who looked like gangbangers, dressed in black jeans and black L.A. Raiders jackets with matching baseball caps—identical to the costume worn by the victim. Their dress, as I'd learned from a narcotics officer, marked them as from the gang KGB, which stood for Kool Gangster Brohs.

"Those dyke cops give me the creeps," said Taneesha, but Bender seemed to ignore the comment.

Bender had more than he could handle. Each of those present would have to be questioned in private, and he couldn't let any of them go until they had given their statements. Some of them would likely end up going back to the station to be interviewed by other detectives. At the very least, Bender's and my presence would prevent them from further corroborating their stories, which no doubt they had been doing prior to our entrance. Why else would they be hiding in their apartment when one of their family had just been killed in cold blood outside their door?

I knew I was being suspicious, but I figured that with this job, it came with the territory. At least five minutes had passed since 911 had received the initial call—ample time for these witnesses to modify their stories if they were going to try to protect someone.

As Bender was asking Taneesha to sit down and relax, one

of the youths sprang from his seat and vaulted to within inches of Bender's face. With the perceived threat, Bender's left arm swung across toward his gun. But he didn't draw it.

"Back off, Kenny," he said. So he knew this one, too. "I said back off!"

Kenny stepped back a pace, shifting excitedly from one foot to the other. "It was me they was after, man," he said, breathing rapidly almost to the point of hyperventilating. "They was tryin' to kill *me*, man! Tyree just got caught in the crossfire."

5

In Bender's way of looking at it, this was his thirty-seventh murder/marriage.

He solved the case over the next two days and charged Kenny Doleman with the murder of Tyree James, with the two other KGB youths charged as accessories. There had never been any crossfire for Tyree to get caught in. Kenny had tried to pass it off as a hit from a rival gang, to the point of providing detailed descriptions of the parties supposedly involved. But there had never been any rival gang in the housing complex that night.

The killing had simply been an execution of one they thought had turned police informant, which, in fact, Tyree had. A narcotics officer confessed to Detective Bender that Tyree James had recently spoken to him, and that Narcotics had taken every precaution to keep his cooperation a secret. Somehow, Kenny Doleman had found out and shot Tyree James once in the back of the head, as well as twice in the chest, from a nine-millimeter semiauto. He and his KGB pals had managed to intimidate even Tyree's family members into cooperating and sticking to a prepared story. One of Tyree's own sisters, either Taneesha or Latricia (it was still unknown which), had made the initial call to 911 and given the bogus description of suspects fleeing in the four-door sedan. None in the James family had yet been charged with a crime, probably because their testimony would be needed when the case came to trial.

Bender's case against Kenny Doleman was rock solid. Special Investigator Terry Holcombe had tested Kenny's forearm for traces of gunpowder and come up positive. Blood spatter found on Kenny's Raiders jacket matched the victim's blood type. The murder weapon itself had been easily found, having been hastily hidden in the Jameses' laundry hamper in the bathroom of apartment 2-F. Kenny's fingerprints remained on the pistol despite someone's attempt to rub them off. The slugs recovered from Tyree's body were marked with striations matching them with the barrel of the recovered weapon. And even though Kenny still maintained he had nothing to do with it, his pals had confessed fully— at the same time and in separate interviews with different detectives—to what had really occurred, and each said that Kenny alone had fired the weapon that had killed Tyree.

"Kenny Doleman and Tyree James," Detective Bender said to me the next time I saw him after he'd got Kenny and company incarcerated in the La Follette County Jail. "From now on, you'll never think of the one without the other."

I stared at him stupidly.

"You understand me now?"

I nodded glumly, and Bender walked away, satisfied.

I understood, all right. I understood only too well. My problem was, I'd never been given the opportunity to learn the name of my betrothed.

Six

1

Will was right; I did look awesome in uniform.

I'd demanded the more expensive cotton garments instead of the polyester we were expected to wear. Normally, the chief's office wouldn't allow us to spend our uniform allowance on the cotton, any more than they would let us spend it on a leather patrol jacket; such items would have to come out of our own pockets. But I faked an allergy to man-made fabrics and managed to get an exemption.

The pants were a little high-waisted, so I'd taken them to a Korean tailor and had her lower the waistline a little. They shrunk up a bit in the wash so that they clung nicely to my flesh, enshrouding my ass and my bulge in dark navy blue. I had my shirts similarly fitted so that they tapered down toward my waist. These alterations I paid for myself; the chief was unlikely to spring for them.

Of course, the overall look was diminished by my having to wear a Kevlar vest underneath the shirt and a bulky utility belt at my waist. The vest made my chest seem bigger but also more formless. I thought that—at least for the male officers—the manufacturer should mold the vest in the shape of a man's well-muscled chest, like the bronze breast-plates of Roman centurions. We could stretch our shirts over them and look like a platoon of goddamn superheroes. The utility belt—with service weapon and portable radio, in addition to expandable baton, handcuffs, extra live rounds, and high-powered flashlight—weighed a good twenty pounds and would make any officer seem wide in the hips. We carried around more shit than Batman. But at least with the alterations I'd got, my pants would never sag around my butt. I had a clear idea of how I wanted to come across on the street. If I looked like I was going to kick somebody's butt, I probably wouldn't have to.

My gun was the last item I'd bought to complete the getup. We had no allowance for buying service weapons and had to shell out the cash ourselves. I still had money in savings from my stint at Glitz and as Simon's midnight cowboy, so I didn't bother cutting corners: I purchased a matte-black nine-millimeter Glock model 17, the most powerful gun allowed under departmental policy. Some of the older officers still relied on Smith & Wesson .38 Specials, maintaining that the Glock was unreliable and could easily jam when most needed, whereas the Smith & Wesson revolver never had this problem. All I knew was that in terms of firepower, a .38 wasn't much better than a .22. The standard clip for the Glock held seventeen rounds; even with a speedloader, a revolver was no match. That was why the drug dealers carried nine-millimeters (and better). If I didn't want to be outgunned, I would have to join the club.

But it would take many hours of practice down at the shooting range in the station's subbasement before I could become comfortable with having the weapon constantly at my side. A semiauto like the Glock could empty its seventeen rounds, one after another, in a matter of seconds.

I was afraid that someday I'd draw it and it would go off in my hand and blow some poor fuck away.

2

"Some of the old-timers don't think you're really gay," said Off. Lydia Kurtz one afternoon out of nowhere, while we were cruising around Hockstetter Park on the northern-most border of her beat. "They think you just made it up so you could get some kind of special consideration."

"I hope you told them to go to hell."

"I told them to take a flying fuck." She laughed.

My first months out on the street were spent with Kurtz as my field training officer. I drove the marked squad, and she tried to sit back and let me do as much as I could on my own. It was real on-the-job training, a totally different learning experience from the tedious classroom work and in-services we'd been doing for months. I'd made good scores on all my exams in the academy, but the real test would come during the requisite probationary period, first with my FTO, then solo. If anyone in the class was found not up to snuff, they would be axed or at the very least have their probation extended. For now, I enjoyed working with Kurtz, but I was anxious to get out on my own, in my own squad, doing my own stuff.

So far, our shift that day had been quiet. We'd been looking for a black Monte Carlo that a woman's boyfriend had "borrowed" without her permission. We also wanted the guy, one Kent Stabin, on a couple of narcotics warrants, and we might be able to charge him with auto theft as well, if his girlfriend's story held up. So far, we'd seen no sign of either car or Stabin. Kurtz had had past contacts with the suspect and would be able to recognize him on sight.

"So, are you and Gunt an item, or what?" Kurtz asked.

"Yeah, you could call us that," I said. "We almost moved in together, but then we decided to take it more slow. We don't even hardly have time to date."

Kurtz was riding shotgun, literally; to the right of the radio console stood an always-loaded single-barreled thirty-gauge, clamped into a rack and pointing up toward the ceiling. It was standard equipment in most Isthmus City squads and, according to Kurtz, "could be a lot better friend to you than your Glock in an emergency situation."

Kurtz sported a short butch haircut of tight curls, the hair itself dark brown but showing gray at her temples and in a stark, unruly shock that shot off from one side of her widow's peak. She wore thick-rimmed glasses and had a squarish, masculine jaw. Out of uniform, she looked like a particularly difficult WSU professor. In full blues, she was an honest, by-the-book professional who took her work seriously, though she also had a good sense of humor and could be a lot of fun to work with.

"Gunt's a good cop," she said. "But then he had a good instructor."

"You were his FTO, too, weren't you?"

"Like I said . . ." Kurtz paused for effect, then emitted a curt laugh. "I guess they're giving me all the gayboys."

"All two of us."

"Well, it's nice to have some, at last, after this slew of young party dykes we've been getting."

Kurtz used the word *dyke* in a deliberately confrontational fashion acceptable among the politically correct because it meant she was supposedly "reclaiming" a formerly hated epithet. This was what people thought I was doing when I used the word *queer.*

"I suppose you and Jodi are just homebodies."

"Yep."

"You've been together how long?"

"Two years, ever since she started academy."

"Congrats."

I'd picked up Kurtz and Sommers at their house one day when their car was in the shop. They lived in one of those pretty Victorian homes across the street from the queer sculpture in Sauk Park where I'd stopped to read *The Stand* that first night in Isthmus City—no more than five blocks from the crack house on Williams Street.

"Will's the one who turned me on to the job," I said. "I figured if he could do it, so could I."

"Now if we could only get a gay chief."

Kurtz herself was currently under consideration for sergeant. Not that she would be Patrol's first dyke sergeant if she made it; we already had three, plus a newly promoted dyke lieutenant, Carol Cowles, who had been assigned to head up IA. In addition, we had several dyke detectives—one a detective supervisor—none of which began to touch the number of dyke patrol officers. What with Isthmus City's being a big college town—and in a state with a progressive political tradition and a statewide gay rights law—it wasn't surprising we had so many on the force. Fully half of our officers were women, and of those, at least half were dykes. Will and I were the only two openly queer guys in the department, though we both suspected there were a few closet cases among our brethren.

"We should have you and Gunt over for dinner sometime," said Kurtz.

"I'll check with Will." I turned the cruiser off from the park, onto Kipling. We'd still seen no sign of the car.

"It's hard to socialize much with civilians once you're on the force," Kurtz said. "The only relationships that seem to work are between cops. You and Gunt are lucky you found each other."

"He's been good for me. A couple of years ago, I wouldn't have even admitted I was a queer."

That, of course, was the understatement of the century. As tenuous as it was, my ongoing thing with Will—whatever you wanted to call it—was the closest I'd ever had to a mature relationship. Until I'd come to befriend the dykes at the police department, women had always frightened me. But women like Lydia Kurtz weren't threatening at all. I often found myself nervous and tongue-tied with nondyke women, including some of my new colleagues. I guess in that sense, I was a male version of a fag hag; I could hang out with dykes all day and not have to worry that they wanted my dick. Straight women had often been sexually aggressive toward me, and I'd never liked it one bit. But I liked my dyke cop friends, especially Kurtz. She was a real pal.

I turned my head and spied the dusty, black Monte Carlo on a side street.

"Hey, look," I said, and pulled the squad around the corner, onto Maugham Terrace, in front of the housing project where Tyree James had been whacked. "There's the car."

"And there's our guy," she said, sitting up higher.

"Where?" As I pulled the squad up alongside the Monte Carlo and stopped, I saw where Kurtz was looking, into the shadowed back alley of one of the projects. A tall white man with long, dirty hair was standing over a shorter black woman, passing her a plastic baggie while she handed him a wad of bills.

"There," said Kurtz. "That's Stabin over there, selling crack to Taneesha James. C'mon."

I radioed for backup. We got out of the squad.

"Police!" I yelled as we ran up. My finger hovered over the

expandable baton on my belt, in case I might need it. "Hold it right there. Hands away from your sides."

Taneesha James dropped the baggie. Stabin hung on to the cash. Both did as they were told and kept their arms away from their bodies. Kurtz snatched up the suspected crack, put Taneesha up against the wall, and began patting her down.

"Watch it, bitch!" said Taneesha.

Kurtz went quietly about her work and managed to get Taneesha in cuffs without my assistance.

"I ain't done nothin'," Taneesha insisted.

"Are you Kent Stabin?" I asked the guy.

"Yeah," he said. "What the fuck is this?"

"Get yo' hands off me," yelled Taneesha.

"You're under arrest," I told Stabin.

"What the fuck for?"

"Turn around. Against the wall."

I performed a quick pat-down search for weapons but found none. I cuffed his wrists behind his back.

"What the fuck for?" Stabin repeated.

"A couple of outstanding warrants."

Just then Officer Sommers pulled up in her squad; our backup had arrived—though Kurtz and I seemed to have the situation well in hand. Sommers helped Kurtz lead Taneesha out to the sidewalk, and together they placed her in the back seat of Sommers's squad.

From Stabin, I retrieved as evidence the cash Kurtz had seen him take from Taneesha. Kurtz came back and helped me walk him back to our squad, where we secured him in the cage in the backseat.

"What about my fucking rights?" asked Stabin. "Ain't you going to read me my fucking rights?"

"Nope," I said, tightening his seatbelt. "You've been watching too much fucking TV."

I shut the door. Kurtz whispered, "Right on," and slapped me on the back.

I was grinning from ear to ear.

Goddamnit, I really *loved* this shit.

3

Back at the station, Kurtz tested the suspected cocaine base and it came up positive—so in addition to his warrants, we booked Stabin for delivery of a controlled substance.

The operations officer on duty was Capt. Richard "Buzz" Rollack. As captain of the South District, he was Kurtz's ultimate superior officer—and mine as long as she was my FTO. His nickname arose from his trademark Korean-era U.S. Marines brush-style haircut, though Buzz himself dated from the time of Vietnam and had never served in the military. Instead, he had already been firmly entrenched in the Isthmus City Police Department by the time civil protest unsheathed its pinko head in the late sixties, and he had served his country at home by bashing flower children at the first Fulton Street Block Party in 1969. None of which meant he was a bad policeman; in fact, he was a plum. But as plums went, he had already had his day in the sun and so become a prune, ripe for retirement as far as I was concerned.

Rollack clapped me on the back in a manly, congratulatory manner. "Good job, Colson," he said.

We were sitting in his office, going over the arrest report I'd just dictated to one of our stenos. With Rollack's blessing, Kurtz and I had decided not to charge Taneesha James with anything, since the delivery charge on Stabin was more important and the D.A. still needed Taneesha's cooperation in the Kenny Doleman case. But the captain wanted to go carefully over my report before we went back out on the street, to make sure none of us had made any grave errors in judgment. Taneesha, meanwhile, was sitting in the lounge, waiting to be taken back to Maugham Terrace.

Behind him, Rollack's computer screen showed most city units busy on calls. Code numbers indicated what type. Most were traffic; rush hour had just begun. Near Rollack's monitor was a radio unit turned down low.

As Rollack was scanning through the final page of my report and I was sitting there sweating, I made out the voice of the dispatcher saying "report of skeletal remains" and giving out an address of "twelve twenty-two Williams."

"What was that?" I said, sitting up with a start.

"David Seven." The responding unit, Dave Brito, sounded laconic, like it was a routine call. "Copy, Dispatch. Responding." Rollack's screen updated itself, now showing D7 in red where before he had been blue, at 1222 WILLIAMS on a code 17—a death investigation.

"Skeletal remains?" asked Kurtz, blinking her eyes harshly as if having just woken up from a long nap. We'd all been taking a breather and chatting over Rollack's fresh vanilla-almond coffee.

"I don't know." Captain Rollack took his feet off his desk and got on the phone, punching the red hotline to Dispatch. "No shit? We got an SI out there? . . . Well, try the lab. Holcombe should be there. . . . While you're at it, get Bender—he's in service. . . . Yeah, I know—the screen's all red. . . . Well, a lot of them are in here on arrests. But I can free up Charlie Four. . . . Colson and Kurtz. . . . Righto. They're on their way out."

Rollack remained on the line but looked our way and shooed us out of his office with a wave of his hand.

"Captain?" I cleared my throat. He was still trying to listen to Dispatch.

Rollack covered the mouthpiece and whispered, "What!"

"Someone's got to take Taneesha James back home."

"We'll take care of it." He grinned at me with condescension—obviously touched by my thoughtfulness.

Kurtz tugged on my arm. We grabbed our clipboards and headed down the hallway and out to the garage.

"What was that address?" Kurtz asked. I couldn't tell if she'd forgotten or was merely testing me.

"Twelve twenty-two Williams," I said, unlocking our squad and getting in.

"And what sector is that?" she asked, getting in. So she was testing me, after all.

"Four-oh-seven."

"Colson, you're slick."

"If you only knew."

We pulled out of the garage and onto the street. My heart was pounding something fierce. I radioed Dispatch that we were responding to the scene.

4

The house was no longer there, exactly.

Huge tread marks like those of a tank had torn up the front lawn. A small bulldozer sat parked on the street. Much of the structure lay in a heap of broken wood planks that leaned precariously against piles of debris. Most of the chimney had come down already; what was left was the tallest thing standing.

Off. Dave Brito was marking off a large area with yellow tape that read CRIME SCENE—DO NOT CROSS. Two workmen from the demolition crew were standing just outside Brito's perimeter, talking excitedly.

Kurtz and I trudged up the muddy lawn to meet Brito, who was climbing over the rubble, wrapping tape around any convenient piece of wood that happened to be sticking up.

"They pulled you guys up from South?"

"We were in the station," explained Kurtz. "So where are the bones?"

"Over there." Brito nodded over his shoulder. "Some of it fell out of the chimney. It's kind of a mess. Bender's going to be pissed."

Kurtz and I climbed past the broken-up planks until we found ourselves in what used to be the living room of the house, standing before what was left of the fireplace. The chimney was now broken off at about six feet, and some bricks on the mantel had been knocked loose. Lying amid scrap wood and dusty bricks just before the fireplace was a greenish-brown skull with yellowed teeth, along with a couple vertebrae, probably from its neck.

"That's it?" Kurtz asked. "Just some old skull?"

"There's more in there," Brito said.

"Does it glow in the dark?" Kurtz went on, as if none of this impressed her.

"Climb on up and see for yourself. But be careful."

Kurtz stepped eagerly onto a pile of brick on the backside of the chimney and looked down into the opening. The sun was getting low in the sky, so the interior must have been cast in shadow. She grabbed her Maglite off her utility belt and shined it down inside. I watched her closely as she scanned back and forth, but her expression didn't change a bit.

All she said was "Wow."

"Wow," Brito mimicked, talking out of the corner of his mouth. "Jesus!"

"Colson, you want to come and see this?" Kurtz called.

"No, that's OK."

"Come on, don't be a wuss. You don't see shit like this every day."

My gaze kept popping back to the skull.

Hey, baby . . .

"Must have been some burglar," said Brito, tying off the last of his tape. "She tries to come down the chimney but gets stuck."

"No way," said Kurtz. "Who'd do a thing like that?"

"No one's lived here for years," said Brito. "She could have kicked and screamed all she wanted in there, and no one would have heard her."

"How do you know it's a she?" I asked.

"Come see for yourself," said Kurtz, still looking down with her flashlight. "She's wearing a dress."

It was the last thing I wanted to do. Yet something compelled me to follow my FTO up that pile of bricks and look in over the rim of the demolished chimney. My foot slipped on the loose rubble. I reached out to catch my balance and scraped up my hand in the process. Kurtz caught me and helped me get to my feet. She held her flashlight while I looked in.

Within was a jumbled pile of brown bones that had settled into a heap, tangled up in the ripped and torn fabric of the slinky dress the transvestite had been wearing. It hardly resembled anything human. I began to wonder how anyone could manage to fit into such a narrow space . . . and even though I'd been there when it had happened, the scene before me took on an eerie sense of unreality.

This is the house; this is not the house.

This is the chimney; this is not the chimney.

This is the corpse; this is not the corpse.

Nothing was the way it had been on that night two years before. I did not recognize the body. I barely recognized the dress. Any bloody boot prints I might have made had long since turned to dust or been scraped away or otherwise covered up in the layers of dust and destruction. By daylight, even the neighborhood seemed not to be the same. It was like I'd been transported to a movie lot and this whole scene was some kind of setup: false fronts, stage tricks, a fake skeleton. I wondered if the radio call and everything else was just an elaborate trap designed to lure me in—to make me break and confess.

Hey, baby, want a ride?

"Jesse?" said Kurtz.

Blood was dripping onto an exposed femur. It was from the cut on my hand.

I shuddered and drew away from Kurtz, putting my cut up to my mouth and tasting the gritty wound.

Kurtz shut off her flashlight and followed me down. "You better put some antiseptic on that. Did you have your tetanus shot?"

I mumbled some kind of answer.

"Come on, Brito," Kurtz said. "Why would she put on a dress to burgle a deserted house?"

"Did I say she was smart?" Brito said.

I closed my eyes hard for a moment and thought, *What's happened to me? What am I doing here, in this uniform? Why didn't I get the hell out of Isthmus City when I had the chance?*

I opened my eyes and felt instantly dizzy. At my feet, the

transvestite's grinning skull was making my head spin. He was getting the last laugh; I'd never escape. Wherever he was, he was hard at work sealing my fate. Everything was going to go devilishly wrong.

My stomach was churning—then came a wrenching spasm. I tasted bile in the back of my throat. I doubled over as if someone had landed a sucker punch to my gut. I caught my balance on a pile of wood. The two cheeseburgers, fries, and low-fat banana yogurt shake I'd had for lunch came hurling out, just on the other side of Brito's police tape.

"Shit, Colson, you OK?" asked Kurtz.

Brito was laughing, but without malice as far as I could tell. He just thought I was a greenhorn learning a new lesson, and he took pleasure in watching me suffer, like I was being put through some kind of initiation rite.

"I'm fine," I managed to get out, shrugging Kurtz's hand off my shoulder. I wiped my face with a black bandana from my shirt pocket. "It was something I ate."

"They probably undercooked the meat," said Kurtz. "Fast food can kill you, you know. Did you know that McDonald's shakes used to contain the same chemicals as embalming fluid, except the formaldehyde?"

"No," I said, and swallowed hard. "I didn't know that."

5

By the time SI Holcombe arrived in his van, my stomach had calmed down. A moment later, Detective Bender screeched up in his unmarked squad. Bender's magnetic flashing red light had fallen off and was dangling out the window by its electrical cord. Bender came up the lawn first, looking his usual self, his gut hanging over his belt; he was dressed in a short-sleeve shirt, his ever-present holster hanging over his right shoulder. He was wearing shiny leather shoes and trying to step around the mud. Holcombe was still gathering equipment from the back of the van when Bender joined us.

"Aw, shit," he said, scratching his head. "What the hell is this?"

As a rookie, I tried to stay in the background and let the other officers handle Bender. I hadn't figured him out.

"You want to hear it from me or from them?" asked Brito.

Bender shouted "Come here" to the two workmen, calling them into the taped-off area. They looked guilty as they approached. "You want to tell me what happened here?"

"We didn't know nothing about it," said one. "The place was a crack house, you guys wanted it torn down. We stopped as soon as we saw the bones, then we called. That's all I know."

"Jesus fucking Christ," said Bender. "Who's in charge of this mess?"

"The city. They contracted us. Nobody told us about no skeleton. How was we supposed to know?"

Bender took in a deep breath. "When did you first see the bones?"

"I was up on the bulldozer, and when I rammed the chimney, my buddy saw the skull come falling out. Then we stopped. I don't know what time it was."

"I got the call at five forty-five," said Brito.

"S'about right," said the workman. He looked all shook up, and I didn't blame him.

Terry Holcombe came up the lawn lugging his camera gear around his neck and carrying a silver case in one hand. He was a bald black man of about forty who kept a closely trimmed beard. He was supposed to be the best special investigator on the force and had reportedly made it clear to his superiors that he was uninterested in any promotion that would take him away from SI work.

"I'll try to get this while the light's still good," he said, looking back at the sun hovering over the horizon. Brito told Bender his theory about the bungling burglar.

"Are you kidding me?" said Bender. "When was the last time you heard of a burglar wearing a dress?"

Kurtz and I exchanged a glance.

"This was a murder," Bender went on, "no doubt in my mind."

"If it's a homicide, you'll never find out who did it," Brito said, perhaps implying that Bender should simply pronounce it an accident and forget about the whole thing.

"Colson?" Bender turned my direction.

"Yes, sir?" I squeaked.

He placed a fatherly hand on my shoulder. "I want you to help Holcombe with evidence collection."

I swallowed hard, still tasting vomit. I must have looked as green as a leprechaun.

"Come on, kid," he said, "it's just a pile of bones."

I wondered if he could tell I was a killer, if he could read it in my face.

"Yes, sir," I said.

Holcombe took photos of the skull and vertebrae that had fallen out of the chimney, then went up top and, using a flash unit, took several more of the chimney's interior.

The deputy coroner, Betsy Cantwell, was eventually called in. She and Bender supervised the recovery of the skeleton. Holcombe snapped photos at every step of the process. The workmen stayed and helped us take apart the chimney without disturbing the bones, until Holcombe could reach in and retrieve them carefully, one by one.

Kurtz and I helped Cantwell bag up everything that she or Bender considered of evidentiary value. We all wore latex gloves and handled every piece with care. Bender paced around behind us, looking over our shoulders and sifting through some of the rubble of the crime scene. The work took time, and it was around sunset that Cantwell made her most interesting discovery.

"What have we here?" she said. The deputy coroner held in her hands a dusty, round mass that jiggled when she moved it. She brushed away some of the dust; underneath, it was a plastic bag of some kind, its contents a pale yellow color.

"Silicone breast implant," Bender said from behind us.

That explained a few things.

"Let's hope there's another," Bender said.

There was. Kurtz found it. We bagged them both separately. I was surprised they had never ruptured.

Aside from the fake tits, the dress, and the skeleton itself, we also recovered the transvestite's wig. No one had yet put forth the notion that it could have been a man. So far, Cantwell hadn't examined the bones closely enough to figure that out.

And I certainly wasn't going to speak up.

Eventually, Kurtz and I delivered the bagged remains to the coroner's laboratory. Then we went to the property room back at the station and bagged and tagged the remaining evidence such as the dress, the wig, and some soil and bricks from the scene.

By the time we were finished, Kurtz and I had packed in some serious overtime, and I had calmed down considerably. What meager evidence they had was a shambles. The remains were over two years old and had been greatly disturbed by the demolition crew. Chances were the coroner's office would never positively identify the corpse. Even if they did, they would never find any evidence to link the crime to me.

I had nothing to worry about.

I was going to get away with it.

Seven

1

What I know about my pa isn't much.

Gene Colson had been a senior at Amarillo High School in 1970, and Margaret Aylesworth a junior. Gene was from a blue-collar family, the son of Archie Colson, a worker at the Pantex plant, the one place in the entire nation where every single atomic warhead in the United States arsenal had to go to have their plutonium trigger installed so they could be armed. The bombs came to Amarillo from all over the country, loaded up on so-called "white trains" and shrouded in secrecy so that upon arrival, workers like Archie Colson could make them war ready. Then they would be carted off on more white trains to their final destination in a missile silo, in the belly of a B-52, or on board a submarine. Archie Colson was necessarily reticent with Gene about his work, for reasons of "national security," and their relationship had always been sour as a result. Gene was so wild and out of control, he might as well have been a minister's son.

Gene owned a red '65 Ford Falcon with a V-8 engine he'd souped up himself. Of all the photographs I've seen of my pa, more showed him posing with his car than with my ma.

Gene apparently spent Friday and Saturday nights cruising Western Avenue with his buddies, unless he was on a date with a girl. Margaret Aylesworth was on the cheerleading squad and normally dated jocks. Gene was a greasy mechanic, so it took repeated requests from him before she accepted his offer to go out to the movies, and even then it was only because the jock she'd got lined up had canceled at the last minute. Gene had got ready for her on short notice but didn't mind.

Margaret herself had been a gangly but pretty girl whose auburn hair was always beauty-shop perfect. She had an undeserved reputation as a bad girl. She got barely passing grades. Her opportunities for the future were few. She'd always sewn well and possessed a natural ability beyond what her mother had taught her; she was active in Future Homemakers of America.

For their first date, Gene took Margaret to the drive-in, which was showing a double feature of two gory British horror films—*Taste the Blood of Dracula* and *Frankenstein Must Be Destroyed*. They'd ended up in the back seat of Gene's Falcon, where one thing had led to another. Sometime during the first feature, I'd been conceived, amid thundering sounds from the speaker hooked over the driver's side window.

"Your pa'd left the volume all the way up," my ma told me once. "All I can remember is the sound of those horses, pounding and pounding in my head, and the sound of a whip cracking, and the horses whinnying while their hooves thundered along the road. They were pulling a great black coach—Dracula's coach—through the forest, and I just kept wondering when they were going to stop. Then it was all over, and your pa collapsed on top of me, smelling like a bottle of Aqua Velva. I didn't really realize at the time what had just happened. . . ."

2

Two months later, Margaret's mother noticed the signs before she did. Margaret was getting sick in the mornings and had inexplicably missed her period. Although furious at first, Fanny Aylesworth took Margaret to a doctor, where the pregnancy was confirmed. It was Fanny Aylesworth who pried the name of the boy out of Margaret and had Gene Colson come over to the house for a talk. Right then and there, Fanny and Daniel Aylesworth demanded that Gene marry their daughter and that they raise the child together like a responsible couple. Dumbfounded, Gene acquiesced.

Archie and Mae Colson accepted the news of the engagement glumly and were none too proud of their son. They kicked him out of the house but helped him make a down payment on a trailer home on the other side of town. Once he was on his own, Gene dropped out of school and took a job fixing cars at a Shamrock station.

Margaret dropped out as well, once the pregnancy began to show. She and Gene were married by a judge, and she was given permission by her parents to go live with Gene in the trailer. They scraped by.

On June 22, 1971, Margaret gave birth to me, a nine-pound baby boy, at St. Anthony's Hospital. My pa named me Jesse James Colson before Margaret had even come out of the general anesthesia.

Somehow, Gene missed being drafted. He went from job to job at different gas stations and spent some time in the unemployment line. Margaret earned some money on the side as a seamstress working out of our trailer. She did good work and charged very little. Word of mouth spread, and she soon developed a regular clientele.

Gene Colson left the trailer on a hot summer's day in

1975 and never came back. His old Falcon had long since been replaced by a black Chevrolet Camaro, which was the only thing he took with him besides the clothes on his back and a fifth of Southern Comfort from the kitchen cabinet.

Ma had never offered me a satisfactory explanation for my pa's disappearance. But having got to know her myself up close and personal over the course of seventeen years, I'd ended up running away myself and, for the first time in my life, felt sympathy for the pa I'd never really known. Gene Colson had set an example for me—simply to vanish, to sever every tie to the world, and to start anew, where nobody knew me. After a few years of drifting, I finally felt like I'd truly come to *know* my pa. Gene had left Margaret for the same reason I had—if he hadn't, he probably would have killed himself.

If my ma thought *she* was a survivor, she didn't know the half of it.

Eight

1

I slept until ten the next morning. The sun was streaming in through my south-facing windows. It caressed my flesh, which lay fully exposed, since my sheet had fallen off during the night and I'd slept nude, as always. I was alone in the bed; Will hadn't come over. I got up, showered, shaved, and shat. I cut up some Spam into an omelette and poured Durkee Red Hot sauce all over it. I did some stretching exercises and then stepped into a jockstrap, cotton fleece shorts, T-shirt, and running shoes and went out for a run. I took the trail that ran along the north shore of Lake Minoqua, a mere five blocks from my downtown apartment. It was a hot day and humid, and I quickly worked up a sweat.

On my way back, I pulled two quarters out of my shoe and bought an *Isthmus City Sentinel*, which I read folded in long leaves as I walked home to cool down. The "SportsEXTRA" section had exciting photos of the Milwaukee Brewers' latest loss. The "CityBEAT" section ran the headline RACE RELATIONS 'NEVER BETTER,' MAYOR CLAIMS, along with an unflattering wide-angle photo of Mayor Beverly Kotzen with her blond bouffant hairdo, overrouged cheeks, and Sally Jessy

Raphael glasses. The "LifeSTYLES" section carried a feature on the annual boat show at the Isthmus City Expo Grounds. The closest the *Sentinel* ever came to a banner headline was running nearly the entire width of the front page:

SKELETON FOUND IN CHIMNEY

That was all. It wasn't very creative; they had simply reduced the story to its barest essence. The lead was particularly awful:

The intact skeleton of a woman was discovered yesterday afternoon lodged in the chimney of a home on the near-east side that was in the process of being destroyed under a recent, controversial city ordinance allowing for the condemnation and demolition of residential properties with a proven link to the illicit drug trade, a police spokesperson reported last night.

The rest of the story wasn't much better, although some had been lifted directly from the department's news release:

The gruesome find was made Wednesday at 5:45 p.m., by Theodore Paducah, 27, and Brent Essenhaus, 23, both employed by Paducah & Sons Construction. According to Paducah, he was operating the bulldozer, and "when I rammed the chimney, my buddy saw the skull come falling out." He and Essenhaus then phoned police from a nearby residence.

Dep. Coroner Betsy G. Cantwell had scheduled a postmortem for early today and said that she wished not to speculate on the cause of death until such time as the postmorten could be completed.

However, according to Det. Harvey D. Bender of

the Isthmus City Police Department, "There's no evidence yet to suggest foul play."

Bender is heading up the investigation of what is, for now, being termed a suspicious death. "She may very well have been a burglar who got stuck trying to negotiate the chimney," explains Bender.

"We have as yet to positively identify the remains or determine how long they've been lodged up there. It's going to be a long haul with this one. We may never know what really happened to the poor girl."

The 80-year-old home, at 1222 Williams, has stood abandoned for years and is alleged to have been used frequently by crack addicts, teenage gangs, and homeless people from the nearby men's shelter. It was condemned and marked for demolition under the city's recent so-called "Seize and Destroy" antidrug law that was championed so vigorously by Mayor Beverly Kotzen and has recently been challenged in court by the Wisconsin chapter of the Civil Liberties Coalition as "racist" and "unconstitutional."

The piece disturbed me. It seemed so blasé, so matter-of-fact. I could imagine people reading it and saying, "Oh, how awful," and then forgetting all about it before lunch. It was one of those freakish kinds of stories that, despite being big news locally, other TV anchors across the country would report at the close of their broadcast as "like something out of Stephen King," and then offer a wry smirk and a stupid, flippant comment to their colleagues: "Don't try *that* at home!" or, "You know, Pam and I once had a dead possum stuck in the chimney of our summer home . . ."

It seemed Bender was deliberately misleading the reporter.

Maybe he wanted to trick the killer into a false sense of complacency.

At first, I wanted to cut out the story, and went to the kitchen to get a pair of scissors. Then I thought better of it. The last thing I needed was a scrapbook lying around filled with clippings about the case.

Realizing this, I placed the paper on top of a stack slated for recycling.

I wasn't going to allow myself to become morbidly fascinated with what I'd done. That was all behind me, and I wanted to keep it there, out of my new life. The Jesse who'd committed the murder wasn't the same Jesse I'd become, nor even the Jesse of old that my ma had raised. The Jesse who'd killed the transvestite had been the Jesse of the moment, the one who'd thought he'd reached the edge of a very flat world. I was a cop now: I had a life. Sometimes it was hard to believe I'd ever killed anybody.

But that other Jesse still lurked within me, somewhere. He was the one who wanted to cut the story out of the paper and save it. It was he who was so fascinated by the unraveling of the mystery, while I wanted simply to forget about it. So long as I could keep him at bay, no one would ever know what I'd done.

It was he that I'd seen in the bathroom mirror at the Greyhound station, he who'd drawn the gun on me without the slightest care as to whether the security guard might stumble in and arrest us. It was he who'd wanted to shoot the driver of the pickup, he who'd nearly shot the hooker, he who'd felt so threatened by the transvestite that he'd had to shoot the poor fuck's head off.

I didn't think he'd be much of a problem anymore. I was in control of myself—of my life—really for the first time. I was even in control of my gun. It was constantly at my side during working hours, and like other officers, I also had a license to carry it concealed on my person off duty, which I sometimes did—and without taking it out and shooting anyone.

I didn't need Jesse the badboy coming back and giving me shit. I knew who I was, and I *liked* myself, which was more than he could ever say. Ever since high school, Jesse the badboy had never allowed people to take his picture, fearing his mother would someday let it be used on a wanted poster that would hang in every post office in the country, after he had committed some heinous crime.

I'd already gotten over that when I'd allowed myself to be photographed for my official police ID card. There I was, smiling what I'd always thought of as my badboy smile— the one I'd seen only in the mirror, in living flesh and yellowed, tobacco-stained ivory—captured striking a pose on grainy Polaroid film.

I had to shower once more after my run. In a couple of hours, I would be back at work, and I didn't want Kurtz to be overwhelmed by my musk. When I emerged from the shower and wiped the condensation off the bathroom mirror, I saw the old Jesse grinning back at me.

You're in the shit now, he told me. *You're not going to make it.*
Shut the fuck up, I told him.

2

Detective Bender sat in on briefing that afternoon at a quarter to three. Once Sgt. Molly Kelly had finished going over the day's ho-hum list of runaway juveniles, stolen autos, and requests for extra patrol, she turned the floor over to Bender.

The bags under Bender's eyes were prune colored. His sparse hair was mussed, as if he hadn't showered that morning or had simply not gone to bed. He had a file folder before him on the conference table, along with a yellow legal pad that was filled with illegible scribblings.

I was seated at the far end of the long table, directly opposite Bender at the other end. Lydia Kurtz sat on one side of me, Will Gunther on the other. Will's foot touched mine and tapped on it impatiently. I withdrew it but gave Will a secretive smile.

"First of all," said Bender, "I hope none of you believe what you read in the papers."

Spotty laughter arose from the assembled second-detail officers. Kurtz elbowed Dave Brito and whispered, "I told you so."

Bender continued: "I spent half of last night picking through rubble. We thought we might find other bodies, but there weren't any. Then I spent all morning looking over the coroner's shoulder."

I could imagine the deputy coroner, Betsy What's-Her-Name, and the county pathologist, their hands encased in latex, working with the bones—laying them out upon a stainless steel table until they somewhat resembled a human figure, picking up the skull and peering into its empty sockets, asking it to give up its secrets. I could also imagine Bender, exhausted from lack of sleep and impatient with the pace of the postmortem, hovering around the coroner and the pathologist while they tried to work, and generally getting in the way.

"I know I've only got a few minutes before you have to go out on the street, so I'll try to save you the whole song and dance."

No, I thought. *Tell me everything you know.*

"Our best guesstimate is that the bones are a year and a half to two years old. The victim was positioned headfirst in the flue, so we've ruled out Brito's idea that it was a burglar in a dress trying to get in through the chimney. That would be more of a suicide than a burglary, anyway."

"Ugh," Kurtz said.

"We know how the victim died, and it wasn't suicide."

Bender paged through his messy notes and wiped his nose with a handkerchief. "The damage to the back of the skull is consistent with a gunshot wound fired anteroposteriorly— that's a ten-dollar word for front to back. This was a shot through the mouth powerful enough to inflict a great deal of damage. It was fired from close range, likely from within the mouth itself—we found powder traces embedded in the teeth. Thus, we're treating it as a homicide.

"The coroner also discovered that these are not the bones of a woman, as we had erroneously assumed because of the dress and the silicone breast implants, but those of a man about six feet tall and probably in his twenties, at least from the condition of the teeth. He must have been some kind of a transsexual. Since all the flesh had decayed off the bones, we can't tell if he still had his penis. He might have had it lopped off. Since Williams is just a block off East Madison, I'd be willing to bet that the victim was a transsexual hooker who picked up a bad trick."

"So what do you want us to do?" asked Sergeant Kelly.

"Not much. Just be aware of the situation for now. David units in particular should keep their eyes open, ask around their neighborhoods, see if anyone remembers anything. If any of you know of missing persons from your beat who fit the profile, let me know. We're going to cull through the files anyway, including the county's, but you might be able to save us some time if you learn something."

I could save him a hell of a lot of time. I could solve his case for him right here, in front of about twenty witnesses.

That's my Jesse, said the voice in my head. *Play it cool, boy.*

"That it?" asked Sergeant Kelly.

Bender shrugged. "I guess so. Just remember, the killer's probably from around here. He probably thought we'd never find the body, and now we have. He may yet give himself away."

"You wish," said Sergeant Kelly.

Briefing ended. I grabbed my clipboard and stood up.

Bender knew more than he was telling. I needed a look at that file and those notes.

But what I really needed was to keep my head. Nobody but me knew what had happened. Bender could only find out so much before he ran into a brick wall. I held the key.

Bender looked up and made eye contact with me. His eyes were bloodshot and bleary. "Hey, Jesse," he said, with a half-smile.

"Detective," I said.

"You and Kurtz did a good job yesterday helping Holcombe."

"I just follow orders."

"No," said Bender. "There's veterans who wouldn't have given a damn and would have done a sloppy job. But what you guys did for me could prove crucial. If you're sloppy, you might miss that one bit of evidence I need."

"Detective, I've still got some interning to do with the Detective Bureau, and I was wondering, do you think we could arrange it so that I could intern with you again? Especially when you're working on this case. I'd like to see how you go about it."

Bender nodded. "I'll talk to your captain, see what I can do."

"Thanks."

"Oh, and Jesse," he said in an apparent afterthought, like Lieutenant Columbo on TV.

"Yes?"

"We're pals, aren't we? Call me Harve."

Nine

1

Kurtz and I were dispatched to assist other units at the site of a multiple motor vehicle accident with injuries. One vehicle was reported to be a motorcycle. Fire Rescue was also responding.

Our second-detail shift went from three in the afternoon until eleven at night. During the slow transformation from stark daylight to bleak nighttime, I would see the city itself change. The daytime gave us shoplifters, schoolyard fights, and a lot of speeders; night gave us drunk drivers, domestic violence, sexual assaults, and armed robberies.

I'd have thought that police officers would be among the most rational and least superstitious of people, but in fact the reverse was true; most of my colleagues genuinely believed that nights of the full moon should have been more heavily staffed than others and that officers asking to have those nights off should be denied their request as a matter of routine. My coworkers carried in their pockets lucky talismans on keyrings, wore lucky jackets, and preferred their squad numbers with sevens in them. Those who worked fourth detail, from eleven at night until seven the next morning, seemed the most superstitious of all—but then their entire lives revolved around the night. Those of us on second experienced the natural shift in perception of any animal going from the safety of day to the hidden dangers of night. We grew more aware—some citizens would say more intense, more dangerous—after sundown.

"I used to belong to a dyke bike club," Kurtz told me en route to the accident scene, over the whining scream of our siren. "Had a big motherfucker of a Harley, until I joined the force. You just see too much carnage, even when riders wear helmets. Kind of ruins all the fun."

When we arrived, we were the fourth unit on the scene. Officer Sommers was already there, as was Capt. Richard "Buzz" Rollack. Will Gunther had come down from Central District; he must have been in the neighborhood when the call came in. All the squads were parked haphazardly, red and blue lights spinning on top, on the perimeter of the scene—one entire block of Minoqua Drive blocked off, traffic being rerouted onto side streets.

Captain Rollack was in charge. He sent Kurtz to assist Fire Rescue with the injured biker, who was screaming his head off; Rollack then asked me to search the area of the felled motorcycle for the biker's severed finger, to retrieve the finger if possible, have it put "on ice," and then get it to the hospital either with Fire Rescue or on my own, if I had to.

"His finger?" I asked, like a perfect idiot.

"Right index finger," said Rollack absently, as if he couldn't be bothered further—which indeed he couldn't.

The accident scene was a royal mess. The two other vehicles involved were a minivan and a small subcompact, both of which had apparently collided after the minivan had swerved to avoid hitting the motorcycle. The people in the cars seemed not to be as seriously injured as the biker but were nonetheless being assessed by EMTs.

When I got to the mangled Harley-Davidson, I found its front wheel still spinning. When I reached out to stop the tire, I saw the severed digit right there, wedged between the spokes, pointing up at me in the illumination of my high-powered flashlight and dripping blood from what seemed to be roots dangling from its base. After first putting on a pair of rubber gloves, I grabbed the finger and asked someone from the gathering throng of onlookers to fetch a cup of ice. A citizen in his bathrobe rushed into his home and returned bearing a highball glass. I placed the finger inside, stirring it like a swizzle stick deep into the crushed ice, and placed the glass on the seat of my squad temporarily while I obtained a witness statement.

The biker, still screaming, was loaded into the Fire Rescue unit thirty feet away, at the site where he had been thrown from his hog upon striking the minivan. The EMTs were already on their way to the hospital before I could give them the finger. Kurtz was riding along with them, probably taking the biker's statement and generally observing him, trying to determine whether he had been drinking any alcohol or what other factors might have contributed to the accident.

Following Rollack's orders, I hopped into the squad, and sped off toward the hospital with full lights and siren. But by the time I reached the emergency room and handed the glass over to the nurse, all that remained was the ice itself, some of it pink and melted from the blood.

"What's this," she asked, "a strawberry margarita?"

I searched my person. I searched my squad. I went back and searched the accident scene. I retraced my movements during the minute it had taken me to drive to the hospital. I searched the drive outside the emergency entrance. Yet in the end, I failed to find the finger.

But by then it no longer mattered; the doctors had gone ahead and sewn up the skin over the biker's bare knuckle, and Captain Rollack already wanted to talk to me.

In the midst of all the confusion, some citizen must have copped the finger from me as a souvenir—probably took it home and put it in the freezer.

Hell—stranger things had happened.

2

Back at the station, after the accident had been tied up and all the officers had made their reports, Captain Rollack reamed me out in his office, in the presence of Lydia Kurtz, since she was my FTO and had to go practically everywhere with me.

"There's no excuse for a fuckup," he said, though I wasn't sure whether he meant my mistake or me.

"I told you, I had it right there in the glass, and it just disappeared."

"I don't think it was his fault," Kurtz put in.

It was just one of those things—nothing to lose any sleep over. The accident was the biker's fault in the first place, and he was lucky his head hadn't been smashed open like a jack-o'-lantern. He'd proved to be a member of the Z.Z. Ryders motorcycle gang and had been wearing no helmet. A blood alcohol concentration of 0.29 showed he had been riding blitzed out of his skull-and-crossbones on the way home from their "clubhouse."

So he was short an index finger. Big deal. The boys in Narcotics would probably be thrilled.

"You blew it. All you had to do was find the guy's finger."

"I did find it, sir. Someone must have taken it."

"You could be found negligent, you know." Rollack stared me down as if he were a father giving a stern lecture. "I wouldn't be surprised if that biker brought a civil suit."

I countered with sufficient disrespect to get Rollack's goat. "Look, *Buzz*, the guy's a low-life, and he hangs around with convicted felons. I pulled up his jail record—we booked him a few years ago for endangering safety, and he's had a number of drug charges. He's probably got access to firearms, but after today, he's got no trigger finger, so the way I figure, it's just as well."

"Wouldn't have done much good sewn back on, either," said Kurtz, who had stayed with the biker all through the investigation. "Once he's out of the hospital, we're hitting him with OWI, operating after revocation, and a probation violation."

"But that's not the point," Rollack maintained. "Low-life or no, you still lost his finger, and I'm still writing you up. I may end up extending your probation."

At this I smiled, to his utter confusion.

Kurtz was seething behind her firm-set jaw. Her arms were folded, and she was breathing heavily through her nose. I was touched by her protectiveness, but then it probably had more to do with her own personal dislike of Buzz Rollack than with any respect she might have for me. She'd already told me of a few occasions in the past when she felt Rollack had mistreated her because of her being a dyke.

But I could even tell that Rollack sympathized a little with our point of view about the biker. When Tyree James had been shot and killed by Kenny Doleman, Rollack had told me it was "no great loss." His writing me up in this instance had to do with his firm belief in the unwritten guiding principle of police work, which is CYA (Cover Your Ass).

The discussion was finished. I rose to leave.

"Thank you, sir." It came out sounding like *fuck you*—as I intended.

Rollack snapped his eyes up to meet mine, too furious to speak. At the heart of that gaze, I imagined, was his realization that no matter what discipline he meted out today, he would be retired within two years, while I had thirty yet to look forward to, and by the time I reached retirement age, he would have long since bit the dust.

"See you out on the street," I said, and flashed my best death's-head grin, courtesy of Jesse the badboy.

3

When I crawled into bed late that night, my mind was spinning and I couldn't get to sleep. I plowed my head under the pillows, trying to hide my eyes from the moonlight that seeped in through the venetian blinds. The cotton sheets retained the accumulated musky odor of my sweat from the past weeks. For whatever reason, I'd always enjoyed the smell and so seldom bothered to wash my sheets. I'd always been hairy—even as a teen—and always perspired with ease, yet I disliked cologne or even deodorants (probably because my ma was a scent freak, and our trailer home had always been filled with feminine smells: bubble bath, after-bath splash, perfume, potpourri, incense, carpet freshener, air freshener, and disinfectant spray). There wasn't a cop on the force who didn't smell after wearing uniform and Kevlar vest all day, and I was no exception.

Though exhausted, I couldn't sleep. I was unable to shake

the finger from my mind. If I'd managed to return it to the hospital in time, the biker might still have functional use of it. As it was, a part of him was lost forever, and it was nominally my fault, though I still couldn't understand how it had happened.

At two o'clock in the morning, I couldn't stand it any longer; I reached for the phone on my night table and punched out the phone number that had grown the most familiar to me since I'd moved out of Simon's house.

"Hello?" said Will's slurred voice. He probably wasn't even truly awake yet. At least he was a good-enough foot soldier to have actually answered his phone rather than leave his answering machine turned on. We all knew we could be called up at any time of day or night for some purpose or other, and most of us believed it was best to pretend you weren't home and then to call them back if the emergency assignment was something that happened to catch your fancy.

"Will?" I said. "It's me."

"Oh, hi."

"I can't sleep." I was rubbing my dick.

"Do you want me to come over?"

"Yeah," I said. I didn't really want to be alone any more that night. Besides which, I was horny as hell.

"I'll be right over. Let me put on some pants."

"Forget the pants," I said.

4

But Will was much too modest for that; he arrived wearing loose-fitting sweatpants and a ratty T-shirt. These, however, soon came off and lay somewhere between the front door and the door to my bedroom.

Even with the air conditioner turned on high, our fucking left us slick with sweat—as if we'd squirted it on each other out of a bottle. I liked Will's scent almost as much as my own; his was more delicate and less brutal, but still wholly masculine and able to give me an instant hard-on. I'd always enjoyed his body, too, because it matched mine so well, muscle for muscle, hair for hair, cock for cock. Despite his blond head, his ample body hair was as dark as mine. Our cocks were both cut and roughly equal in size and had come to know each other very well.

By four in the morning, Will and I had gone through my last four condoms and quite a lot of lubricant and were completely exhausted. At that point, I broke out a fresh pack of cigarettes. I was smoking less than ever; before he met me, Will had never smoked at all, and I did feel a little guilty about having corrupted him.

"Feel better now?" Will asked. I stuck a Camel in his mouth.

"Yep," I said, and lit first his cigarette, then my own.

"You've picked that up from Kurtz."

"What?"

"That 'yep' and 'nope.' Sometimes she can sound like Gary Cooper without half trying."

"Oh, I guess I have. I hadn't noticed."

Even with bags under his bloodshot eyes and a look of utter exhaustion across his face, Will managed to look at once angelic and elfish. He did sometimes remind me of an elf from the depths of the Black Forest, what with his fair hair and dark, arched eyebrows. With him lying back against my pillows and looking at me down the bridge of his nose, with his hair splayed back off his forehead, his face held an especially mischievous quality I found slutty and appealing.

"Why couldn't you sleep?" he asked. "Was it because of the finger incident?"

"Yeah," I said, now self-conscious about the *yeps*. "I can't finger it . . . I mean, figure it out."

Will burst out laughing, then said, "I'm sorry."

"Freudian slip."

"You can finger me out if you like."

"I already did that."

If Jesse the badboy was the devil on one of my shoulders, Will was the angel on the other. I was lost somewhere in the middle. All I could try to do was listen more closely to Will than to the voice in my head.

I'd been giving in to all these queer desires, all because of Will. At first, I'd kept it up, thinking I had to keep everyone in the department thinking I was queer. But the further things had progressed with Will, the more I came to realize I was probably just as queer as he was—and probably always had been. Somehow, he made it OK.

"Look," Will said, reaching up to stroke my hair, which was drenched in sweat. "They're just giving you shit because you're gay. I told you they were going to look for any little thing they could find, hold you up to a higher standard. Rollack's a real prick. I'm glad he's not my captain. Every time I've ever dealt with him, he's always been confrontational, always second-guessing everybody. He doesn't trust his own officers. He used to stake out Night-Owl Donuts to time how long his officers were spending on break. When the chief got word of it, Rollack got his ass chewed off."

"Good," I said. "But he's not all that bad. He just doesn't want to have to put up with any bullshit."

"But it wasn't his job to check up on them. Listen, if you

hadn't been on the scene, he wouldn't have even bothered with the finger. He had all these officers there and wanted to make use of them. He had you look for the finger because there was nothing else to do. He probably never even expected you to find it. He's got no right writing you up for losing it. The way I figure it, it's just a tough break. I don't think my captain would have written me up."

"Well, it's no big deal. Kurtz doesn't think it'll extend my probation. She even says she'll take the case to the chief if Rollack wants to be a real jerk about it. But I bet you anything he'll wake up tomorrow and change his mind. Even if he is a homophobe—which I'm not sure he is—he knows I'm one of the best new cops in his district. He won't want to let me go, because he might end up with some incompetent instead."

Will yawned. "You're probably right. Let's go to sleep."

"I'm going to get a glass of water," I said. "Want some?"

"No, thanks." He already sounded like he was drifting off.

I got up and went to the kitchen. The blue moonglow coming in through the window was sufficient to see by, so I left the light off. The cool black-and-white checkered floor tiles felt good under my bare feet. I let the water run in the tap for a while so it would get cold. I grabbed a clean glass from out of the cupboard. I opened the freezer to get some ice.

As I reached for the ice cube tray, I saw a fishstick lying there in the front, out of its box. But upon looking closer, I saw that it wasn't a fishstick at all: it was the biker's blue finger, the severed end caked with dried, frozen blood.

The glass I was holding fell to the floor and shattered.

"What happened?" Will called from the bedroom.

"Nothing," I responded. "I'm just a klutz. Go back to sleep."

126

I stood quietly for a moment, listening to see if Will was stirring, but I heard nothing. I turned on the light and swept up the broken glass.

I tried to think of something to do with the finger. I couldn't just take it out and throw it in the garbage. Homeless people went through garbage these days looking for returnable bottles, and someone was bound to find it. For now, I would simply have to keep it in the freezer but keep it well hidden. I tore off a sheet of aluminum foil and wrapped it up, then hid the small package in the back of the freezer box, behind some TV dinners.

I told myself it was I who had done this, not Jesse the badboy. I couldn't go on blaming him for everything.

But for the life of me, I couldn't remember how the finger had come to be in my freezer. If I'd had anything at all to do with it, that part of my mind was a complete and total blank.

Ten

1

I was interning again with Harve Bender at the Detective Bureau. We'd been sitting inside all afternoon at the conference table with our coffees, poring over a stack of missing persons files loaned to us by the La Follette County Sheriff's Department, in addition to our own. None of the men in the photos came anywhere close to the one I'd killed, even when I tried to imagine them in full makeup and wig. But more important, none of the files made any mention of the missing person's having had breast implants. We were drawing a complete blank.

Bender got on the phone with Johns Hopkins University, where they did a lot of sex-change operations, but whoever he'd ended up talking to hadn't been very cooperative. The mere fact that we'd come up with two silicone breast implants on a male skeleton didn't help them to help us. They had done hundreds of sex changes—many involving breast implants—and their files were confidential, anyway. Besides which, Johns Hopkins was hardly the only place in the country where one could get such an operation—and there were plenty of other doctors in foreign countries who did it as a matter of routine—in Amsterdam, Singapore, Rio de Janeiro. Bender came away convinced that the breast implants would not lead him to an identification of the skeleton.

While he had been talking on the phone, I'd been staring at his gun in his shoulder holster. I had never seen Bender indoors in anything more than a short-sleeve shirt, and his harness was always exposed.

"I thought those were for dicks in suit jackets," I said, motioning toward his shoulder holster. I was in plainclothes like him, but I preferred to wear my gun on my belt.

"I can draw faster from this than you can from your belt," he said, casually removing his snub-nosed .38 Special and weighing it in his hand.

"I bet my Glock kicks your thirty-eight's ass."

"Oh yeah?"

Bender's reliance on a revolver was outdated when you considered the kind of firepower we could run up against from these gangs, which had emigrated from Chicago carrying whole arsenals with them—weapons we weren't even allowed to use.

"Wouldn't you be better off with a longer barrel so you could at least aim the damn thing?"

Bender nodded grudgingly, sliding open the fluted cylinder and dumping all five rounds out on his desk. When he closed it up and spun the cylinder, it made a ratchety sound.

"Listen, kid," he said, handing it over to me. "It's not the gun, but he who uses it."

"Or she," I added. Kurtz had trained me to speak without gender bias.

I hefted his .38 Special in my palm. It was a Smith & Wesson model 36 with a two-inch barrel and a round butt—

heavier than my Glock, with a shiny but scratched-up stainless finish.

"You're probably right," I said. "I couldn't kill anyone with this unless they were standing right in front of me."

"While your nine-millimeter will hit practically anything if you hold the trigger down long enough."

"You want to see it?" I said, aiming his gun toward the wall and looking down its sights.

"I wouldn't even want to touch your Glock," Bender said. "No offense."

With one eye closed, I scanned my targets on the wall until I alighted upon a photographic portrait of the president, then suddenly had a vision of myself as assassin and pulled the trigger. The hammer slammed against the empty chamber with a surprisingly loud noise that made me jump, as if Bender had tricked me and secretly left in one bullet. The president would have been a dead man, and then we would have been married forever. That was about how long it took.

"Would you touch my Glock if your life depended on it?"

"I guess," he said, taking back his gun. He opened the cylinder and replaced the rounds. "But I hope to hell I'll never have to. Call me sentimental, but this little piece of shit has already saved my life a couple of times. If I'd happened to have been wearing that other piece of shit of yours, my ex-wives would have long since been collecting survivors' benefits."

Bender closed up his gun again and spun the cylinder before replacing it in his shoulder holster.

"You ever killed anyone in the line of duty?"

"Yes," he said. "Jesse, let me give you some advice that might save your ass."

"All right."

"Avoid ever having to draw your gun if you can help it."

"OK."

"But if some bastard's left you no choice, you'd better be prepared to shoot him."

"OK."

"And kill him."

"OK."

"If you can't do that, you're in the wrong line of work. Maybe they don't tell you that in the academy. Maybe they think they're training social workers instead of cops. But I don't think we should be out there holding people's hands. We should be trying to keep our citizens from killing each other. Any cop that thinks he can fire a warning shot or shoot somebody's kneecap is going to wind up dead. We haven't had a cop killed in the line of duty since 1931. Not that we haven't been shot at and even hit—just ask Carol Cowles—but we've sure been skating for a long time. Jesus, I shouldn't even be talking like this—I'm jinxing the hell out of us."

"I didn't think you were superstitious, too."

"I'm not," said Bender. But then he showed me that his fingers were crossed, and he let out a hissing, snakelike laugh. "I just don't believe in tempting fate."

2

A few days later, I brought the biker orchids because they are supposed to be the most masculine of flowers. I wasn't sure he would take to them but figured it was the least I could do.

I poked my head into the hospital room, which was a double with an empty bed in addition to the biker's. So his room was private, at least until they checked someone in. The biker looked as if he might be here a while. He had one leg and one arm in a cast and was in traction. He also had a brace at his neck, as well as bandages on his head and exposed arm. The other leg was hidden under the sheet.

"Axel Brightman?" I asked, though I was pretty sure it was him. His fingers poked out from the end of the arm cast—only three, with a wide gap separating them from his thumb. The heavy door closed firmly behind me.

"Who are you?" He was awake but groggy, squinting at me and probably unable to see clearly. I'd noticed a shaggy beard on him before he was put into the ambulance, but that had now been shaved off, for whatever reason. He was probably forty years of age and could easily be mistaken for an accountant or a car salesman.

"Officer Jesse Colson, Isthmus City police," I said. I'd come in my street clothes, both because I was off duty and because I figured a biker with a criminal record wouldn't respond well to me in my kick-ass uniform. "I was sorry about what happened. Thought I might ought to pay you a visit."

"Sorry my ass," said Brightman. "Soon as I get out of here, I'm going to jail."

"I'm sorry about your finger."

"Why?" he asked. He wouldn't know what I'd done until he read my report—to which he wouldn't have access until his case reached court.

"I mean, I'm sorry you lost it," I said.

"Oh, well," Brightman said, and sighed. *"Que será será.* You can put the flowers over there. When the sun comes up in the morning, it should hit them."

"All right," I said, and set the glass vase down upon the small table. I pulled at a couple of the flowers until the arrangement looked good enough. "How's that?"

133

"Perfect."

I couldn't help staring at the gap where his index finger should have been, and thinking of the little foil-wrapped package in my freezer. I still hadn't thought of anything to do with it. If I threw it in Lake Minoqua or Lake Winoma, it would wash up somewhere. If I threw it in a field, someone was bound to stumble across it. I kept thinking of Kyle MacLachlan finding that severed ear in *Blue Velvet*, and all the dark mysteries its discovery had revealed. And until I could figure out how the finger had gotten in my freezer to begin with, I wasn't entirely ready to let it go.

"Well, listen," I said, "I really got to go, but I wanted to stop by and see how you're doing. You looked banged up pretty bad."

"Yeah, I guess I really bit it this time." Brightman chuckled, deep and throaty, with a smoker's timbre to his voice. "Maybe it'll teach me a lesson."

"If you want me for any reason, you can call me at this number." I removed a business card from my pocket and handed it to him.

Brightman grabbed it with his free arm but winced in the process. He held the card up to his face and peered at it suspiciously. It was my official police department business card, with the Patrol Bureau phone number on it.

"Why the hell should you care?" asked Brightman. He sounded confused rather than bitter. Obviously, no cop had ever given him the time of day. "What's the deal? You some kind of Christian cop?"

"No," I said, but couldn't really tell him why I'd come.

"Oh, I get it," he said, sneering. "You're just looking for information. Drug tips, other dirt. Well, I'm not telling you *jack shit*, so you can take your fucking business card and shove it up your ass." With that, he threw it on the floor.

Within half a heartbeat, I was at his bedside with my hand on his throat. He feebly tried grasping at it but either his arm was too weak or he was in too much pain. I squeezed just enough to make him panic.

"Listen, asshole," I said, grinning my badboy grin. "I came here because I was trying to be some kind of goddamned angel of mercy, but I could just as easily break your neck, and there wouldn't be one goddamned thing you could do about it."

Brightman's eyes were wide and staring, as if my squeezing his neck had inflated his eyeballs like little balloons. I'd succeeded in completely terrifying him.

I released my grip and withdrew my hand. He gasped for air at first but was breathing normally within a minute.

"Motherfucker," he said, and began to cough.

"That's right," I said.

"I'm going to tell my lawyer about this."

"Go ahead. It'll be your word against mine, and who's going to believe a Z.Z. Ryder over an honest cop?"

"My lawyer will," Brightman said.

"Maybe so," I said, "but he's paid to believe you."

I left the room thinking how much I *really* loved this shit, and happy that he'd managed to erase whatever guilt I might have had about losing his goddamned finger.

3

I interned with Bender again that week, and we ended up out on the street doing "footwork" that was largely conducted by car. Since I was basically along for the ride, Bender drove—though more often than not he was jotting down a note or handling a cigarette and, characteristically, driving with his knees. Our windows were rolled down, letting in a warm and humid wind. Bender went through three cigarettes before we'd been gone from the station more than twenty minutes, and I began to realize that his footwork was, in part, an excuse to get out of the smoke-free building and into the great outdoors so that he could kill himself with a chain of Pall Malls.

I joined him, but only for one cigarette, and I stuck to my Camels. He accused me of falling victim to advertising.

"What do they call it? Subliminal seduction," he said. "They design Joe the Camel to look like a big cock and balls so that homos and closeted fratboys will go running out to buy them. A Pall Mall is a real man's cigarette. Nothing subliminal about it. Just death in a box."

"Whatever," I said. It wasn't worth provoking him further.

"Now you'll call me a homophobe."

"No," I said. "In fact, my money says you're a closeted fratboy."

"Sigma Epsilon Chi," said Bender. "But only for one semester, before I dropped out and joined the army."

"You enlisted?"

"Uh-huh."

"You some kind of patriot?"

"No, just a fatalist."

"Now *that* I believe. So where are you taking me?"

"We're going to go pay a call on Miss Taneesha James," he said.

"Oh, swell," I said. Even though I'd barely begun my career as a cop, I'd already had frequent contact with her. "So what's the trouble?"

"She is," Bender said. "She fries her brain on crack all day and calls me with these paranoid fantasies. Everyone's out to get her. She thinks Kenny's got some friends in Chicago who're coming up here just to kill her."

"Doesn't sound that paranoid to me," I said.

"Maybe," Bender said. "Maybe not."

He took his eyes off the road momentarily, fiddling with the squelch button on his scanner. We passed through a red light at the intersection of Kipling and Conrad, though I suspected Bender had somehow already seen there were no cars coming and ducked his head down just to freak me out.

It didn't faze me.

But then I was something of a fatalist myself.

4

Crack cocaine, as I'd learned in academy, was preferred by users because it was a far purer form of the drug. Most street cocaine was actually cut to the point where 60 to 80 percent of it was filler matter—most commonly inositol or mannitol but sometimes even baking powder or nondairy creamer. Cocaine base or crack, on the other hand, was 80 to 100 percent pure and relatively easy to make. First, you added street cocaine to water to dissolve both the cocaine hydrochloride and the cutting material. You then made the solution basic by adding baking soda. Since cocaine was itself basic, it formed solid lumps and precipitated out like the stuff you saw around the rim of your glass when you drank Alka-Seltzer. You heated up this solution so that it became super-saturated, and then removed the cocaine base in the form of lumps, which you then dried to form a rock. To ingest it, you cut off a chunk and, as the saying goes, put it in your pipe and smoked it. Since it was highly concentrated and al-most totally pure, you'd wind up with a much more powerful high, and smoking it gave you a faster and far more efficient rush than you could get from snorting street cocaine up your nose.

This was what, according to Bender, Taneesha James was "frying her brain on." In my short time on the force, I'd seen the way people could act when high on crack, and the idea that Taneesha could have become paranoid was not hard to believe. It was probably crack addiction that had got her and her brother mixed up with gangbangers like Kenny Doleman in the first place.

"Kenny wasn't that big an operative," Bender explained to me as we pulled up into Maugham Terrace. "These were real small-time gangbangers. Kenny killed Tyree James over peanuts. I don't think he really knows anyone in Chicago who's willing to commit another murder just to shut up his ex-girlfriend. Besides, the D.A.'s case is fairly solid even without Taneesha, so it wouldn't do him one damn bit of good to have her dusted, and he knows it."

"But what if something did happen to her?"

"Listen, Jesse, just because I think she's delusional doesn't mean we aren't taking her seriously. Narcotics has got undercover officers working Maugham Terrace on routine drug surveillance, and we've asked them to keep their eyes open. The project is serviced privately by Badger Security, and they're also supposed to be looking out for potential trouble. I've told Taneesha we can't give her a twenty-four-hour-a-day guard, but we've done whatever we could to provide extra protection."

Maugham Terrace and the surrounding neighborhoods on the south side had been built as middle-income housing in the fifties and sixties, but for some reason, by the midseventies these initial residents had migrated to the white-collar west side and blue-collar east, lowering property values and rents to the point where the south had became a refuge for low-income households and people on welfare, attracting families from the worse-off inner-city neighborhoods of Milwaukee and Chicago by its relative comfort and less-depressing atmosphere. Families fleeing gang violence in the cities had unwittingly brought it along with them, not realizing the extent to which their children were already involved.

In the late eighties and early nineties, crack had quickly become the most widely available drug in Isthmus City. Most of the gang activity centered around its distribution out of Chicago and the local turf wars fought by the different factions of youths stupid enough to be duped by the big, ruthless warlords—who didn't care how many of their foot soldiers died in shootouts with rival gangs, so long as their product reached the customer and the money kept flowing. The warlords were businessmen first, always keeping their eye on their bottom line and their return on investment. They'd never seen anything quite as profitable as crack; the main drawback was it was so easy to make and to obtain that they had to fight hard just to maintain their market share.

Bender parked his cruiser in front of 1516 Maugham Terrace. Young black children were running around on the yellowed lawn that wrapped around the side of the building, screaming and poking each other with sticks. Bender paid them no mind. We went into the building and up the stairs, to apartment 2-F, and knocked on the door.

"Go away!" came a woman's voice.

"Taneesha," said Bender, turning to give me a wink. "It's Detective Bender."

I looked at the peephole and saw a shadow pass before the small pinpoint of light.

"Who's that with you?" Taneesha wanted to know.

139

"Officer Colson," Bender said. "He's with me. Don't be afraid of him. He won't bite."

"You got anyone else out there?"

"Just us."

I heard the sound of the chain lock being unfastened, then the turning of two deadbolts.

"Get in!" Taneesha said, opening the door wide and motioning us inside. "Go on, quick!"

Bender stepped inside, and I followed. Taneesha slammed the door closed and refastened all the locks. She was breathing rapidly and had dark stains of perspiration at the front and back of her loose-fitting T-shirt. She looked more drawn and gaunt than when I'd first seen her the night of Tyree's murder. Her skin was shiny with sweat, her eyes wide and bloodshot. She'd tied her hair back with a scarf.

The apartment was stuffy and hot. No windows were open, and although one contained an air conditioner, it was turned off. The kitchen area was a mess of filthy pots, pans, and dishes. The carpet was hidden ankle deep in dirty clothes—which, along with the dried food on the dishes, added pungent and mildewy smells to the already close air. I could hardly breathe.

"Taneesha," said Bender, stepping haphazardly across a stream of socks, blue jeans, and other garments, "you should really get some air in here."

"No," she said, shaking her head. "They'll come in."

"Nobody's coming in through the window, and you're keeping your door locked like a good girl."

"Detective, you gotta help me," she said. "They want to kill my baby."

Bender walked casually around the apartment. I tagged along on his heels like an adoring dog. We wandered into the bedroom, which was likewise carpeted with dirty clothes. The sheets had been stripped off the waterbed and were tangled up on the floor, exposing the rubbery mattress. The curtains in the bedroom were drawn and fixed shut with a safety pin. I followed Bender into the bathroom, which was tidier than any of the other rooms even though the tub and shower curtain were both thick with mildew. The lavatory was cluttered with makeup and hair-care products.

"Where is your baby, Taneesha?" Bender asked.

"My mama's got her over at her place. It ain't safe here no mo'. I seen Kenny's boys lookin' in through the windows, wantin' to kill my baby."

"Taneesha, you're on the second floor. No one can look in through your windows."

"I seen them, Detective."

"Come on—"

"Now what are you going to do about it?"

"Do you think your baby's safe at your mother's?"

Taneesha's face fell in horror with some sort of sudden realization. I don't think this was the response Bender had been looking for. "Do you think they gone over there? Oh, my God, my baby! Why would they want to hurt my little girl?"

Bender reached out gingerly and laid a hand on her shoulder. "Calm down, Taneesha. I'm sure she's totally safe over there. You know, you really need to clean up this place. When was the last time your social worker came over?"

"That motherfucker," she muttered.

"What's his name?"

"Jimbo."

"Out of the south office?"

"He's a motherfucker."

"Jimbo? Jim Lawnberger?"

"Jimbo! Fucking Jimbo! I hate him. I don't want to see him around here no mo'."

"Was there something that happened today that made you call?" Bender asked.

"What?" said Taneesha, looking at him like he was the one who was crazy.

"What made you call?"

"You want to know what he said to me? He said he was gonna kill me and my baby."

"Who said this?"

"Kenny."

"When did he call?"

"I don't know. Leave me alone."

"Was it sometime today?"

"Yeah, sure," Taneesha said. She sat down on her sofa and folded her arms like a small child in a pout.

"Taneesha, if Kenny called you from the jail he's going to be in big trouble, you understand? You signed that form, remember? He's not supposed to have any contact with you. If you get a call from him, you shouldn't call me, you should call nine one one, all right? If anyone threatens your safety or that of your child, you call that emergency number, not me. You got that? Now give me your mother's address. I want to go talk to her and check on your baby, is that OK?"

At that point, Taneesha began sobbing into her hands. "I'm sorry, Detective."

Bender touched her head lightly. I thought she'd react violently and shrink away, but she just kept sobbing. "It's all right, Taneesha. I'm going to call LCSS and see if we can't get someone other than Jimbo to come and see you, is that OK?"

Taneesha nodded.

"Good. Now are you going to be OK?"

She nodded again, still holding her face in her hands. "Yes, Detective. God bless you."

Bender rolled his eyes at the ceiling, then glanced down at his watch. It was my impression he'd been through these scenes with Taneesha before and didn't want to waste too much more time here.

"You feel free to call me anytime, Taneesha. But if you feel in danger, call the nine-one-one dispatchers, and they'll help you out. Now, how about giving me your mama's address?"

5

We checked on the welfare of Taneesha's two-year-old girl, Felisia, at her mother's, which was a little bungalow on Conrad two blocks from Taneesha's apartment. Bender told me that the kid was from a past boyfriend, not Kenny Doleman. We then went up to the La Follette County Jail and talked to the deputies, who told us Kenny Doleman had been in solitary for the last two days because of uncooperative behavior and had been denied access to the phones. Bender nodded with a smug look on his face, as if he had known all along that Taneesha hadn't received any calls from Kenny. We contacted La Follette County Social Services, and Bender tactfully suggested that they have Jim Lawnberger's supervisor go out and talk to Taneesha, perhaps get her some psychological counseling through La Follette County Mental Health.

By the time we were finished dealing with Taneesha James's problems, Bender's shift was over, and he invited me out for beers at Fightin' Bob's by the Lake.

"Jesus Christ," he said, once we'd finally sat down with a pitcher of Leinenkugel draft. He poured me a foamy glass, then one for himself. "I should have sent some Patrol officer out to check on Taneesha, but I was afraid she'd shoot anyone other than me."

"Has she got a gun?" I asked, alarmed. I'd dealt with her a few times in the past without expecting her to try and kill me.

"Who knows?" Bender said. "But she could certainly get one if she wanted to, and who's going to find it buried under all those clothes? Anyway, now that's eaten up the rest of my shift. I'm sure you thought we'd be working on the chimney case all day."

"Yeah," I admitted.

"There's not much we can do right now. We'll check the dental records of the missing persons against the skull, see if we get a match. If that doesn't work, I'm going to send the skull off to the Smithsonian and have them reconstruct its facial features. The first thing we've got to do is get an ID. Without that, we're screwed."

"What about the dress?"

"Nothing," Bender said, and took a deep gulp of beer. "We haven't figured out where it was bought. For all we know, it could have been picked up in Boston or L.A. or through the mail. I don't think the dress will prove significant."

"So what else have you got?"

"Nothing. Not a clue. But if we can reconstruct the face and get a sketch out of it, maybe someone will recognize him and come forward."

"If you have to send it off to the Smithsonian, how long will that take?"

"A few months," Bender said. "Maybe longer."

"Do you think it'll work?" I asked.

"Lots of old cases have been solved this way."

144

"Really?" I said, suddenly apprehensive. "I remember when I was a kid seeing an episode of *Quincy* where they reconstructed this guy's face from his skull and solved a twenty-year-old murder. But I figured that was just TV."

"Oh, no, it's real," said Bender. "And it works."

"Well, that's good to know, I guess." I downed a large gulp of Leinenkugel.

"I want to close this thing."

"You don't want some crazy killer out on the streets."

Bender nodded. "That, and I don't want an unsolved case lingering for years in my case files. As if I didn't have enough work. But I *will* solve it, even if I have to work on my own time. Unless I give myself a stroke in the process."

"You don't have to try *that* hard," I said.

Eleven

1

"Your English teacher said *what?*" Ma's eyes are aflame, her jaw grimly set. Her breathing is deep, her nostrils flaring—like a bull preparing its charge.

"She said I stuff my jeans with a sock—and in front of everybody!" I'm leaning back against the wall, folding my arms in front and looking down at my ma, who is seated at her sewing machine. It has stopped in midstitch and is emitting a high-pitched whine. Ma's small hands remain placed lightly upon the cloth, in front and in back of the stalled needle, while her eyes stare up at me, wide and alert like she's just downed a pot of coffee.

"Why, that bitch!" Ma says.

The needle begins to creep. Without Ma's looking down at her fingers, they respond to the movement and begin guiding the cloth. Then her eyes return to her work, and she presses her thigh against the throttle underneath the sewing table, allowing the needle to pick up speed.

Gene lies asleep at Ma's feet, snoring. His ears and front paws twitch; he's lost in a dream.

"I should have—" I begin. "I mean, I really should have—"

"What?"

I laugh. "I should have stood up, unzipped my jeans, whipped it out, and—"

"Jesse!"

"And proved it to her!"

"You certainly should not have done anything of the sort!" Ma's sewing becomes furious, the bobbing needle moving too fast for my eyes to make out. "You did right keeping your mouth shut. Now I can take this to the principal, and he won't have any choice but to take our little Miss Ginseng aside and—"

"Jensen," I correct shortly. "Pamela Jensen."

"Oh, Pamela, is it? You're on a first-name basis with her? Have you been ogling her in class, is that it? Did you give her some reason to strike out at you like that?"

"Ma!"

"You mean to tell me she just says this out of the blue, entirely unprovoked?" Ma smiles and bats her eyes like she's proving herself no fool. "She simply walks up to you and starts accusing you of padding your crotch?"

"That's right. I didn't do nothing. Can I help it if I . . . I mean . . . if I stand out?"

"That's Gene Colson's fault."

The dog wakes up and pricks up his ears, then realizes Ma isn't talking about him and goes back to sleep.

"He passed that down to you," Ma adds, gesturing vaguely toward the fly of my jeans.

"Ma!"

"Ain't nothing to be ashamed of, Jesse. Why, you should be thankful to that sewer rat. Look at you—those gymnastics have filled you out so you're the spitting image of your father—from the neck down. You look nothing like him in the face. That's where you take after me."

"Ma, about Miss Jensen?"

"What?"

"What do you mean about talking to the principal?"

"We'll get her fired, sugar."

"Fired?" For the first time, I worry about what I might have set in motion. I mean Miss Jensen no harm—I was simply unable to keep my mouth shut.

"I, for one, don't want my son attending a school for 'higher learning' where an unmarried teacher with what we might call a reputation is allowed to make sexual advances willy-nilly toward the children."

I swallow hard. "You mean she'll lose her job?"

"Of course, stupid."

I feel like I've been struck in the face, as I always do whenever she calls me such a name. I wonder why I even spoke about Miss Jensen in the first place.

I step away from the wall and turn to go.

"Jesse, darling." Ma stands up and grabs some girl clothes from off a rack standing beside her machine. "I've mended these Sunday dresses for Opal's little wretches. Would you be a dear and run them over to her? I've already called. She's expecting you."

"Yes, ma'am," I say dutifully, and grab the pink frilly dresses by their hangers.

I feel sorry I never opened up *All Quiet on the Western Front*. I've got to start reading it for Miss Jensen, so that I can save her, somehow, from Ma's wrath.

"Now, Mama's going out tonight with Frank," she says, cheering up suddenly and touching her hair. "So you're on your own for supper. Opal was a dear and offered to feed you, and I said you'd be happy to join her. She's fixing your favorite."

"Lasagna?"

149

"Go on," says Ma, shooing me away and sitting back down at her sewing table. "I've got to finish this up and go prepare for my date."

"OK. Have fun, Ma."

"You too, hon. Don't let Opal get off without paying. Tell her I don't operate on credit."

2

It's twilight as I walk through the narrow streets of the trailer court on my way to Opal Femrite's. I've put a pine-green plastic garbage bag over the dresses so no one will see me carrying around something so girlish. I can smell the lasagna wafting out of an open window before I even get up the steps of the Femrite trailer.

"Hello?" I call through the screen door. "Opal?"

"Come on in, Jesse!" she says from down the hall. "Don't let the cat out!"

I block Julep's exit with my boot as I open the door and come inside. Julep meows, annoyed at me. I make sure the door is closed. Julep arches her back, sticking her tail straight up in the air, and stretches her front claws on the hooked rug just inside the door. I reach down to pet her, but she flinches away and races off down the hall.

"Fine," I say. "Fuck you, too."

The smell of food is stronger inside. I lay the dresses down on the living room couch and wander into the kitchen. The lasagna sits cooling atop the stove in a large glass baking pan. I lean over and take a good whiff.

"Smells great, Opal." She still hasn't appeared from wherever she is. "Opal?"

"Be out in two shakes of a lamb's ass!"

I go back into the living room and sit on the La-Z-Boy recliner, on top of which lies a fancy doily crocheted by Opal herself. Upon the coffee table sit two of Opal's handmade candles. One is a square block of white wax containing an assortment of seashells, its wick unburnt. The other is a large brown mushroom painted with goldenrod polka dots, also with a clean wick. On the couch across from me is stretched a crocheted afghan in a southwestern pattern, done in various shades of earth-colored yarn. Some of Opal's needlepoint adorns the walls in wooden frames.

Opal Femrite emerged from the hall momentarily, dressed in a bright canary-yellow bathrobe, fixing a towel turban upon her head. "Just let me get dressed," she says, before disappearing once again. I pick up the latest issue of *Family Circle* and leaf through it briefly before setting it down and then looking at my watch.

"Is there anything you want me to do?" I call to her.

"No, you just sit tight. I'll be out before you can say Jim Johnson."

Jim Johnson, I say to myself. "Where are the girls?"

"Over at Hilda's, playing with little Shannon. I've got you all to myself tonight, you might say."

"Oh."

Opal Femrite finally comes out wearing a pink cotton blouse and black jeans, her feet in moccasinlike house slippers. Her hair is cut short and spiky, with frosted tips still slick from setting gel. At least three conflicting perfumelike odors emanate from her person.

"Well, look at you, Jesse, you are really growing up! Let me take care of these first, then we can eat." Opal grabs the bag with the dresses without even looking at them and takes them into a back bedroom. "I remember when you were yea-high, and now will you look at you?"

I've got nothing to say to her as she comes back down the hall. She's talking like she hasn't seen me in years, when in fact we see each other all the time in the company of my mother.

"I suppose you want to eat."

"Yes, ma'am."

"Please, none of this 'ma'am' shit! You make me feel twenty years older. It's just Opal, please!" She blushes convincingly. "Now have a seat at the table, and we'll get right down to it."

Over dinner, which consists of a salad and many helpings of lasagna, we discuss my ma and how school is going. All through the meal, I hold back what Miss Jensen said to me, but afterward, when I'm helping Opal with the dishes, it all comes tumbling out in detail. She'd hear it from Ma, anyhow.

"Well, is it true?" Opal asks.

"Of course it is. That's exactly what she said."

"No, I mean, do you really stuff your crotch with a sock?" Opal wipes off the last of the dishes and sets it to finish drying on the rack. She turns and looks not at me but down at my bulge.

"No, ma'am—I mean, Opal." My voice quavers.

"You mean this is the real McCoy?" Opal reaches out slowly and presses her hand against the fly of my jeans.

I simply stand there, propped against the Formica countertop, barely breathing. Opal's fingers squeeze my crotch. I can feel myself getting hard. Then Opal hooks her finger into the waist of my jeans. I think she's going to tear my fly open, but instead she says, "Come with me," and pulls me along behind her, down the hallway and into the master bedroom. She pushes me down onto the bed.

"Opal, I—" I don't know how to finish.

"Shh," she says. "I want to show you something."

I think she's about to take off her clothes, but instead she opens up the trunk that lies at the foot of her bed. Rummaging around inside, she brings out several objects and places them on the coverlet. They are of all shapes, varieties, and colors—wax candles, each shaped like a cock and balls, with a quarter-inch wick poking out of the tip. Their colors are gaudy purples, blues, greens, and oranges—like a box of crayons—none look natural.

I laugh. "Where did you get those?"

"Made them," Opal says proudly. "This one belonged to Bob, my ex." She lifts up one that's short and thick, with a ballsac the size of a dried apricot. Most of the others prove longer, though none as long as mine.

Opal pulls out a creamy white box slightly smaller than a shoebox and hands it to me. It's made of plaster, sliced in half; when I open it up, I find inside the clear indentions of an erect cock, complete with bulging veins and mushroom-shaped head. This one is larger than her ex-husband's. Written in red magic marker on the outside of the mold is RICK FEATHERSTONE, 4-29-84.

"Jesse, I want to make a candle of your dick."

"What if my ma finds out?" I say—the first thing that pops into my head. "She'd kill me."

"Don't worry about her," says Opal, dismissing the thought with a wave of her hand.

"I don't know."

"I bet yours is bigger than any of these."

"But how do you . . . I mean, I gotta stick my dick in plaster?"

"Oh, it's nothing, trust me."

"That's easy for you to say."

"Let me take off your pants."

I feel my heart skip a beat. I've never had sex before or shown anyone my hard cock. Yet I lie back on the bed, propped up on my elbows, my legs dangling off the edge, and let Opal Femrite stand there and unbutton my jeans—*pop, pop, pop, pop, pop!* She grabs the elastic band of the forest-green bikini briefs my ma just bought me and pulls them open just enough for my cock to spring out, practically hard, its head already a deep purplish red. Opal pulls off my cowboy boots and socks, and yanks my pants completely off, together with my bikinis. I pull off my T-shirt myself, so that now I'm completely naked except for my cheap wristwatch.

"See?" I say. "No sock in my crotch."

"You're darn tootin'!" Opal says, grabbing my cock in her fist. She holds it at the base, squeezing tightly enough that the veins bulge out and the head balloons to larger than I can remember ever having seen it. "How long? You ever measured it?"

"Ten inches."

"Then you get the blue ribbon, boy."

"You ever burn any of these?"

"Sure do. I can always make a new one. I keep all the molds."

"How many have you done?"

"You'll be number thirty-seven."

"Does it hurt?" I ask, as if she would know.

Opal shakes her head. "You just have to stay hard for a few minutes while the plaster sets. You're young, you can do it. It won't hurt unless your cock never goes down—then you'll never get it out!"

I'm suddenly horrified that just such a thing might really happen, and that the paramedics might have to come and cut the thing off of me. . . .

"Just kidding," Opal assures me. "Don't worry. I know

154

what I'm doing!" She takes a rawhide bootlace from a drawer and ties it around the base of my cock, underneath my scrotum, just tight enough that I can feel a constant pressure, but not tight enough to cut off the circulation. "That'll help you stay hard—not that a boy your age needs any help. Now stand up."

I stand. For some reason, I feel totally in her power. I'm not even all that attracted to Opal Femrite, but the thought of anything even remotely sexual keeps me aroused. As far as I'm concerned, there is nothing she might ask me to do that I won't do.

"You've got a great ass, Jesse."

"Thanks, ma'am . . . um, Opal."

"That's more like it." Opal grabs my ass with both hands and squeezes. Her fingernails dig into my flesh. She gives one of my cheeks a sharp slap. "I remember watching Margie spank you out on your stoop one day. You were just the cutest little thing!"

I feel the warm rush of blood to my face; for the first time during our encounter, I'm truly embarrassed.

Opal grabs the end of the rawhide and yanks on it like a leash. "Come on, Jesse. Now there's a good boy." Opal leads me back out into the kitchen and has me sit down at the table. "Now you just sit here and keep yourself hard while I start mixing up the plaster of Paris."

Closing my eyes, I grab my cock and begin stroking it, thinking of Miss Jensen. If this really works, I can give her a candle of myself as a present, instead of an apple.

Twelve

1

Lydia Kurtz grabbed me by my shirtsleeve as I was coming out of the men's locker room. "Hey, Colson, you got to come see this."

"What?"

It was my last scheduled day with my FTO, and briefing was supposed to start in five minutes, but Kurtz was dragging me off in the opposite direction, down the hall, toward the Detective Bureau. I imagined she had arranged some kind of surprise celebration for me, with cake and accouterments. Even before we got there, I was thinking, *Aw, Kurtzie, you shouldn't have.*

It was two-forty in the afternoon, and half the detectives on duty were in the station. They'd gotten up from their desks and were gathered in a tight circle around Harve Bender's desk. Then I realized it wasn't Kurtz who'd gotten me the cake, but old Harve. But none of the detectives bothered to turn around as Kurtz and I approached.

"Get a load of this," Kurtz said to me.

"Jesus Christ, Harve," said Alison Donohue, another person crimes detective. "How'd they do that?"

"You should draw some lipstick," said Tony Pallone, a youth services detective. "Maybe put on a wig."

By this time, I'd decided it wasn't a cake; I felt a slight disappointment. I nudged my way into the circle to see what all the fuss was about.

Sitting before Harve Bender upon his desk was a full-size replica of a human head in heavy white plaster. Bender turned it my direction so that I could see its face. I would have recognized it anywhere; despite the masculine features and lack of makeup or earrings, it clearly belonged to the transvestite. The face stared back at me, a disembodied head resting upon one of the stacks of paper and files that covered Bender's desk. It was crude, like a death mask.

The eyes opened; the lips parted.

Hey, baby, want a ride?

"Fuck!" I said. I backed away from it suddenly and into Kurtz standing behind me. The eyes hadn't opened; the lips hadn't parted. I felt like a hippie having flashbacks of a bad trip. I was lucky I hadn't drawn my Glock and blasted the head to smithereens.

Relax. It can't hurt you.

Bender and all the assembled detectives turned to look at me. "What's the matter?" Bender asked.

"Nothing, Harve," I said hurriedly, wiping the sweat from my brow.

Now close your eyes and open wide like you're going to suck my dick.

"You look like you recognize him."

"Oh, no." I tried to laugh it off. "I was just shocked, is all. Kurtzie dragged me back here, and I thought maybe it was going to be a surprise cake."

"Colson," said Kurtz, "it's the FTO who's supposed to get the cake. German chocolate, please, with cooked icing."

Bender was still staring up at me with a crooked grin on his face. "You're sure you don't recognize him?"

Look at you! You're the rough trade poster boy.

"They did a great job—very lifelike." I was amazed at how fast the head had been turned around. Bender had sent the actual skull off to the Smithsonian less than two months before. As in that episode of *Quincy, M.E.*, they must have reconstructed the facial features directly on the skull itself using modeling clay, then made a mold of that and created a fresh replica in plaster from the mold.

"I was hoping someone around here might have had contact with him before," Bender said, turning the plaster head around to look at its face. He seemed grossly disappointed that no one had yet identified it, although it was my impression he had just unpacked the head sometime that afternoon. "We're still looking for an ID."

"Sorry I can't help you," I said. "I'm still looking for a piece of cake."

"Oh, well. Ask Will Gunther to come take a look at it, too," Bender said.

"What's Will got to do with this?" Like a good boyfriend, I was suddenly defensive.

Bender shrugged. "Listen, I don't mean anything by this, but I figured you guys might have run into more transvestites and transsexuals than the rest of us. Especially you, Jesse. Didn't you used to bartend at Glitz?"

"Yeah, but—"

"Isn't that where you and Will met?"

"Yeah."

Trying to hide my nervousness, I looked around at the faces of the other detectives, none of whom I'd gotten to know as well as I knew Bender. I didn't mind if they figured I was queer, but I was none too comfortable discussing it in front of them. Bender was simply focused on the matter at hand—his so-called "chimney case"—and probably hadn't given a second thought to my feelings.

"Correct me if I'm wrong," Bender went on, "but isn't Glitz where they hold the annual Miss Gay Isthmus City pageant? I've always been under the impression that drag queens like it better than the other bars—not as rough."

"Yeah, I guess so. But how long ago did you say this guy was killed?"

"We've placed it at a little over two years."

"I didn't even come to the city until two years ago, and I didn't start working at Glitz until later. Your victim was dead before I ever would have seen him."

"Damn," said Bender, as if he'd really been counting on my being able to recognize the head. Did he know something else he wasn't telling me? "But maybe Will saw him, sometime before you came to town."

"I doubt it," I said, though I didn't have any reason to suspect anything one way or the other. I supposed I didn't like the idea that Will might have known the transvestite. But then, Will had claimed when I met him not to have had much time to go out to the bars and that he wasn't much of a social butterfly, anyway.

Kurtz tugged on my shirtsleeve again. "Come on, Colson. We're late for briefing."

As we left the Detective Bureau, I said to Bender, "I'll tell Will to come take a look, but don't expect him to know anything just because he's a queer."

The detectives laughed good-naturedly. They all liked me; they thought I was a real cut-up, talking like this about me and my boyfriend.

Alone among them, Bender didn't notice Kurtz and me

leaving the room. He simply sat there, staring puzzledly at his prized head like it was some kind of hunting trophy.

This is only the beginning, said Jesse the badboy. *I told you, kid—you're not going to make it.*

"Shut up!" I said.

Kurtz turned around and, in her best Robert DeNiro voice, said, "Are you talkin' to me?" as we entered the briefing room to the annoyed stare of Captain Rollack. Will looked up at me with a worried look from across the table, as if he'd thought I wasn't going to show up.

"Sorry, Capper," said Kurtz. "My fault." She sat down without a further word and began going over the photocopied daily report. She was chewing gum and smelled strongly of cinnamon.

Rollack glared at us—probably more for having interrupted his train of thought than for being late.

I was happy Kurtz would take the blame for me. It was my last day of probation, and since I'd already skated on the finger incident, further gaffes were likely to stand out. I smiled innocently back at Rollack and then began going through my copy of the daily report.

"Now, where was I?" the captain asked.

One more word and I'll blow your balls off.

I wanted to tell the voice in my head to shut up but was afraid that I'd accidentally speak aloud again and that Kurtz would figure something was wrong with me.

2

"Kurtz," I said, "did Harve Bender ever kill anyone in the line of duty?"

"You didn't know that?" She made it sound like I was the only person in the entire world who'd never heard.

"I don't know the story, no."

It was midafternoon. We'd parked our cruiser and begun a foot patrol through Hockstetter Park. It was a hot day, and large groups of people were having cookouts in the picnic shelters. Some were playing Frisbee, while the younger kids terrorized each other with water guns that looked more like bazookas, with huge plastic tanks strapped on their backs.

Even in my all-cotton uniform, I was sweating like a pig—which is exactly what Jesse the badboy had decided I'd become. *You're gonna be bacon on a meathook,* he told me. *Fucking queer cop.*

"Bender was doing undercover surveillance one night," Kurtz explained. "Out with Carol Cowles. She was a detective then. They'd been staking out some guy's house but hadn't seen any action, when this pickup truck goes by at a high rate of speed, scraping the side of a car that was parked along the curb. They pull out and chase the guy down, figuring he's probably intoxicated and at the very least they've got a hit and run. They call in a high-speed chase. Cowles is driving. They end up on Wisconsin Avenue, heading east. They're nearly to the city limits before the guy pulls over for some reason. They figure he's come to his senses. Cowles approaches the driver's side. Bender stays behind the vehicle as her backup. The driver's the sole occupant. Bender gets a bad feeling, so he reaches for his gun. Just then he hears a gunshot and sees the flash coming from the driver's hand, and Cowles falls to the ground. Bender aims at the back of the driver's head through the back window of the pickup and fires three times, shatters the glass. The driver falls onto the seat, and Bender's not even totally sure he even hit him, but he goes back to the car and radios for Fire Rescue. When he goes to check on Cowles, she's getting up on her own. She's got blood coming from her head, but it turns out to be superficial; the bullet just grazed her. Bender opens the door to the pickup and looks in."

"And the driver was dead." I had this horror-movie image in my mind of the driver springing up from the seat to attack Bender as he opened the door.

"Oh yeah," said Kurtz. "Good and dead. Only he's real small and skinny, and he'd been sitting on top of a phone book. There's blood all over the cab. Bender checks the guy's wallet for ID but finds only a learner's permit and a high school ID card. The kid was only fifteen."

"Shit," I said. "But he had a gun. He shot Carol."

"I know," said Kurtz, "but I think Bender still feels guilty about it. At the time, his own son was also fifteen. Bender was in line to become a detective supervisor. If he had, he might even have made lieutenant of detectives by now. But ever since, he's taken his name out of the running, says he doesn't want a promotion. Which is just as well, if you ask me. Detectives like him shouldn't end up administrating. We need them out on the street."

"Man," I said, "that's tough."

"I think Bender had a little breakdown, too."

"What do you mean, 'little'?"

"I'm not sure, really." Kurtz gave me a quizzical look as we tramped across the unmown grass. "All I know is, he left one day and took an indefinite leave of absence. He said he was too stressed out. We all thought we'd never see him again. He took worker's comp for it and just seemed to disappear for a few months. Then one day, about three months later, there he was, back on the job, acting like nothing had happened. He wouldn't talk about it."

"No one knows what he did all that time?"

Kurtz shook her head. "He'd just gone through his third divorce. None of his kids were living with him. He was all alone. I don't even really know if it was a breakdown, or if he just took a three-month vacation to Acapulco—and I guess I don't really care. He's been fine ever since. It obviously did him some good."

"God damn," I said. "That's too bad. I really thought he had his shit together."

"Hey, don't knock him, Colson." Kurtz was defensive. "It could happen to any of us. We could go off the deep end like *that.*" She snapped her fingers to illustrate the point. "This is a high-stress job, and sometimes things can get a little unreal. About six years ago, one of our officers barricaded himself in his house with his family as hostage. He was a gun collector, and we knew he had a shitload of guns lying around the house. There was a standoff for about twenty hours before he came out unarmed and turned himself in. We were lucky no one was hurt. He could have shot his family, himself, or one of us. Up until then, he'd been a perfectly normal guy."

"He must have had some deep, dark secret."

"We've all got secrets, Colson."

"I mean something hideous, horrible."

"Maybe we've all got something like that."

"Even Bender?"

"Especially Bender. Hell, he was in Vietnam."

"Even you?"

"Maybe," she said with an enigmatic smile.

"I don't believe it," I said. But I was merely being chivalrous.

"Shit, Colson, probably you, too." Kurtz punched my shoulder, like a real pal.

"No, not me," I said, trying to pass it off as a joke.

"Go on, let it out."

"I can't."

Kurtz became thoughtful and said, "Did you ever read *The Picture of Dorian Gray?*"

"No," I said. "Why?"

"Oh, I don't know. I think you'd like it. It's all about secrets—secret sins. There's a lot of things about me I wouldn't want anyone else to know."

"Even Jodi?"

Kurtz nodded. "Are you kidding? Especially Jodi."

3

The next morning, two police sketches based on the plaster head cast appeared on the front page of the *Isthmus City Sentinel*, one of the victim as he might well have appeared every day, with a short, neat haircut—he looked masculine and athletic; the other had him garishly made up with lipstick and mascara, with a big head of blond hair that made him look like Diane Sawyer. Neither struck me quite so profoundly as had the cast itself. The sketch as a woman didn't do him justice; in real life, he had been more beautiful (for a transsexual) and less clownish.

I had the next three days off. When I returned to work, it would be shift change, at which time I'd finally be on my own and riding Charlie One, the northernmost beat in the South District. Will Gunther and I were both switching to nights on fourth detail and had somehow managed to get the same day-off rotation. Although he and I belonged to different districts, my new beat actually abutted his David Three, Central. Lydia Kurtz was also switching to nights, merely because Jodi Sommers had been bumped to fourth detail due to the seniority of another officer who had switched to second. Kurtz and Sommers were still riding Charlie Four and Charlie Three, respectively, in South.

The district distinctions themselves were a kind of ridiculous. Each of the four districts—Central, North, South, and East—operated out of the same primary police station just off the courthouse square. We had no West District because directly west of downtown lay huge Lake Minoqua, and whatever other territory might have been considered west made up the campus of Wisconsin State University, which had its own police and security. Our four districts had sprung up under the guise of decentralization; each captain had his eye on a separate stationhouse of his own within the actual territory of his district, but until such time as the city council approved funding, we were operating under a supposedly temporary arrangement called "centralized decentralization"—an Orwellian concept whose net result was to make the department top-heavy with captains and lieutenants, who spent much of their time fighting petty territorial battles over equipment and, more often than not, simply bumping into one another.

Will came over around noon, and we walked from my apartment down to Strand Street, an eight-block-long pedestrian mall sandwiched between the La Follette County Courthouse at one end and Old Main, the oldest building on the WSU campus, at the other. We ate gyros at Athenae for lunch and then, after browsing in a few used-book stores, entered the campus and bought a pitcher of Leinenkugel at the student union. We took our brew out onto the expansive terrace overlooking Lake Minoqua. It was a hot, humid day, but with a cool breeze off the lake.

"Did you see the paper today?" I finally asked him.

"Yeah," said Will.

I told him how Bender had wanted him to go and have a look at the plaster head, to see if he recognized it.

"I saw the sketches," Will said. "The guy does look familiar."

"He does?" I was shocked.

"If it's the guy I'm thinking of, I used to see him at Glitz all the time."

So Bender was right, merely from his facile judgment of Will's character. No wonder he was a homicide detective.

"I thought you didn't get around much," I said with a twinge of jealousy. "When we met, you gave me the impression you'd never been there before."

"I never said that," Will said. "Anyway, I didn't go that often." He set down his glass of beer and removed his shirt. Many of the people hanging out here were likewise scantily clad and soaking up the sun's rays. It was near the end of summer, and Will was already deeply tan. Over the past few months, his hair had become bleached an even lighter shade of blond, and the sun had even lightened up his dark eyebrows. With his bronzed skin, he looked less like an elf than a California beach bum.

I removed my shirt as well. I wasn't quite as tan, because until this year I'd never been much for sunbathing. Will and I had sunned together in the city parks and on the beaches of Lake Winoma, which were better than those along Lake Minoqua. On those occasions, we'd worn skimpy Speedo swimsuits, but today we were both in comfortable cotton bermuda shorts, seated on iron chairs around a café table.

"Did you know his name?" I asked. I enjoyed the warmth of the sun on my skin. I was already sweating and could smell the familiar, friendly odor wafting up from my armpits.

167

"No," Will said. "But it seemed almost every time I went, he was there, like he was a regular."

"In drag?"

"Always. And he was always with this woman. She wasn't a transvestite but, you know, real. I never met her, either. I never talked to them. But it was hard not to notice them. For a transvestite, he was kind of big in stature."

"Really?" So Will had noticed, too.

"You should talk to Simon Scales. He might have known their names."

"When was the last time you saw them?"

"I don't know," Will said. I couldn't make out his eyes behind the glare of his Ray-Bans. "But it was before you started working there."

"Have you told any of this to Harve?"

"Shit, Jesse, I practically just woke up and saw the paper. It's not that pressing. I'll call Bender later."

"You should tell him about that woman," I said. "Maybe she's the one who killed him."

"And stuffed him up a chimney?" Will said, shaking his head in disbelief. "She was short and scrawny. I doubt even I could do something like that."

"Oh, I bet you could," I said, and meant it. Will wasn't any bigger than me, and when I'd done it, I'd been starved half to death from an acute money shortage. "You sound like you remember them pretty well."

"Just their faces, Jesse."

"Have you ever seen that woman again?"

"Not that I can remember."

"I wonder if she's still in town."

"Talk to Simon."

"Good idea," I said. "I think I will."

I didn't bring up the subject again while we sat there

drinking beer and vegetating in the sun. We finished the first pitcher quickly and then got another. Luckily, my shorts were loose enough to hide the hard-on I had from staring at Will splayed out in his chair. His dark brown nipples were erect, standing out from his taut pectorals and surrounded by a swirl of light brown hair. The skin at his neck was stretched tightly around his jaw and Adam's apple, while his head lay back facing toward the sky, his hair dangling behind.

What a fucking queer.

My cock stirred further. It wouldn't go down. It felt constrained by my briefs. Something had to be done about it.

Look at him, he's just asking for it.

"Hey, Will," I said, when I'd finished the last of my beer. "What do you say we go for a walk along the trail?"

"Sure," he said. He seemed very groggy getting up off his seat. Drinking beer in the middle of a sunny afternoon could do that to a guy.

We both put on our shirts and left the union terrace, walking west along the trail until we'd passed the boathouse and the dormitories. From then on, the trail went through dense forest along the lakeshore as it headed into the arboretum. It was slightly cooler in the forest, in the shade. Sometimes I would walk a few steps behind Will so I could catch a glimpse of his butt. His cotton shorts stuck to his skin, forming themselves around the muscular globes of his ass. The occasional bicyclist or jogger would pass us along the trail, until we took a fork that led us away from the shore and deeper into the forest.

"There's no one else here," I said.

"That's right," he said, slightly out of breath.

My cock was still rock hard. I reached into my pocket to stroke it.

"I want to fuck you," I said.

Will laughed like he thought I was crazy. "Right here?"

"Yeah," I said. I motioned off the trail, toward a secluded spot in the woods. "Let's go over there."

"Are you serious?"

I took off my sweat-drenched shirt and held it firmly against his face. "Smell that," I said, standing behind him and pressing my crotch against his ass.

Will closed his eyes and breathed deeply. I reached around and grabbed his crotch, only to find he was already getting hard. I led him deeper into the woods.

"Strip," I said, rubbing my crotch through my shorts. "I want to see you naked."

Will smiled, said, "All right!" and quickly removed all his clothes, down to his socks and athletic shoes. He looked gorgeous, all tan except for the thin line made by his Speedos. His pale cock shot out like a rocket from his pubes. "Come and get me."

I took his shoes and quickly removed their lacings, grabbing them up in my fist as I headed toward Will.

"What are you doing?" he wondered.

"Just be quiet," I said. I grabbed him and pressed him up against a tree. "Hug the tree."

Will was able to wrap his arms completely around its trunk so that they met on the other side. I went around and tied his wrists together tightly with his shoelaces, just above a branch so that he was raised up off the ground and standing on his toes.

"Jesse, you motherfucker," he said lightly, as if he admired me. "You got me all trussed up."

"That's the idea," I said. "Now shut up."

I made a gag out of his socks and stuck the knot in his mouth, tying the ends around the back of his head. I grabbed him by his hair and pulled his head back. Will's eyes were wide and staring. Pressed up against the bark of the tree, his cock was the hardest I'd ever seen it. He was squirming back and forth on his toes, having a hell of a time. I threw his T-shirt over his head like a hood and tied it off at his neck by its short sleeves. Will groaned into his gag.

I'd turned him into a nameless, faceless hunk of meat, bound to a tree, up on its toes, flexing its muscles, and sticking out its butt. It was begging to be fucked.

God, he's such a queer. Look how he wants it.

I yanked down my shorts and briefs and pressed my cock up against his crack. I held one hand over his mouth while I grabbed my dick with the other.

"Do you want it dry?" I whispered in his ear.

"Mmm-hmm," he said through his gag.

"Yeah, I bet you do. You want it nice and dry like a good little queer. You want it bad, don't you? You want this cop's cock up your tight hole."

"Mmm-hmm." Will was breathing heavily, his heart beating fast. I could feel it thumping within his breast.

I pressed my cockhead against him, guiding it with my fist. Will groaned as I forced my way in.

"This is just how you want it, huh, queer?" I asked.

"Mmm-hmm."

I thrust my hips, and Will made this really wild sound while I went in deeper and deeper, until my balls were pressed up against him.

We fucked like that for a long time, until I pulled out and spent myself all over his back. Then I untied him and let him down. Will, totally exhausted, had to lie down on the grass for a while.

When I removed the gag from his mouth, he said, "God, Jesse, that was the best fuck I've ever had."

"I never knew you liked it like that."

"Jesse, you were so hot," he said, grinning from ear to ear. "Talking dirty, calling me a queer."

"Well, you are a queer."

"My butt's sore. I don't know if I can walk!"

"I only gave you what you deserved," I said.

He liked it. You raped him, and he liked it.

The thought made my cock grow again. Will was still naked, and so was I. I grabbed his legs and pushed his knees back against his chest.

"Jesse, what are you doing?" said Will as I grabbed his ankles and spread his legs high in the air. He looked up at me with an elfin grin and then said, "Oh yeah."

I gave it to him again nice and rough, just the way he liked it.

4

That night, I took Will out to Glitz. I wanted to talk to Simon, and Will had been falling all over me all day for the love of my cock—so I thought I'd treat him to some drinking and dancing and kill two birds, you might say, with one stone.

It was early yet—about ten o'clock—so only a few couples were out on the dance floor and not every seat around the bar was taken. Some lone men stood by themselves, sipping drinks and scouting around. The music pounded, but I didn't recognize the tune or the artist. I'd been out of the music scene for a while.

"Jesse, darling," Simon said when he saw me. He had been hanging around the bar, chatting with his new bartender, a scrawny waif with a crewcut who looked barely old enough

172

to drink. Simon's feathered gray hair glistened, reflecting the colors of the flashing lights. He offered his arms in a hug. I embraced him briefly and noted he'd gained weight since last I'd seen him. He was wearing a flashy mustard blazer that covered him like a set of drapes. "Where's your cute uniform?"

"It's our night off," I said. "You've met Will?"

"Yes, how are you?" Simon gave Will a tepid handshake and sat back down on a barstool.

"Nice to see you again," Will said, ever the gentleman.

"I'm sure," said Simon, and turned to me. "What are you having?"

"Beer?" I said, looking at Will.

"Beer," Will echoed. "Leinies."

"Haven't got it," Simon said coldly. "How about a nice Michelob?"

Simon's new bartender served us each a glass and bottle. "You must be Jesse Colson, the cop," said the bartender. "I recognize you from Simon's photo."

"Then you must be Simon's new boy."

Suddenly, for some reason, I felt sick to my stomach. I wondered if this strung-out kid had phoned Simon from the Greyhound station rather than slitting his wrists on the john. Then I wondered if I'd looked like this when Simon had picked me up from the truck stop. I wondered if I would have offed myself if I'd had no one else to turn to.

"Billy," the bartender said. His eyes were slate-gray, lifeless. I wondered if he'd ever killed anybody.

"How much?" I said, brandishing my wallet.

"Please, hon, it's on me." Simon touched my shoulder.

"No, we want to pay," said Will.

"Suit yourself," said Simon, waggling his fingers in the air and rolling his eyes.

I gave Billy the bartender a ten, and he gave me some change.

"Listen, Simon, I came looking for information. Did you see the paper this morning?"

"I've already talked to a detective about that."

"Who?"

"I don't know. Detective Bend-*over* or something."

"Bender," I corrected, but Simon knew this and was just fucking with me. "What did you tell him?"

"That's confidential."

"Come on, Simon. You can tell me. I've been working with Bender on this case."

"Then you can go ask him, can't you?"

"You knew the victim, is that it? You recognized him."

Will, perhaps against his better judgment, jumped in: "He used to come to Glitz all the time with some woman. I saw them myself."

"Well, you know me," Simon said, and downed the last of a Mai-Tai he'd been nursing. "I can't keep a secret to save my life. Yes, I remember her."

"When was the last time you saw her?" I asked.

"Since before I met you," Simon said. "But I never knew either of their names. Not their *real* names, anyway. She went by the name of Alexis, but I think that was just a trade name."

Will threw Simon a glance. "What was she," he asked, "a prostitute?"

"Not really. I always thought she was some kind of domi-natrix." Simon sat back and smiled and let this sink in.

Will didn't seem to get it, poor thing—but I was beginning to understand.

"She always called *him* Vanessa," Simon added.

"Do you think she did it?" I asked.

Simon asked Billy for another drink. "I don't know. She was very petite, and he was so big. But sometimes she could make him look like a very pretty girl."

"She'd dress him up?" I asked.

"Oh, yes," Simon said. "She did everything short of putting a leash around his neck."

"Did they live together?"

"Probably, but who knows? Sometimes I saw Alexis here with other transvestites. I'm not even sure if all of them were gay. I always thought she was dressing them up like women and taking them out in public to humiliate them."

Will laughed. "Sounds pretty kinky."

"Oh, you're cute," said Simon, and rolled his eyes.

"Did they pay her for it?" I asked.

"I think most of them did," said Simon. He took a gulp from his fresh Mai-Tai, and winced; Billy had made it too strong. I could make a Mai-Tai that Simon would like. "But the reason I remember *Vanessa* is that he/she was with Alexis far more often than the others. He probably did live with her. She did a better job dressing him up than she did with the others. Vanessa had a beautiful wardrobe. The dresses and shoes didn't always fit the others so well."

"So you don't know any of this for sure."

"Well, you know," Simon said, "one hears *rumors*. I don't know where I picked some of this up. Maybe I'm just bull-shitting and some of this isn't exactly right. But it's what I told your Detective Drop-the-soap—er, Bend-over."

"Bender."

"Whatever." Simon didn't care; he was having his fun.

"What did Alexis look like?"

"Small, with big black hair that was always piled up on her head. She always looked a little gloomy, with pale skin, dark mascara, scarlet lipstick."

"How old?"

"About thirty. She always wore these tall, high-heeled black leather boots that went up to her knees, and her boobs were always, you know, boosted up in a bustier."

"Sounds creepy," said Will. "I bet she did kill him."

"You're probably right," I said.

I hoped that Bender thought so, too. If he could ever identify the victim and track down Alexis, it would only lead him away from me, and perhaps he could even find cause to charge her with the crime. Now he actually had a suspect, even if he still hadn't identified the corpse.

"Thanks, Simon," I said. "I owe you one."

"That's not all you owe me," he said significantly.

I gave him a kiss on the cheek. "Nice to see you again. But Will and I really came here to dance."

Simon patted my back. "Go on, then!"

Will and I went out onto the dance floor, which was more crowded than before. I recognized the song as something new by Madonna. I looked up and saw Simon ascend the spiral staircase and disappear through the door to the DJ's booth.

"How could you ever stand living with that old queen?" Will shouted into my ear over the blaring music.

"Kept me from getting into trouble," I shouted back. "Now shut up and dance."

Simon was looking down at us from the DJ's window, frowning and drumming his chubby little fingers on the windowsill; he didn't look happy. *You know me,* he'd said. *I can't keep a secret to save my life.*

Bender knew I used to work at Glitz. I wondered if Simon had told him the true story of how we had met—none of this crap about Brian Bellman's garden party. Despite his past good grace in letting me go, Simon now seemed bitter over it and jealous of Will. I could see him deviating from our agreed-upon story to get back at me. But if Bender was ever to learn of the battered and bloodied condition Simon had found me in just a little over two years ago . . .

"What's the matter?" Will yelled in my ear as we danced.

"Nothing," I said, smiling disingenuously.

Simon Scales might have outlived his usefulness. I wished my pasta carbonara had killed him after all.

Thirteen

1

I went grocery shopping the next morning, and although hungover and without a shopping list, I still had the presence of mind to stop at the specialty coffee stand, as I'd planned before getting blitzed. I would be going back to work in two days and wanted to bring my own coffee with me. Before, I had simply schnorred off my FTO.

Lydia Kurtz had always brought along a thermos from home on our tour of duty and had got me addicted to her gourmet joe. But I had taken her to task over her preference for what I called "women's blends"—stuff like Island Mocha or Vermont Raspberry or Chocolate Hazelnut—after which she began bringing me French Roast, Norwegian Blend, and something called Columbian Supremus Est.

"Is this macho enough for you?" she had asked.

"Yes," I'd said, my tongue tingling from caffeine overload. She'd brewed the CSE especially strong—or else laced it with speed—because it had kept me awake for the next thirty-six hours, keeping me bright eyed and bushy tailed not only for my entire shift, but all through the night and a court case the following morning and up until the end of my next shift, after which I had collapsed at home on my bed and slept the sleep of the dead.

It's a common-enough joke that cops liked to drink old, bad coffee out of large, church-social–size percolators and consume massive quantities of jelly doughnuts. But the truth of the matter—at least at Isthmus City—was that gourmet coffee reigned, while the doughnut had been permanently dunked in favor of microwave popcorn or a fresh bagel. Even some of the old-timers had changed their ways.

Capt. Richard "Buzz" Rollack, however, had drunk only bottled mineral water for as long as anyone could remember, because his parents were John Birchers who had instilled in him a firm belief that fluoridation was a communist plot. He had recently taken to eating an oat bran bagel every day to keep himself regular. Buzz had confided to me, once when we were alone in his office, that his whole outlook on life had changed after the fall of the Berlin Wall and the collapse of the Soviet Union.

"I'm not afraid of communists anymore," he told me. "Only cholesterol."

I stood there in aisle 2 at the supermarket, unable to choose between First-Thing-in-the-Morning Blend or Kona Bona. My capacity for reaching a decision seemed diminished by the aftereffects of the beer and tequila Will and I had poured down each other's throats all night. In fact, he was still zonked out back at my apartment, sprawled naked on the bed.

"Jesse?" some woman said.

I turned around in search of the voice, one eye half closed, the other with eyebrow raised.

It was Jodi Sommers, dressed in an orange T-shirt and blue jeans and standing at least a foot shorter than me. Her dark hair was cut short—not so much a bob as a Prince

Valiant. She was holding out her hand for me to shake and had a smile on her face.

"Congratulations on graduating the academy," she said.

"Thanks," I slurred.

Sommers laughed, too loud for my headache. "I was in the class just before yours."

"Will's class."

"That's right." She stood there for a moment saying nothing. "That's where I met Lydia."

"Yeah," I said. "I know." I wondered if she was jealous I'd got to spend so much time with her lover.

I was suddenly self-conscious of the way I was dressed. I had thought I would only be stepping out for a few minutes and coming right back home, so I had simply thrown on an old T-shirt and tight spandex biker's shorts over a jockstrap. I realized that as I had stood there looking at the wall of coffee beans, Sommers had been standing behind me. I wondered if she'd been checking out my ass.

"Buying some coffee?" she asked.

"Yeah," I said, and emitted a probably rancid yawn.

"What kind do you like?" she asked.

"Columbian Supremus Est," I said. "Kurtzie turned me on to it."

Sommers examined the wall for a split second, then grabbed an empty bag and began filling it with Decaf Cocoa Coconut. "I like this one."

"Decaf?" I said.

"I don't like to pump my body full of stimulants."

Then why drink coffee? I wanted to ask, but didn't want to invest too much in the conversation. I felt off balance, like I was naked, exposed, taken by surprise. I didn't feel much like talking to people today. Sommers was pressing her luck.

She dumped her bag of beans into the coffee grinder and

turned the selector knob to AUTO-DRIP. She had a little difficulty getting the bag correctly under the spout, but once she
had, she flicked the switch and the grinder whirred to life.
The smell of freshly ground coffee jolted me out of my
stupor.

"See you around, Jesse," said Sommers, neatly folding the
top of her bag. "We should have you and Gunt over sometime for dinner."

I grunted.

As she left the aisle, I turned toward the grinder, opened
the lid, and looked to see how big the hole was.

Perfect, I thought.

I'd finally figured out how to dispose of the finger.

2

Will, in striped boxer shorts, came into the kitchen
scratching his neck and yawning.

"Leave me alone," I said. I was putting away groceries and
didn't want to be disturbed.

But Will must have thought I was joking, because he sat
down at the kitchen table, reaching inside his shorts to
scratch his crotch. "Wow," he said, "what time is it?"

"Quarter to three. Why don't you go watch TV or something?" I grabbed a huge can of crushed tomatoes and put it
up on the top shelf of the cupboard.

"I just got up," he said, with another yawn.

"You're in my way."

"I'll help you." Will started to get up.

"It's a one-man job," I said, pushing him back down. My
fingers came away slickened with his sweat. "They've got
male strippers on *Donahue*."

"Don't care." Will had a silly grin on his face.

I still had some frozen fish and ice cream to put away but was somehow nervous about opening the freezer door in front of Will, like I was worried the biker's finger was going to come jumping out at me. I didn't know why I should be so anxious; Will had been over many times while the finger had been hidden, frosted over behind the TV dinners, and I'd never given a thought to his discovering it. He wouldn't see it now, either, if I opened the door.

"You were out like a light," I said. I grabbed the ice cream and fish together, opened the freezer, and stuffed them inside. The interior walls were covered with two inches of ice; I'd put off defrosting it until I could get rid of the finger.

"Let me make a pot of coffee," said Will, standing up. He grabbed the sack of coffee I'd left on the table and opened it, sticking in his nose the way a dog might. He inhaled deeply like he was taking a hit off a joint. "Mmm," he purred.

"Kona Bona," I said.

I put away the grocery bags while he started brewing. I couldn't imagine ever living with him—or with anyone, for that matter. I needed more elbow room. Will was already starting to act like this was his apartment, too—but because I liked him, I'd never been too stern. I would try to drop the occasional broad hint, which Will missed, because by his very nature, he took everything at its most superficial level and was hopelessly gullible. I didn't think there was a thing I could say that he wouldn't believe. It was nice to have a "boyfriend" like that, except in these particular situations when I really wanted him to *go*.

Will poured me a mug and I offered him half 'n' half; he took his light. I took it black.

He grabbed the remote and turned on the TV. It beamed to life instantly, presenting us with the picture of a middle-aged transvestite holding his wife's hand. "I love him," the wife told Phil Donahue. "I just want him to be happy."

I was eager for Will to leave so I could go out and get rid of the finger. If it looked like he wasn't going to go home, I might have to sneak out while he was in the shower.

"I thought you said there were male strippers," said Will, heartbroken.

"So I lied," I said.

But Will turned the channel and found some oiled-up, long-haired muscle hunks parading around in tiny thongs and wiggling their naked ass-cheeks in front of the faces of screaming grandmothers.

"I found them," he said. "They're on *Sally Jessy*."

3

Will wanted to drag me into the shower with him, but I'd already taken one while he was asleep, and I told him I had to run back out because I'd forgotten to buy beer, which, I suppose, was true. I opened the freezer and reached behind the TV dinners and, for a moment, had a terrifying presentiment that the finger would be gone. But there it lay, right where I'd left it; I had to dislodge it from the encroaching frost. I placed the foil-wrapped thing in the zippered pouch of my fanny-pack and hurriedly left the apartment, to the sound of Will singing a George Michael song above the roar of the water.

When I reentered the grocery store, I worried I might run into Jodi Sommers once again—but we'd met at least an hour ago, and surely she was finished shopping by now. Not many other shoppers were around, anyway. At midafternoon, the store was at its slowest; it served mostly the WSU student population, and its busiest hours were in the evening, after class.

I went directly to the coffee aisle and pretended for a while to choose between blends. I suspected that store security or even a video camera might be watching, and I wanted to figure out a way to do my deed in secret. I certainly wasn't going to unwrap the foil and expose the frozen digit.

I wondered why I was even bothering to do this. After all, the finger had nothing to do with the real crime I'd committed. Even if someone was to find the finger on me, it was not evidence of a murder; the biker was alive and well and had been discharged from the hospital.

Don't kid yourself, kid. You'd be in the shit.

I grabbed an empty coffee bag off the shelf and snapped it open. I took a good look up and down the aisle, even though I knew I'd look suspicious for doing so. But nobody was watching and I could detect no security camera. I unzipped my fanny-pack and casually dropped the foil package— which had now grown soft—into the bag. Then I placed the bag under the spout of a coffee bean dispenser—Vermont Raspberry, I noticed—and poured in about a pound's worth. I set the grinder to the ESPRESSO/FINE position and poured the contents of my bag into the lid. One end of the foil was poking up out of the beans. I closed the lid, placed the open bag underneath, and turned on the machine. The grinder snarled at me like it was having some kind of trouble but soon overcame this and ground everything up. I made sure it was finished before removing the bag, then took a peek inside. Aside from ground coffee, I could see flecks of shredded aluminum foil, along with what looked like bread crumbs and small white flecks. At first, I thought these white things might be maggots—although how maggots could come to be in frozen tissue was beyond me—but as I took a sniff of the bag, I realized the flecks were ground bits of fish, and the things like bread crumbs *were* bread crumbs.

It hadn't been the finger; it had been a fishstick, after all.

Taking another whiff of the coffee-raspberry-fish smell, I broke out into laughter. The coffee grinder smelled of fish now, too. *There was a fish in the percolator,* I remembered—a line of dialogue from *Twin Peaks*, which had been my favorite TV show when I was living with Tom Latimer.

After buying the coffee and leaving the store, I wandered onto the WSU campus and poured everything out at the base of a Douglas fir—coffee, foil, fish, and all.

It bothered me that I could have deluded myself into seeing a severed finger where there had been only breading.

Unless someone took the finger from your freezer in secret and replaced it with the fishstick.

But there was only one person who could have done that, because ever since signing the lease, I'd had only that one person over, and by now he was probably wondering where the hell I was.

Fourteen

1

"Jesse?" came the gruff voice on the phone. At first, I thought it was Kurtz.

"Yeah?" I said. It was ten o'clock in the morning and I hadn't yet truly woken up.

"Harve Bender. I was wondering if you could help us out. We're staging a little reenactment."

"Of what?"

"Finding the bones in the chimney."

"That wasn't me, that was Brito. The construction workers, even."

"Brito's on vacation. I want you and Kurtz." Bender hung there on the phone; I met him with silence. "That is, if you don't mind."

"What's this for, *Crimestoppers*?"

"No," said Bender. "There's a crew out from California. They're setting up right now in the station to interview me. You ever seen *Mysterious Disappearances*?"

"Oh, yeah," I said, "on NBC, with Raymond Burr."

"I thought you didn't watch TV."

"Not much, but that's a pretty good show."

"They get a lot of tips."

"You think it'll help you any?"

"Maybe, maybe not," said Bender. His pride was getting the better of him. "They might give us a lead we can build on, point us in the right direction. All I'm really looking for is a positive ID on the victim."

Yeah—me, too, I thought.

"He's got to have family, friends, somebody," said Bender. "No one can just totally cut themselves off."

"My pa did." It just came flying out of my mouth. I don't know why. "He vanished into thin air, left my ma and me when I was four. Nobody's seen or heard of him since."

"Oh, yeah, I guess I remember something about that."

I thought I'd thrown him a curveball, but if I had, he'd caught it and thrown it right back. I'd never told him anything about my pa. "How do you know?"

"Your mother told me."

"My ma?" My head was swimming. "When did you ever talk to her?"

"Last year," Bender said, with a curt chuckle. "Didn't Buzz ever tell you? I was the one who did your background check."

"You're shittin' me."

"Scout's honor."

"You know everything about me, then."

"Hardly."

He knows too much.

"I can't believe you talked to my ma. Must have been rough going."

"She was pretty nice," Bender said. "I got the impression she was crazy about you."

Crazy is right.

"Listen, Harve, I got to run," I said. I didn't feel much

like talking to him anymore. I felt somehow violated. He'd never told me he was the one who'd checked up on my history. He must have known about Tom Latimer back in Denver and about the accident we'd had up on the roof. Of course, the inquest had ruled that I'd had nothing to do with it, so Bender shouldn't be *too* suspicious.

"Oh. OK." Bender sounded disappointed, almost forlorn. I wondered if he was lonely.

"When they shooting this thing?"

"This afternoon, around two, at the site. Twelve twenty-two Williams. It's still pretty much as we left it, at a standstill."

"Yeah, all right. Gotcha. 'Bye."

I hung up, then slammed my fist so hard into the drywall above my bed that it collapsed into a small crater. My hand came away covered in a fine, powdery dust.

2

While we stood around waiting for them to set up their camera and lights, I asked Bender how the case was progressing. He'd got the same information as I had from Simon Scales but hadn't yet been able to do much with it. I didn't let on that I knew Simon's story. Bender had only a vague description of this Alexis woman; no one could tell him her real name or current whereabouts, much less anything about Vanessa. Bender seemed not to have much of a clue as to what to do next, but he very much wanted to grill the mystery woman. She was his only suspect, such as she was.

I hoped he would find her and charge her, and that she would be found guilty and put away for life.

"OK," the producer called. "We're ready for you."

"Where's Raymond Burr?" Kurtz asked facetiously.

"Mr. Burr doesn't participate," the producer said condescendingly. "He just introduces the segments."

"I knew that," Kurtz told me, and nudged me in the ribs. "I did."

"I believe you," I said, and smirked.

I suddenly had this vision of Raymond Burr in the early years, as the black-and-white Perry Mason, towering over me as I sat on the witness stand, prying the truth out of me with those cold lawyer's eyes. . . .

—Isn't it true, Officer Colson, that on the night in question, you had, in fact, just arrived in town on the bus, no more than two blocks from where the victim was slain?

—Yes, Mr. Mason, that's correct.

—And isn't it also true that you were carrying a loaded pistol that you'd stolen from a farmhouse in Minnesota?

—I don't know what you're talking about!

—Your honor, if I may, I'd like to present into evidence exhibit A, a thirty-eight caliber revolver recovered from the crime scene. Ballistics tests prove that the bullets that killed the transvestite were fired from this selfsame weapon.

—Come on, Mason! You can't prove that I ever handled that gun. My fingerprints aren't on file.

—Your honor, if it would please the court, I would like to submit into evidence exhibit B, which I have in this plastic bag. It is—if you'll pardon me, sir, and ladies and gentlemen of the jury—a single pubic hair recovered from the sightpost at the end of the barrel of the murder weapon. A DNA test performed by Dr. Witherspoon of the State Crime Lab proves beyond a shadow of a doubt that this pubic hair belongs to Officer Colson, and that he was, in fact, the last person to handle the gun before it was disposed of behind the Mertz Paint warehouse.

190

—No, it isn't true, I tell you! It was her—that Alexis woman!

—*No! And I put it to you, Officer Colson, that it was you who killed the transvestite—*

—Transsexual.

—*Pardon me. That it was you who kept the revolver shoved down your jeans. That is was you who grabbed it so fast that the sightpost snagged on this one measly little strand of pubic hair, just before you fired twice—with deliberate and malicious intent—directly into the mouth of the transsexual. It was you, Officer Colson, who brutally murdered this poor, helpless transsexual in cold blood.*

—Stop it! Stop it! Yes! Yes, I can't bear it any longer! I did it! Take me away where I won't cause any more harm to anybody! Take me away, for God's sake!

"Officer Colson?" asked the unit director.

"Huh?" I was jolted out of my reverie. I'd been giving myself goosebumps.

"We're ready. I want you right over here."

3

Later that week, Lydia Kurtz and Jodi Sommers invited Will and me over to their house to eat takeout and watch the show. They didn't run our segment until the end of the broadcast; by then, I'd spent the better part of the hour keeping Kurtz and Sommers's three cats away from my pizza.

"In a moment," came Raymond Burr's voiceover, "a gruesome murder in Isthmus City, Wisconsin, that has police baffled. You may be able to help identify the victim—and catch the killer—when *Raymond Burr's Mysterious Disappear-*

ances returns. . . ." They then cut to a Burger King commercial that showed a waitress bringing your Whopper out to your table.

"Do they expect a tip?" asked Sommers.

"They're not allowed," said Kurtz, a strand of greasy mozzarella cheese dangling from her lips.

My knee was jumping up and down, but I wasn't aware of it until Will placed his hand there to calm me. "Hey, stop it," he said. "You're really jumpy."

"Too much coffee," I said, but I was really worried about the show. Someone out there in TV-land was going to recognize the victim, and then Bender would finally be able to get the ball rolling.

"Here." Will handed me another slice. "You're not fat enough."

As I began nibbling at it, the show came back on. The four of us sat transfixed.

Raymond Burr, resplendent in a dark suit, wine-red tie, and full gray beard, stood before a brick fireplace in which crackled a cozy blaze. He slammed shut a leatherbound book he had been holding.

"Fire has long fascinated man," Will said in a basso voice, before Raymond Burr could open his mouth.

"Cut it out, Gunt," said Kurtz.

"In 1841," said Raymond Burr, "Edgar Allan Poe wrote 'The Murders in the Rue Morgue,' which featured no black cats, no premature burials—but did contain perhaps the most gruesome murder in the annals of fiction. Some hundred fifty years later, a similar crime took place in Isthmus City, Wisconsin, and went undetected for two full years. Now local police are seeking *your help* in solving the murder, and in catching a psycho killer—"

"Psycho killer?" I said, my mouth full.

"A psycho killer who has come to be known as . . . the Chimney Sweeper."

At this point Raymond Burr faded away to footage of Lake Minoqua and beautiful downtown Isthmus City.

"The Chimney Sweeper?" I blurted. "Where the hell did they come up with that?"

"Probably Bender," said Sommers.

"Isthmus City, Wisconsin," came Raymond Burr's voice-over. "A quiet college town, home of Wisconsin State University, known for its two lakes and surrounding farmland, the heart of the dairy industry. . . ."

Fairyland of the Dairyland, I thought.

Bender had done my background check, which meant he knew that I'd worked as a chimney sweeper for Tom Latimer. In fact, he probably knew all about Denver. Maybe he actually suspected something more than the official story.

"It was in this house that the body was found—or, rather, what was left of it. . . ."

They showed a photograph someone had taken of the abandoned house on Williams before it had been torn down. The camera zoomed in slowly on the boarded-up windows. The dark music in the background was eerily effective.

"Skeletal remains were discovered during demolition, when workers saw a skull fall from what was left of the chimney. The workers then called police. . . ."

"Here we come," said Kurtz.

But the reenactment only showed me and Kurtz picking through the rubble, tagging bones, scratching our heads at the dress. They seemed to have cut the interview Kurtz and I had sat for. The next thing we saw was Bender seated at his cluttered desk in the Detective Bureau, describing the condition of the remains and the results of the postmortem, including the victim's presumed transvestism, transsexualism, and possible sex change.

"But the identity of the victim still remained a mystery, so Detective Bender shipped off the skull to the Smithsonian Institution in Washington, D.C., where, with the assistance of high-tech computers and a little old-fashioned modeling clay, experts in forensic anthropology were able to reconstruct the facial features of the victim."

Cut to a bespectacled geek from the museum offering a brief demonstration of what must have been a weeks-long procedure.

"This is what they came up with," said Burr's voiceover, as the plaster head appeared on the screen, revolving slowly as if set on a turntable. "The museum also provided these computer-enhanced images of how the victim might have appeared, both in and out of drag."

They flashed the sketches that had already run in the *Isthmus City Sentinel*, which had a circulation of about a hundred thousand. The ratings for *Raymond Burr's Mysterious Disappearances*, on the other hand, regularly placed it among the weekly top twenty, with an audience of over 20 million viewers. Right now, each one of them was staring at the sketches and the 1-800 number at the bottom of their screen. Out of those 20 million, it seemed unlikely that none had ever met the guy I'd killed.

"Operators are manning the phones," Raymond Burr reminded us.

"Sexist," said Sommers through a mouthful of pizza.

"What do you want them to say?" said Will. "Personing the phones?"

"If you have any information about the identity of the victim or his killer, *please call now*."

"Did you ever hear anything suspicious?" Will asked Kurtz. "You're right in the same neighborhood."

"We don't even know when it was," said Kurtz.

Kurtz could have seen me sitting on the bench right along with the queer sculpture. All she would have had to do was look out her front window that night. She would have remembered that—a grungy young man sitting there reading, so late at night. She would have thought it odd.

"With your help," Raymond Burr concluded, "Detective Harvey Bender may be able to apprehend the Chimney Sweeper before he strikes again."

"Before Bender strikes again?" said Will.

The scene returned to Raymond Burr standing before the raging fire, a dim orange glow illuminating his face.

"In his tale, Poe wrote that this manner of thrusting the corpse up the chimney was 'something altogether irreconcilable with our common notions of human action—even when we suppose the actors the most depraved of men.' "

"Food for thought," Will said.

"Food for thought," said Raymond Burr with a raised eyebrow; it wasn't his fault but his writers'. "For *Mysterious Disappearances* . . . I'm Raymond Burr. Good night."

Kurtz turned off the set.

"Bender thinks he's still in the city," Sommers said.

"Who, the killer?" I asked.

"Either of you men want the last slice of pizza?" Kurtz asked. "Otherwise, I'm just gonna throw it away."

Will shook his head, so I said, "I'll take it."

"He must be long gone by now," said Will. "Nobody could be that stupid." He looked over at me, and I jumped. But of course there could be nothing significant in his look.

"No, you're right," I said, taking the cold pizza wedge

from Kurtz. One of the cats pleaded with me to give it to him. "If I was him, I wouldn't have stuck around. No way."

4

I spent the rest of the night alone in my apartment, chain-smoking. I had thought I was turning my life around, building a new start. But it wasn't so—I was just a big fake and my whole life a fraud. I'd finally found some real friends—our sitting around the TV making obnoxious remarks reminded me of what I'd always imagined real brothers and sisters did together—but it hurt real bad to keep this secret all balled up inside me. There I was in their midst—the very guy *Mysterious Disappearances* was looking for—and they'd welcomed me into their tight little circle. Will was head over heels in love with me, I could tell. And I had never before had a friend like him that I felt I could trust. I'd always had to rely on myself . . . and on Jesse the badboy, always there to protect me.

5

The phone rang.

I snapped out of sleep and picked it up.

"Yeah?"

"Jesse? Harve Bender."

"Harve?" I squinted at the alarm clock. "It's two in the morning."

"Sorry, I've been working. We got a possible ID in the chimney case."

"Really?"

"No, not really." Bender chuckled. "Yes, really. From the poor bastard's poor mother down in Chicago. She was watching the show but didn't get around to calling us until an hour ago. You don't have court tomorrow, do you?"

"Why?"

"Because I need someone to come with me down to Chicago to ask the lady some questions, and all the other dicks are tied up. I've let you in on enough of this case, I thought you might want to keep up with it."

"Yeah, sure."

"And I could use the company."

"All right, I'll go."

"Be at the station at seven-thirty," Bender said.

"In the morning?"

"Don't ask stupid questions. 'Bye." Bender hung up.

Fifteen

1

Despite having been up most of the night, Harve Bender looked damn good. I'd never seen him looking this swell. His hair was freshly cut and shorter than his norm. And today he was actually wearing a suit jacket, the kind that his shoulder holster was designed to be hidden by. He had on a broad mustard tie that looked fairly snazzy, for him. He'd even shined his shoes.

"Her name's Matilda Hess," he told me as we climbed into his unmarked cruiser. "Lives on the South Side, near the University of Chicago. Bad neighborhood."

"So I've heard."

Bender had wanted me in plainclothes, too. With my OK cop's salary, I'd picked up some nice duds, but I hadn't tried to look too fashionable for this trip. We weren't exactly the guys from *Miami Vice*. I wore a gray jacket speckled with black like dots of pepper, a lighter color of gray slacks, and a plain black tie—very thin, like you see guys wearing in those old photos taken during JFK's time in the White House. At the last minute, I'd stuffed a gray hankie in my breast pocket. I didn't have a dot of color on me. I was going to be in the background, anyway. I was just along for the ride, pretty much, and wasn't even packing a gun.

"We look like a couple of goddamned Christian evangelists," Bender said once we were on the interstate.

I laughed. I felt at ease around him—one of the more ironic things about our working relationship. I suppose he had become something of a friend, too, despite the generational difference.

"How'd you like the show?" I asked as we left the outskirts of Isthmus City.

"It worked, didn't it?" He grinned happily. He wanted to solve this case in the worst way. "And Raymond Burr kind of adds some class."

"He scares me," I admitted. "Did you ever see *Rear Window*?"

"Right, where he's the ax murderer. Puts the pieces of his wife in a suitcase, carries her out of the apartment bit by bit."

"And he comes around to get Jimmy Stewart."

"Who's in a wheelchair."

"And he's this big hulk of a guy, coming at him with his hands out like this."

I demonstrated the classic strangler's outstretched hands, reaching across the seat at Bender.

"Yeah?" said Bender. "So?"

"Scared the shit out of me," I said. Bender wasn't impressed. "What about *A Place in the Sun*?" I said.

"What about it?"

"Where he's the evil prosecutor?"

"Evil prosecutor?" Bender repeated, stupidly.

"You haven't seen it."

"No, of course I've seen it. Elizabeth Taylor, Montgomery Clift."

"And Raymond Burr in the courtroom. He's got a boat in

200

the middle of the floor, and he climbs in and shows the jury how Monty Clift must have been sitting when he killed Shelley Winters out on the lake."

"But maybe he didn't kill Shelley Winters," Bender pointed out.

"Yeah, sure," I said, thrown off track. "And Raymond Burr raises the oar, stands up, and crashes it down against the boat like it's Shelley Winters's head, and the oar splits in two, and he asks Monty Clift if that isn't the way it really happened."

"So that makes him evil?"

"He's the heavy," I said. "That clinches the case right there. Monty Clift goes off to the electric chair because of that. You said yourself that maybe he didn't kill her."

"But he *thought* of killing her. He *wanted* to kill her. That's what scares me," Bender said, and lit a cigarette from the now-sprung car lighter. "When Shelley Winters is there in the boat with him, and she says, 'You wish I was dead,' or some such thing. *That's* the scary part. Because that *is* what he's wishing. He's wishing she was dead. He wants to kill her. The boat capsizes and she drowns. So is he guilty or not?"

"I don't know."

"Raymond Burr was just doing his job."

"I liked him better as Perry Mason," I said.

2

"Didn't you used to sweep chimneys?" Bender asked during a lull in our conversation, as we went through the first toll booth across the Illinois border, at South Beloit. "I seem to remember something about that."

My background check again, coming back to haunt me.

"Yeah," I said. "Back in Denver."

"I didn't know people still did that."

"Well, it's not like little urchins on the streets of London, but yeah, people still do it. It's a sucky job. I hated it. I fell off a roof once. Didn't break anything, luckily."

"Isn't that how your boss died?"

Bender was pretending vaguely to remember the details he had dredged up, but he must have gone back recently to look again at my background file. His check had been over a year ago; he shouldn't have remembered this shit.

"Yeah," I said, "that's right. Tom Latimer. Slipped and fell and broke his neck."

"You were up there with him," he said.

Was he trying to bait me? Was he up to something? Why was he bringing this up now? Did he think he'd found a connection to the Chimney Sweeper case? Or was he just trying to make innocent conversation?

"He just fell off," I said defensively. "He was dead before I could call nine one one."

"Wasn't there an inquest?"

This was beginning to sound like one of Raymond Burr's cross-examinations. Bender was trying to see if I kept my story straight, or if it even matched what he'd dug up on his own.

But I had it all down pat.

"Yeah. The inquest was pretty awful, but I guess it was routine for something like this."

"Tragic accident," Bender said.

"That's right. He hit a spot of ice. I reached out and tried to catch him, but he slipped and went sliding down over the edge. There wasn't anything I could do about it."

"He owned the business?"

"Yeah," I said.

"And when he died, you were out of a job."

"Yeah."

"Then I guess it was pretty tragic for you, too."

"I don't know," I said. "If he hadn't slipped like that, maybe I'd still be working for him. Then I wouldn't be a police officer."

"You like being a cop."

"Yeah, Harve, I like being a cop. That's a stupid fucking question."

"I know what that's like," he said, and at first I thought he was talking about being a cop, but he went on: "Seeing a buddy die right in front of you, nothing you can do about it. You feel helpless—guilty, even—as if it was all your fault. Do you ever feel like that? Do you ever feel guilty?"

"Yeah, sometimes." It seemed like what I was supposed to say.

"Or you wonder why you're still alive and he's all blown to pieces. You get to where you don't like yourself much anymore. I never have liked myself much since 'Nam. That's why my wives bugged out; they said I was 'too self-destructive.' "

"You didn't ever try to kill yourself, did you?" As long as he was asking me about Tom Latimer, I figured anything was fair game. I wanted to hear *his* story.

"Sort of," Bender said. "I'd rather not get into it."

"I heard you had some kind of breakdown."

"You did, huh? Well, I suppose everything gets around, doesn't it?"

A weird thought hit me: my life was in his hands. At least his car was equipped with a driver's-side airbag. If he wanted to kill me or cripple me for whatever reason, all he had to do was crash us. He'd walk away a little winded, but I'd be thrown through the windshield, all cut to ribbons, with

203

every bone in my body broken. I figured I shouldn't try to provoke him.

"I'm sorry," I said. "I shouldn't have brought it up. It's none of my business."

"Sure it is," he said. "I'd rather you heard it from me, anyway."

3

"Kurtz thinks you took a three-month vacation to Acapulco," I said.

"She's closer to the truth than most. Some in the department think I checked myself into a sanitorium or a fucking VA hospital. I encourage this. It makes me seem a much more romantic and desperate figure. I play this little game with them. I've never told anyone the truth."

"So why are you telling me?"

"Who says it's the truth?" he said, and offered a sly grin, taking his eyes off the road the way he often did while driving around town. The closer we got to Chicago, the thicker became the traffic. He was going to rear-end somebody if he kept this up; he was going faster than most of the other cars.

"Watch the road," I said. "You're making me nervous."

He turned back and started spinning his tale, which may or may not have been true but was certainly crazy enough to qualify.

"I suppose Kurtz told you about the kid I killed. I'd just got the divorce papers on my third wife. So I was sitting there one day writing her first alimony check, when I had this blackout. More than a blackout. I had this hellish pain at the back of my neck and then my eyes rolled up and I fell flat on my face across my desk. I was at home, alone. Any-

204

way, I came to about fifteen minutes later figuring I'd just had a small stroke. The alimony check was only half written out. You'd think I'd go see a doctor, right?"

I took this as a rhetorical question.

"But no. I got up, grabbed my car keys, and went to the airport."

"Acapulco?" I said.

"Virgin Islands," he said. "Sounds like the place to go, doesn't it? That's the first thing that popped into my head after I had this little episode. The Virgin Islands. Island of Virgins. I had this vision in my head that I couldn't shake. I just had to go there. So I withdrew all my money from the bank—in cash—went out to the airport, parked my car, and headed for the first ticket agent I saw. I didn't care what airline it was. While I was waiting for the little puddle-jumper plane that would take me to Chicago, I realized I ought to call the department. I got on the phone and told Captain Bork that I was going on an indefinite leave of absence for medical reasons, and hung up."

"I bet that went over well."

"Bork was shitting bricks for the next three months. They figured I'd gone into a forest somewhere and shot myself in the head, that they'd never find my body. I was a little hurt to find this out, later. But in the meantime, I was having a hell of a time. On the DC-10 from Chicago, I was like a little kid, flirting with the hostesses, getting drunk, you know, acting like a perfect asshole. I didn't even care that they wouldn't let me smoke. I regaled my seatmate with gory details of the murder cases I'd solved, then went on to telling him about plane crashes involving DC-10s. When I ran out of real crashes, I started making them up. By the time we reached the islands, he was in a real state. So was I. I stumbled off the plane, down the staircase, and out into the sun.

"I rented a little bungalow. It was actually in kind of sad shape, but what the hell did I care? I had a line from Pink Floyd running through my head: *Nobody knows where you are—how near or how far.* I was on my own and ready to party. I hadn't ever taken a real vacation. At this point, I was thinking I was never going back. I figured on just hiding out and vanishing off the face of the earth. Oh, they might be able to trace me, but anyway I was going to just bug out of everything. No more alimony checks, no more murders, no nothing. Just virgins and islands."

" 'Shine On You Crazy Diamond,' " I said.

"Huh?"

"The Pink Floyd song."

"You never cease to amaze me, Colson. You must have been about four years old when that came out."

"Didn't mean to interrupt," I said. "Go on. You'd just got up to the part about the virgins."

"I doubt there's a one," Bender said. "Unless they're sixteen, and I wasn't looking for trouble. But I went to a lot of bars, went dancing a lot. Got high a lot. I hadn't smoked any pot since 'Nam. In the islands, I was doing it daily. I'd bring girls home to my ratty place. Sometimes they were kind of ratty themselves, but I was so drunk I didn't much care.'

"I kept expecting that stroke to come back, or whatever it was, but it didn't. I thought this was the end of my life. I was just going to lie back and enjoy myself, and then I was going to have this massive pain in my head and drop dead on top of some poor girl."

"But you're still here."

"I'm still here. No matter how hard I tried, I couldn't bring on the stroke. Aside from the pot, I was smoking even more than usual. I gave up on filtered cigarettes. Slugged back a lot of whiskey. Fried my brain on Mary Jane. Went snorkeling."

"Snorkeling?"

"It can be dangerous when you're as fucked up as I was. But those islanders, they didn't care. As long as I had the money, they'd take me anywhere. If I'd wanted to pay someone to take me out into the ocean and push me off the boat, I could have found someone to do it. But I wasn't quite that far gone. I blew a lot of money gambling. I blew a lot of money, period. It was like a three-month fucking all-nighter."

"Once a fratboy, always a fratboy," I said.

"Closeted fratboy, remember?"

They design Joe the Camel to look like a big cock and balls so that homos and closeted fratboys will go running out to buy them. . . .

My money says you're a closeted fratboy. . . .

Sigma Epsilon Chi. But only for one semester, before I dropped out and joined the army. . . .

"You're not serious, are you?" I said.

"You be the judge," he said, and took a healthy drag from his Pall Mall—his real man's cigarette. "It wasn't all girls I took back to my bungalow. The guys weren't virgins, either."

He threw me a look. It was a challenging look, as if to say, *You want to make something of it?*

"I can tell you, Jesse," he said. "As I said, I've never talked about this with anybody. But I think I've got to know you pretty well, kid. You're not going to be judgmental about it. I think I read you well enough for that. I mean, there I was, blowing off the alimony to my three exes, blowing off my children. I was just thinking about myself, wasn't I? There on the Virgin Islands with nothing but me. You wouldn't cast a cold eye on that, now would you?"

I didn't say anything. I was half expecting Bender to make a pass at me, because that had always been my experience when someone told me they were queer. Not that Bender was admitting to being queer, exactly. He wasn't saying what he was. He certainly would have been the last guy in the department I would have pegged as a closeted queer. Maybe he'd simply gone through a phase. He didn't care anymore, he was getting toasted every day, he was looking for sex—he probably hadn't cared who or what he was having it with.

"No, Harve," I said, to answer his question that had been hanging there in the smoky air of his cruiser. "Why would I care?"

"That's what I thought," he said. "I mean, it doesn't make me a shit, does it? Shirking my responsibilities?"

"I wouldn't know. I've never had a wife or kids. For all I know, your wives were shits, too. Maybe your kids. Who cares?"

We stopped and paid another toll. Bender rode through the exact-change lanes and didn't even come to a full stop but instead tossed his change into the catcher and sped on through as the automatic gate opened itself in the nick of time.

"There was this one kid, though," Bender went on. "Not really a kid. A young man. Chocolate brown, shiny, smooth skin. Georgie was his name. I met him on the beach. He came right up to me and sat down and started talking, like he'd known me all his life. I liked him instantly. I felt so at ease. He looked so great, I can't tell you. Not muscular but not scrawny, either. Beautiful dark skin, the nicest smile. Terrific accent, very appealing. Looked great in his striped bathing suit. And here I was, a fat middle-aged guy with gray hair on my chest and an all-over sunburn. If he was looking for his opposite, well, he got it."

I was staring intently at Bender; he was staring straight ahead, really focused on the road now for the first time.

"I took Georgie back to my place. We started meeting every day. It wasn't the first time I'd been with a guy—I'd had a few experiences at college and then in the army—but it was the best sex I'd ever had. He was very experienced, knew some great tricks. I really fell for him. I mean *really* fell for him. I started to straighten out a little. Stopped smoking pot, drank less, lost some of my self-destructive urges—lost some weight. Georgie practically moved in with me. I kept expecting to wake up and find that he'd stolen my money, but he was on the level. He wasn't a hustler, just a sweet kid."

I'd been wondering about that. I would have taken his money in an instant if I'd been in Georgie's shoes. I might even have conked ol' Harve on the head in the process and left him for dead. I paled in comparison with Bender's little brown friend.

"But one day I woke up. I mean, I came out of my stupor, realized I'd dropped out of the world. I had child support, alimony, house payments to make. I had pending investigations sitting on my desk. I had real responsibilities I couldn't just throw away. Georgie wanted me to come back to bed. We'd been up late the night before, and he was still sleepy. I took a shower, and by the time I was through, Georgie was back asleep. I grabbed my stuff and sneaked out of there. I didn't even leave anything for him—no money, not even a note. I went to the airport and got a ticket home. The day after I got back to Isthmus City, I went straight in to work and pretended like I'd never left."

"And no one asked any questions?"

"They asked, all right. I just smiled."

"Do you think about him?" I asked. "About Georgie?"

"Every day, Jesse," said Bender. "Every fucking day, just as I think about Ted Axelrod, my fuckbuddy in 'Nam. Last time I saw him, he was walking right in front of me and stepped on a mine. I got his blood and shit all over me. I still wake up and have to take a shower to try to get it off—but it was twenty years ago. Shit."

"Sounds like you got a lot to think about."

"I'm the most fucked-up guy I know," Bender said. "But I just keep on." He laughed, but it sounded very sad. "You know, I never did have that stroke."

Bender rapped the knuckles of his left hand on the vinyl dashboard.

"Georgie's probably still there," I said. "You could go back."

"You're young, Jesse. You can never go back. You dig your grave and you lie in it. But sometimes it's a long wait before they start dropping the dirt on your head."

"I'll keep that in mind," I said. Now, at least, I knew why Bender had wanted me along for the ride. He'd been aching to tell me this shit. He'd been working closely with me and smelling my scent all the time and sneaking peeks at my ass and priding himself on acting as my mentor, and all because he probably wanted to get into my pants.

Fucking queer cop, I thought, and snickered to myself.

Just like the rent-a-cop.

Just like me.

4

Matilda Hess's house was in what probably used to be a nice area but which now looked rundown, beseiged. The chocolate-brown boys in this neighborhood weren't little Georgies—they were little Al Capones armed with Uzis. Gang graffiti marked several buildings and even some homes. Some of the people hanging out on the streets struck me as drug dealers or lookouts—or generally just up to no good. They all had their little gangland uniforms on—on this street, the color seemed to be red, whatever that meant. This was their turf, these red-clothed youths. They were in charge of this pathetic little 'hood.

I'd heard that the Chicago police put their homicide reports on three-by-five cards, and I believed it; this was one tough son-of-a-bitch of a city.

We walked up the weedy lawn and up the concrete steps of the Hess house. Bender rang the doorbell and then turned around, took a whiff of the air, and crinkled up his nose.

"Dog shit," he said.

The door opened, and Bender turned around to meet the woman behind the screen.

"Ms. Hess?"

"Are you the detectives from Wisconsin?" she asked.

"Yes, ma'am," said Bender, holding out his badge. In his other hand, he was carrying a briefcase. "Detective Harvey Bender, Isthmus City Police Department. And this is Officer Jesse Colson."

"Ma'am," I said, and gave a little nod.

She held open the screen door and said, "Come in. My husband's at work."

As if it wouldn't have been OK otherwise.

She closed the heavy front door behind her and turned the lock with tremulous fingers. Bender was already on his way to the living room sofa when she said, "Have a seat."

I parked myself next to Bender on a slightly worn sofa in front of the TV set, which was on and turned to *Live with Regis and Kathy Lee*.

"Let me get you some coffee," said Matilda Hess. Bender asked her for a touch of milk—skim if she had it—while I asked for mine black. She skittered into the kitchen and came back a minute later with mugs. We thanked her. She sat down

211

in the La-Z-Boy recliner across from us. The coffee table was strewn with issues of *McCall's* and *Good Housekeeping*.

There was nothing particularly special about Matilda Hess's appearance. Her hair was shoulder-length, a dirty shade of blond. Her face was beginning to show lines and chicken scratches that placed her in her mid- to late forties. She had purple bags under her eyes and was wearing no makeup except for some subtle lipstick. Her nails were not polished, and she wore no earrings. She was dressed in polyester slacks and a white cotton blouse. She wore sneakers and white athletic socks.

"I want to get right down to the case, Ms. Hess," said Bender. "Have you got a photo of your son?"

She found her purse nearby and pulled out a worn color snapshot. "That's him," she said. "That's Tommy."

Tommy, I thought. *Thomas Hess.*

Bender was writing on his notepad, so she handed the photo to me.

"Full name?" Bender asked.

"Thomas James Hess," she said, lifting her eyebrows and peering across the coffee table to see that Bender got it down right. "He went missing three years ago."

The photograph showed a young man of eighteen or nineteen with blond hair and tanned skin, smiling into the camera. He was out in the sun, wearing a purple tanktop and black running shorts. He had a solid frame with muscular shoulders and arms and—as far as I could tell—a normal man's chest.

Even though I'd seen him in darkness and made up as a woman, there was no mistaking the face. This was the man who had looked up at me with those doe eyes and thick eyelashes while I stood there with my gun in his mouth.

Hey, baby . . .

I handed the photo to Bender.

"I'd like to see others, too," he told Matilda Hess. "But maybe later. This does pretty much resemble our sketches."

She swallowed hard and closed her eyes for a moment. "Yes, I know. I was shocked to see them on the TV. I jumped right up and said, 'That's Tommy!' "

"Do you mind if we keep this?" Bender asked as he placed the photo in his inner jacket pocket. "Thanks."

I wondered if Bender thought Tommy Hess was attractive. I didn't, but that was because I was imagining him in drag, the way he'd looked as he approached me. I tried not to think of him the other way—how he looked later. But I couldn't help but wonder why he had wanted those breasts.

"Did your son ever dress in women's clothes?" Bender asked.

"He certainly did not," said Matilda Hess. "He was a normal boy like any other."

"So, to your knowledge, he never leaned toward transvestism?"

Matilda Hess grabbed a pack of cigarettes—Virginia Slims—from her purse and tapped one out. She didn't speak again until she had lit the thing and taken a healthy drag off of it. "No, Detective. He wasn't like those people you see on *Donahue*, if that's that you're thinking. He was in the Boy Scouts. He made the all-state wrestling team in high school. He dated girls. He wasn't a homosexual."

"One doesn't have to be a homosexual to be a transvestite," Bender said. If I'd thought he was going to handle her with kid gloves, I was wrong. "Many heterosexual men like to dress up in women's clothes. Tommy never said anything about wanting to be a woman, or having a sex-change operation?"

"Of course not." She got up and grabbed a large book

from the bookshelf. It was a high-school yearbook. "Here, see for yourself."

Bender began leafing through it, then turned to the index to look up the kid's name. HESS, THOMAS, it read, and was followed by several page numbers. I looked over Bender's shoulder as he found all the pages. There was his senior photo, retouched to perfection and looking like half the other white faces on the page. We also found him in photos of the wrestling team, the track team, the newspaper staff, the science club, as well as among photos of couples representing their respective clubs in the running for homecoming king and queen. Tommy Hess hadn't won, but there he was with his date, looking as average and straight and masculine as anyone could want, all dressed up in a blue tuxedo, his date wearing an orchid corsage.

"What were the circumstances leading up to his disappearance?" Bender asked.

"He was working with a construction crew that summer, still living at home. He kept saying that he wanted to move out, into his own place. But I wanted him to save his money, and there was no reason why he should leave home when he had a perfectly nice room right here. He was difficult sometimes, argued a lot with his father. He never was easy to raise, but boys will be boys."

"Did he get into trouble? Any problems with drugs?"

"Yes," she admitted. "We caught him smoking marijuana sometimes. It was all because of the friends he hung around with. He would stay out too late, and sometimes he would come home and you could smell liquor on his breath. Sometimes his eyes were puffy and bloodshot, and we figured he'd been smoking pot. But that was when he was a junior. By senior year, he'd turned around and was doing a lot better."

"These friends of his—what were they like?"

"They weren't fags, if that's what you're thinking," she said. "He knew them from wrestling, mostly. Some of them were long-haired types, washouts. Those were the ones who gave him the pot."

"Was there anything significant that happened just before he went missing?"

"No," she said. "I've been over this before with the Chicago police."

"Yes, I'm sure," Bender said. "We'll be heading down there later to pick up a copy of their report. But anything you could remember now might prove useful."

"All I knew was, one day he was gone."

"Did he leave a note or any explanation?"

Matilda Hess shook her head. She was looking at Bender. I stared straight at her eyes and thought she was hiding something—either from us or from herself. I began to wonder if she'd ever touched her son in a way that she shouldn't have, or if her husband had. It was easy for people to live in denial; I knew this for a fact.

Bender got the address of Tommy Hess's dentist. We were going to need his dental records to confirm the ID. It would do us no good to drag Matilda Hess up to Isthmus City to look at her son's bones.

"Would you like to see his room?" she asked brightly.

"You wouldn't happen to have kept it the way he left it, would you?" Bender asked grumpily.

"How did you know?"

Bender and I followed her down the hall, to the farthest bedroom. She opened the door and let us in.

If we were expecting anything strange, it didn't present itself to us. It was the room of a typical, red-blooded American teenage boy. The walls were plastered with posters of sports cars and bikini-clad women. On one shelf sat several wrestling trophies. The single bed was made up, but when I touched it, my finger came away with a thin coating of dust. No doubt Matilda Hess, Miss *Good Housekeeping*, never came in here. The curtains remained closed to the sunlight. The overhead light was a frosted-glass, squarish thing with figures of cowboys and various ranch brands—clearly something they'd bought when Tommy was a boy.

"Was Tommy your only child?" Bender asked.

"Yes."

"You must have been very proud of him."

She didn't say anything. She hovered around the doorway, arms folded, like she was waiting for us to finish quickly. But Harve Bender was looking around, fascinated. He opened drawers to find socks, jockey shorts, T-shirts. He thumbed through the cassette tapes by Tommy's small stereo: Van Halen, Def Leppard, Megadeth, Aerosmith, Guns 'N' Roses, Bon Jovi. Maybe there was something in that. Guys in heavy-metal bands wore long hair, makeup, and multiple earrings. Bender held up a cassette of a band called Twisted Sister, who had taken this feminine angle to the extreme.

"Hmm," he said, and put it back. He found another one by a band called Hanoi Rocks, whose members also looked like gaudy whores, pouting in their lipstick, eyes blackened with mascara. Whatever Bender was thinking, he didn't want to say it out loud in front of Matilda Hess.

"Do you mind if we make a thorough search of Tommy's room?" Bender asked suddenly.

"Well . . ." she began.

"It would really help us a lot to get to know him as best we can. You don't have to hang around if it's too painful."

"Well, all right," she said. "Go on ahead. I'll be in the living room if you need me."

"Thanks."

She gave a curt smile and went back down the hallway.

"Come on, Jesse," Bender said. "Help me out. We're looking for a secret place where Tommy might have hidden his secret things."

"What secret things?" I asked.

"I don't know. Lingerie?"

There were record albums in addition to the tapes. Bender held one up by the Lords of the New Church—a cover of Madonna's song "Like a Virgin." The band's lead singer was dressed in white frilly women's undergarments and a wedding veil. The other band members were holding him up by his legs, so that his crotch was spread and his pubic hair was sticking out.

"Everybody wants to be a rock star," Bender said.

5

We tried not to turn his room upside down, but we did manage to look everywhere. I thought that at the most, we might find some issues of *Vogue*, like Tommy had kept in the back of his car, or even *Playboy* and *Penthouse*; if he wanted to be a girl, maybe he liked looking at girls and secretly envied the way they were built. Maybe he got turned on looking at them and wishing he were them. But we didn't find anything like that.

Tommy had no women's clothes in his closet—at least hanging up and visible. We looked through some boxes of junk he kept on the floor of his closet, but they were mostly old comic books and car magazines. At last, Bender pulled down a big old typewriter case from the topmost shelf, hidden behind a pile of blankets. He handed it to me. It was heavy, but when I shook it, it felt like it was stuffed with loose items rather than a typewriter. I set it down on the bed and found it locked.

"Harve?" I said. "Do you think we can jimmy this?"

"Here," he said, and took a pocketknife out of his pants pocket. He opened it up to its smallest blade, crouched before the typewriter case, and stuck the tip of the blade in the hole. It looked like a simple lock, and within a minute or two, the latch sprang open. "Here goes nothing," he said.

He turned it upside down so that everything wouldn't fall out, then lifted the base of the box. The first thing we saw was an assemblage of feminine underthings—panties, garter belts, stockings. But underneath were the magazines.

"Holy shit," Bender said, setting aside the panties and things.

They were bondage magazines, all having to do with dominatrixes enslaving men and torturing them. But when we began thumbing through them, we found something more to the point: many of the photos were of men being forced into women's clothes and turned into transvestites. The titles were things like *Humiliated Husband, Transvestite Reform School, TVs in Bondage, Mistress Karla's TV Dungeon,* and *She Made Him a Girl.* Many of the men in the photos were average-looking, somewhat chubby, older guys who were turned into pathetic-looking transvestites wearing lingerie and blond wigs. But in some of the magazines, the men were younger and already had long, straight hair. Bondage and humiliation were integral to most of the pictures, with the men in dog collars with leashes attached. Some of the "mistresses" were women, while others were transvestites themselves. The men were generally dressed up in padded bras or bustiers, but in some cases their naked chests looked more like a woman's than a man's.

"Hormone injections," Bender said, looking at a photo of a busty man with long hair and rouge on his face. The man was naked from head to toe and had a penis in addition to his womanly tits. "He's probably a preop transsexual. They start off with hormone injections before they lop off the guy's dick."

"Ouch," I said. "Shit! Do you think Ms. Hess knows about this stuff?"

Bender gave me a look like *Are you for real?* "We're the first to jimmy the lock."

"She could have the key," I said.

"Maybe," he agreed. "But she would have told us."

"Would she?"

Some of the magazines were also contact magazines that had classified advertising from "mistresses" and "slaves." I started thumbing through them, looking to see if there was one from a mistress named Alexis—or from a slave who called himself Vanessa.

But Bender found it first.

"Hey, look," he said.

The ad had been marked with a highlighter. It was listed under the "Great Lakes" section:

Seeking handsome, macho jockslave with monster dick for TV treatment, forced feminization. He-man turned into a groveling pussycunt. Castration, emasculation—what I say goes. Right slave will be given real tits and pussy. Serious only. All considered. Write to: Occupant, P.O. Box 913, Isthmus City, Wis., 53947.

"Alexis?" Bender asked.

"Maybe," I said.

"Shit. The post office will never tell us who keeps that box."

I felt a clutch in my throat at the ad's wording, where it said "monster dick." I wondered if Simon Scales had ever seen Alexis's ad. He was the one who'd put us onto her and told us about her transvestite friend. Maybe Alexis was a friend of his.

Or maybe Simon was Alexis. In which case, I was lucky to still have my dick. But that was crazy. It couldn't be true. My head was beginning to swim with the idea. I had to put it out of my mind.

At the very least, I couldn't voice my suspicions to Bender, because I would never be able to explain how I had guessed.

Besides that, the closer Bender got to the truth, the closer he would get to me. Even if Simon was Alexis, he wasn't the one who had killed Tommy Hess.

"Damn!" Bender said. "This is it, I'm sure of it! Tommy answered this ad and got mixed up with this nut."

But, said the voice of Jesse the badboy in my ear, *if he finds the person who placed the ad, he'll think he's found the killer.*

"Things must have got a little carried away. They went too far. Maybe it was just a fantasy for Tommy, and when it became too real, he got cold feet, didn't want to go through with it, and his 'mistress' killed him."

If Simon is Alexis, he could take the rap, and you'll get off scot-free. This is your ticket out.

"We're going to have to confiscate this stuff," Bender said. "This is amazing!"

"You're a genius," I said. I had to drill his own brilliant idea into his head. "You find Alexis, you'll find your killer."

When Bender turned to face me, I had to wipe the badboy grin off my face.

Bender himself looked positively gleeful. Then he went out into the living room to talk to Matilda Hess.

I opened up the magazine and looked at the guy with the girlish tits.

I had the sudden, sad thought that I might have actually put poor Tommy Hess out of his misery.

Sixteen

1

Miss Jensen wants me. She wants me bad, just like those pets in *Penthouse*. She's begging for it. That's why she made that crack about my stuffing a sock in my pants—she knows it's no sock, and she wants to know what it feels like.

I've actually gone and read *All Quiet on the Western Front* now. My ma thinks there's something wrong with me, because I've been holed up in my room all weekend reading a book. I pop out every now and then to go to the bathroom or eat, but otherwise, there I am in bed, reading every goddamned word of the thing. And I'm liking it pretty much.

I know that Miss Jensen will be happy when I talk to her about it. She'll be proud of her Jesse-boy.

So I go to school on Monday carrying my paperback copy, now well creased and dog-eared and bent along the spine. All day I can't wait for English class. Miss Jensen is going to be in for a big surprise.

"Welcome back, Jesse," she says to me just before the bell rings. She's got this funny smirk on her face, but now I know that she's not laughing at me—she's playing some kind of game.

All during class, I sit there as usual, in the front row, legs splayed. I'm wearing my best pair of tight jeans. They're faded a little extra in the crotch, where I often rub my dick through the fabric while I'm watching TV when my ma isn't around. The faded spot highlights my bulge, and even though Miss Jensen's trying hard not to look at it, she can't help herself every now and then. I see her eyes dart down when the class is busy writing down the answer to some question.

And for once, I know the answers, too. I really *concentrated* on that book. I know the characters: Müller, Tjaden, Kat, Detering, and the rest. Better, I know the story, and it's really kick-ass. I can understand these guys and this fucking war they're fighting, even if they are Germans. It's the first time that I ever enjoy a book just for its own sake, the first time I ever realize that reading beat watching TV hands down. I'm already wondering what I'm going to read next, thinking that I'll go down to the bookstore and pick up something—maybe a Stephen King book, since everybody seems to like them so much.

Miss Jensen is giving us a pop quiz. We're only supposed to be three-quarters of the way through, but I've finished the whole damn book. I'm actually ahead of half the other kids in class.

When the next class bell rings and I rise to leave, Miss Jensen takes me aside.

"Jesse," she says. "Do you have a minute after school to come and talk to me?"

"Sure," I say. *Do I ever!*

But after school, when I find her alone in her classroom sitting at her desk, all she wants to do is apologize.

"I'm sorry for what I said to you last week," she says, smiling a truly sorry-looking smile. "It was wholly inappropriate, and I should never have opened my mouth."

222

"That's OK," I tell her. "Maybe I needed it."

"I made myself look like a fool," she says. "Word of it's gotten around the school, even to the principal. It's put me in a bit of trouble. I do hope it doesn't turn into a big issue. So I just wanted you to know how bad I felt afterward. You skipped the rest of that day of school, didn't you?"

"Yes, ma'am," I say. It's the sexiest "Yes, ma'am" I've ever said, my eyes downcast, then darting up to meet hers. My cock feels like it's straining to burst my jeans.

"And it's all my fault," she says.

"I guess," I say. I want her to feel sorry for me. It'll make her want me even more, if that's possible.

"Well, that's it," she says. "I've got to finish grading these quizzes."

"How did I do?" I ask.

"I don't know. I haven't looked at yours yet."

"Because I read it," I say. "I spent the whole weekend reading it. I liked it."

"Good," she says. "I'm glad. I'm sure you did fine, Jesse."

But she doesn't have any more time for me. She's busy.

So I have to go. I go down to the bowling alley for a couple of hours and play the pinball machine. The manager gives me hell again for abusing the machine, but it's the only way I know how to play, roughing it up like that.

I call up my ma and tell her I'm eating over at a friend's house. Then, when I leave the bowling alley, I start heading for Miss Jensen's place. I know right where she lives, and I know she'll be there, because I've gone there before at this time of day and watched her through her windows.

2

"Jesse!" she says with an odd laugh. "What are you doing here?"

"I wanted to talk to you about what you said. You want to let me in?"

I'm standing there on her front stoop, and Miss Jensen is there in her doorway, one hand up against the doorjamb. She's attempting to smile but not very successfully; it keeps falling, and she has to pull the corners of her mouth back up.

"You had a chance to talk to me after school," she says.

"You were too busy grading papers," I say. "You didn't have the time for me."

"I didn't know you had anything else you wanted to talk about." She looks flustered and drops her hand from the jamb, then swings her door open wider and says, "I'm sorry, Jesse. Come on in."

I know from the movies that Dracula can't cross a threshold unless he's invited; this is what I feel like as I enter Miss Jensen's place.

It's small, furnished with the basics: sofa, chairs, lamps, a table in the kitchen, some bookshelves with books, some prints on the walls. Teachers don't make much—especially when they're just starting out—but Miss Jensen seems to live comfortably, at least.

"Do you want something to drink?" she asks. "Pop?"

"You got beer?" I ask.

"Jesse, you know I'm not going to get you a beer."

"Coke, then," I say. But my mouth is tasting beer.

I sit down on the sofa and plop my cowboy boots up onto the coffee table, crossing my legs.

"Off," she says, handing me my Coke.

I don't budge, so she grabs my boots and lifts my feet gently off her precious coffee table. I wasn't hurting it any, but it's her place. So I've got my feet planted on the floor, and my legs naturally fall into their widespread pose. The fizzy Coke feels good on my throat.

She doesn't sit with me on the sofa but across from me in a chair. She's got herself a glass of water.

"So what can I do for you?" she asks.

"I think you know," I say.

"I told you I was sorry," she says. "I was way out of line. A teacher shouldn't say such things to her student."

"But you noticed my crotch," I say. "You were looking all that time, just like I wanted."

"Jesse," she says, "we shouldn't be talking like this."

"Why not?"

"Because I'm your teacher, and you're just a kid."

"Oh, yeah? Then how come you were staring at my cock?"

Miss Jensen laughs uncomfortably. "Jesse, there's no way I couldn't have noticed. You were much too obvious about it."

"You didn't have to look."

"Well, listen," she says, "you're not the only one who does it. What I said is true, isn't it? Someone's been spreading a nasty rumor around the school that I'll give guys good grades if they do that. I don't know where it started, but it isn't true. Someone told you that, didn't they?"

"Yes, ma'am," I say. A judicious "Yes, ma'am" every now and then never hurt anybody, and it gets me all hot talking to her this way.

"Kids can be cruel," she says. "Sometimes I think teenagers are the worst. I mean, younger kids don't know they're being cruel. But teenagers are smart enough to know. They just don't care."

"I care," I say, but she acts like she doesn't hear.

"It's sexist, is what it is. Just because I'm young and single and I don't look like an old spinster, people treat me like I'm a loose woman."

I laugh at that. *Loose woman!*

"And it's not just the kids," she admits. "It's the administration and the other teachers, too. They're always hinting that I should get married. Well, I don't have to get married if I don't want to."

"Do you have a boyfriend?"

"No."

"You sound lonely."

"I am, sometimes," she says. "But that's my business. I'm nothing like what people think. I lead a pretty boring life, actually."

"So how come you've got this reputation?"

"I don't know," she says. "Look, I think you'd better go."

"I don't want to. I want to be with you."

"Jesse, it's just a crush, OK? A schoolboy crush. I'm flattered, really I am, but you need to be going out with girls your own age, not thinking about me."

"It's not a crush," I say. "It's something else."

But she doesn't know what I'm talking about, so I get up and act like I'm going to leave.

"Thanks for the Coke," I say. "Oh, can I use your bathroom?"

"Sure, down the hall." She gets up and points me the way.

As I walk down the hall, I know she's staring at my ass. She can't help herself. What they all say about her is true—I know it is. She wants my cock. She's begging for it.

I go into the bathroom and shut the door. I really do have to pee, so I take care of that first. Then I wash my hands and splash some cold water on my face. I slip off my cowboy boots. I peel off my jeans and drop them on the floor. I take off my shirt and my red bikini briefs. Even before I've got all my clothes off, my cock is rock hard.

I walk out into the hallway. No sign of her.

She's in the kitchen, cutting up vegetables for her dinner, and she's got her back to me. She doesn't even hear me approach; she's expecting to hear cowboy boots, anyway.

I come up behind her, grab the knife from her hand, and clamp my other hand over her mouth. I lay the knife down; I'm not going to need it. She struggles and tries to scream, but I'm stronger and she's smaller and I manage to pick her up and carry her kicking and squirming into the living room. My cock is pressed up against her skirt.

I set her down on the carpet and lie on top of her.

She bites my fingers, so I hit her across the face.

My fingers run up under her skirt and pull down her panties. She's trying to squirm away, but I've got her pinned down. She isn't going anywhere.

"No," she says.

"Does this feel like a sock?" I ask. Now she believes me.

"Stop," she says.

"I love you, Pamela," I tell her, over and over and over.

3

The next day it's plastered all over the newspaper: TEACHER'S DEATH A SUICIDE.

Miss Jensen had slit her wrists in her bathtub.

I can't deal with the news, and of course I have to keep to myself that I'd gone and seen her yesterday. But when I'd left her, she was alive. A little upset, but alive. Who would have thought she'd go and do a stupid thing like this? She must have had more problems than she'd been letting on.

The story in the paper alluded to her not exactly fitting in at the high school, and how the administration hadn't been entirely happy with her performance, and how she had recently had "a lot of personal problems," according to one source.

But still, I can't pretend I had nothing to do with it. Somehow, my coming over must have triggered something. Maybe she thought I was going to brag about it around the school, tell everyone how I'd scored with Miss Jensen. She *had* seemed pretty insecure about this reputation of hers. I guess she was pretty fragile, after all. Anyway, now she was dead, and I'd never see her again.

"Isn't that your teacher?" Ma asks, pointing at the photo of Miss Jensen in the paper.

"Yeah."

"Oh, Jesse, I'm sorry," Ma says.

"Why?" I say. "It's not your fault."

"It was a stupid thing for her to do. She's a teacher. She should be setting an example."

"I guess she wasn't thinking about that."

"Oh, honey, you must feel awful."

Ma comes over and places her hands on my shoulders, starts kneading my muscles. I flinch away from her touch.

"Jesse," she says. "Don't be like that."

"Just leave me alone," I say.

Gene Colson looks up from his dog dish, where he's been eating his morning kibble. He lets out a little bark.

"I'm just trying to make you feel better. You're all tense. You let your mama work out those kinks."

"I don't want you to."

"Ain't nothing wrong with a mother touching her son," she says.

I don't say anything.

"Isn't she the one who said that awful thing to you?"

"Yeah."

"You should go talk to one of the school counselors," she says.

"Why, you think there's something wrong with me?" I snap back. I'm staring at Miss Jensen's face in the paper, thinking about yesterday afternoon. It hadn't been as fun as I'd thought it would be. Maybe I shouldn't have done it.

"Hon, it says right there the school's offering counseling for kids who want to talk about it. It's obvious you won't talk about it with me. I'm just trying to be helpful."

"Just stop it," I say, and stand up. She tries to touch me again. "I said stop it!"

I grab my backpack and start heading for the door.

Gene gets excited, running around and yapping. He always gets this way when I leave for the day.

"Where are you going?" she says. I don't like the tone of her voice. It sounds desperate, clinging.

"School," I say. "I'm already late."

"You can stay home if you want," she says. "I'll call you in sick."

"I don't want, OK?" I open the door, and then I turn around. "There's nothing wrong with me. I'm fine, OK?"

Now my ma's getting all teary eyed. "Jesse . . ." she says.

Suddenly, when I look at my ma, I think I'm looking at Miss Jensen. I'd never before noticed the resemblance, but there it was, plain as day.

Gene heads for me, hoping to sneak out of the trailer when I leave. Maybe he doesn't want to be left alone with her.

I slam the door and try to put it all out of my head.

Only, instead of going to school, I head for the bowling alley. I end up wasting what money I have on pinball, and this time the manager doesn't give me any shit, because I give him this look like I want to rip his head off.

Seventeen

1

"Charlie One," I radioed to Dispatch. There was no radio traffic. I wasn't interrupting anything.

"Go ahead, Charlie One."

"I'm going ten-seven for lunch."

"Copy."

It was weird having a lunch break at one-thirty in the morning, and it wasn't exactly lunch I was having, unless cigarettes counted as food. Most nights, we never actually got to take lunch, because we were tied up on calls. Some nights, the less important calls got backlogged and wouldn't even get dealt with until the first-detail shift took over at seven.

But this was one of those nights that was *too* quiet, when you just *knew* something was going to break. The air was hot and sticky, barely a degree or two cooler than the day—or what I'd seen of it. Such oppressive summer nights usually brought the crazies out of the woodwork, so our only saving grace was probably the fact that it was a Monday, and everybody—crooks and cops alike—was tired from what had been a busy weekend.

I met up with Will Gunther in a parking lot on the bor-

der of our beats. We were each in our vehicles, facing in opposite directions and talking through our open windows,
each of us with a cigarette in hand. Like good boys, neither
of us would smoke within an enclosed squad car, because
that was against the rules. In that respect, Harve Bender was
the least coplike of all my colleagues, with a total disregard
for any small regulation that didn't quite suit him.

I was Charlie One now, fourth detail, on my own, and I
loved it. It was a lot more fun than hanging around with my
FTO—as wonderful as Kurtz had been—and more fun than
interning with Bender. I'd never before found a job that so
matched my temperament. Chimney sweeping had been the
worst—filthy, grubby work, and I'd never quite gotten used
to climbing up on people's roofs and tromping around with
all those tools. Falling off that one roof hadn't helped, and
neither had working for Tom Latimer—a creepy, unscrupu-
lous old shit. His falling off that other roof and breaking his
neck had been a godsend, because otherwise I might have
been trapped in that job forever, for lack of alternatives.

But life had given me a lot of second chances. In police
work, I'd finally found my calling.

It was an old cliché that, personality-wise, cops weren't
that far from criminals. Cliché or no, I found it largely to be
true. We both saw ourselves as apart from the rest of society.
We both believed that you had to stick with "the gang" if
you wanted to belong; to the extent that there was honor
among thieves, there was honor among police, as well. We
both knew that success in life hinged on how well you could
fuck the system. The difference was, cops had a fear of vio-
lating the rules; some of them joined the force because they
thought it gave them license to do things they couldn't ever
do as mere civilians. Crooks, of course, thought they had the
liberty to do whatever they liked—specifically because they

never believed in rules. Cops supported capital punishment because they knew it would deter *them* from committing murder; but the true criminal was never deterred by even the harshest law. Those cops who went bad did so because first, it was in their nature, and second, they lacked the necessary restraint. Those who stayed on the straight and narrow had the most self-discipline; they managed, somehow, to resist the temptations that cropped up every time they turned around. The only rule a crook ever followed was, Don't get caught. And smart crooks had to resist temptation, too—the temptation to commit a deceptively simple crime when there was a great risk of being found out.

Having seen both sides of the coin, I felt better prepared than my colleagues. Despite my past, I knew that I would remain an honest cop. I had nothing to gain by being crooked, and everything to lose.

"Want to meet for breakfast at shift change?" Will asked. The summer sun had darkened his skin and further bleached his hair so that it was nearly white. Even in the dim light of the parking lot, he looked damn good. He had one of those mischievous, elfin looks on his face.

"Sounds good," I said. "Where at?"

"Peggy's Blue Plate?"

"All right."

"So," Will said, exhaling a cloud of smoke, "you went with Bender to Chicago. He got a line on that skeleton."

"Yeah," I said. "It's all too weird for words. The guy wanted to have his cock lopped off is what we think. Bender's still waiting to get the dental records, so the ID isn't confirmed yet."

"You talked to the victim's mother?" Will had this very intense look on his face, like he was totally into hearing about all this. I figured he was interested because of my own

233

interest in the case. We had often talked about it, lying to-gether in bed. The danger of discussing it had always kind of thrilled me.

"It was all pretty creepy," I said. "She's in total denial, still thinking her son was some macho wrestler. I bet there's a history of sexual abuse there." I was gearing up to tell Will the rest of the story of our meeting with Matilda Hess, when an alert tone sounded over the radio.

Will and I held our breath; our first suspicion was that one of our own was down.

"City and listening units," the dispatcher began. That meant it was bad, that they needed all the help they could get. "Ten thirty-two"—man with a gun—"at 1719 Conrad. Suspect is female black and has barricaded herself with fam-ily members inside. Tactical unit en route. Charlie Four?"

"Charlie Four, copy," squawked Lydia Kurtz.

"Charlie Three?"

"Charlie Three, copy," said Jodi Sommers. Over the radio, I could hear her siren already on.

"Charlie One?"

"Charlie One," I said. "Copy. On my way."

I tossed my cigarette out the window, waved good-bye to Will, and sped off, deeper into South District. Shortly after, I heard Will dispatched, along with others. We were switched to a tac channel.

"Suspect has made threats to harm those in the house as well as herself," said the dispatcher. "Trying to raise suspect on the phone to begin negotiations."

That address on Conrad sounded familiar, but I couldn't quite place it. This kind of situation was a very big deal and could be highly dangerous. It usually sprang out of some kind of domestic quarrel, when there were guns in the house and someone temporarily lost control. Barricaded persons happened every three or four months in Isthmus City, and I'd heard of two different occasions when the suspect had proved to be an ex-policeman. The difficulty in these situations was trying to take the suspect alive, or at least without harming the others in the house. It could turn into a shoot-out, dangerous not only for those inside but also for the cops on the scene, not to mention the neighbors. That was why we had a tactical unit specially trained in hostage negotiations. Without them, the whole thing could turn into a massacre.

But it was likely that they wouldn't arrive until after Kurtz and the rest of us got there.

I stepped on the gas and responded with red lights and siren.

2

"How we doing?" I said to Lydia Kurtz, as I drew up beside her and Sommers. Our squads were parked along Conrad, visibars casting the neighborhood in an eerie red-and-blue light show. Our radios squawked with the voices of the tac team, who were just getting their shit together.

Kurtz had her service weapon out and ready, aimed at the ground. The suspect was still inside the house. I drew my Glock out of its holster and kept it pointed at the ground as well.

"She's screaming and hollering in there," Kurtz said. "I think she's on the phone with Dispatch."

"No shots fired?" I asked.

"Nope."

The house was a small bungalow with an unkempt lawn overrun with dandelions and crabgrass. The paint on the clapboard siding was peeling off, and parts of the roof needed patching. An early-model Toyota Celica was parked in the drive; its muffler was hanging down and touching the gravel. Children's toys and a tricycle sat in the yard.

"Why does this house look familiar?" I asked.

"It's the James house," said Sommers. "Berniece James lives here."

"Taneesha's mother," I said.

Now I remembered. Bender and I had been here once to check on Taneesha's baby. The first time I'd run into Berniece James was at Taneesha's apartment the night her son Tyree was killed. She'd always struck me as a well-meaning but frightened woman. Her family was totally out of control, involved in gangs and drugs. She had moved here from Chicago to try to keep her children away from all that shit.

"Taneesha must have the gun," I said. "She's been having paranoid delusions. Who else is in there?"

"I don't know," said Kurtz. "Berniece, Latricia, probably Taneesha's baby, maybe Latricia's kids, too."

"Shit," I said.

Will pulled up, adding to the collection of marked squads parked haphazardly along Conrad Street. He came out of his squad with his gun drawn; he was pumped up. The four of us spread out and tried to cover the house as best we could until the tac team arrived.

We could see lights on through the curtains but couldn't make out much of what was going on aside from the screaming, shouting, and crying. I heard an object crash against a wall.

Harve Bender pulled up in his unmarked squad. He was one of the leaders of the tac unit—probably the only one who was actually on duty on a Monday night. Within a few minutes, the other members of the unit were all mobilized around the perimeter of the James household. We had the street blocked to traffic. Some officers were going around to neighboring houses and advising people to stay out of their windows. We were armed to the teeth. There was no way Taneesha could get out without being taken into custody or being shot. Technically, Kurtz, Sommers, Will, and I were all there to assist the tac team, and Bender was in charge.

I was stationed near Bender's squad. Bender was standing just outside his open door, talking to Dispatch on his cellular phone. I could hear what he was saying.

"You've got her on the line?" Bender said. "Try to get her to come out unarmed."

We stood there in wait, aiming our weapons at the front door of the bungalow. It was several minutes before anything happened.

During that time, a crowd began to gather around our perimeter. They came from houses along Conrad, as well as from the nearby housing projects at Maugham Terrace. The crowd was mostly black and Latino. The city had had problems before in this neighborhood with mobs of people ganging up on police. The last thing we needed tonight was a riot.

Finally, the door of the bungalow opened and Taneesha appeared, waving her gun around inexpertly.

"Don't let them take my baby!" Taneesha shouted. "I'll kill them! Don't let them touch my baby!"

She took a few steps closer. Her eyes were wide and frightened. She was in a worse state than that time Bender and I had paid her a visit. I was glad Bender was here, since Taneesha had dealt with him often in the past. If anyone could talk her down, it was him.

Bender reached for his bullhorn. "Put the gun down, Taneesha," he said. "Throw it down in front of you."

"Get back!" Taneesha said. "Leave me alone! If I throw you my gun, you're going to take my baby!"

"Taneesha," came Bender's voice through the bullhorn. "It's Detective Bender. No one's going to take your baby. Now, come on, Taneesha. We don't want anyone to get hurt. You're scaring your mother and your sister. Throw the gun down and put your hands up where I can see them."

"Fuck you!" Taneesha said, waving her gun around. "Fuck you, Bender! I don't want to hear no more of your bullshit!"

The crowd began cheering her on and jeering at us.

"Dispatch," Bender said quietly into his cellular phone. "Did you tell her to drop her gun?"

Bender swore. Apparently, Dispatch had not.

"Look, try calling her back. This time explain that she's got to come out unarmed," he told them.

I had a bead on Taneesha. Any second now, I could take her out. Any second now, she could shoot any one of us. And if one of us was shot, there would be a lot of Monday-morning quarterbacking when it was all over.

The phone rang in the James house.

"Answer the phone, Taneesha," Bender ordered through the bullhorn. "Go back inside and answer the phone."

Looking around as if not knowing what to do, Taneesha suddenly went running back into the house.

"Jesus," Bender said to me. "That was close."

We waited for a long time. Bender talked strategy with some of the tac team—alternative plans in case Taneesha decided not to come back out. They would use tear gas as a last resort: that would mean gassing not only the James family but also us and the rest of the neighborhood.

Finally, the door opened once more.

Taneesha came out again, but she was still armed. I tried to determine what kind of gun it was. It looked like a nine-millimeter of some kind, black and sleek, perhaps a Smith & Wesson. It didn't look like my Glock.

"You can't fool me!" she shouted. "You're up to your old tricks!"

"Drop the gun, Taneesha!" Bender said into the bullhorn. "Drop it or we'll have to shoot."

Taneesha held the gun straight out, her arm shaky but not so much that she couldn't hit one of us. She took a few steps closer, slowly and with assurance. She was aiming right at Bender, who was armed only with a bullhorn in one hand and a cellular phone in the other.

"Kill me, then!" she said. "I don't give a fuck!"

"What about your baby?" Bender asked her. "Think about her, Taneesha. Do you want her left without a mama?"

This was going on much too long. One of us was going to get killed. Taneesha was going to start with Bender and then finish with the rest of us. We had a dozen guns drawn on her, including the rifles of the tac squad, but she could easily get off a few rounds before any of us could respond. By then, Bender could be dead. I had no doubt Bender was wearing his bulletproof vest, but Taneesha was aiming high, for Bender's head.

"Leave my baby alone!" Taneesha shouted, coming closer. "Just go away and leave us the *fuck* alone, *motherfuckers!*"

I had her right in my sights, and I knew no one else was going to do it. I aimed at her head; I aimed for the kill, as I'd been trained. Her frightened eyes made an easy target, lit up for me by the flashing red and blue lights of our squads.

I squeezed the trigger gently and heard a loud series of reports as my service weapon fired off several rounds.

Taneesha fell to the ground still clutching her gun. No

one else had been hurt. Taneesha hadn't managed to get off a shot. I'd got her just in time.

Berniece James came running out of the house, screaming. A policewoman in tac-team garb ran out and held her back.

Latricia James stood in the doorway, holding Taneesha's baby. Latricia's kids stood alongside her, clutching onto her legs and crying.

The officers holding the crowd back at the perimeter had their hands full. Some extended their collapsible batons, just in case. The crowd was roaring, cursing at us and spitting at the nearest police officers.

"Murder!" they cried.

Bender went running out to Taneesha, took the gun from her hand, and felt for a pulse.

I was certain she was dead; I'd hit her at least twice, right in the head, and the rounds I'd used were powerful.

"Fuck!" Bender shouted. "Goddamn!"

Something was wrong—something beside Taneesha's being dead. I had a feeling what it was, even before Bender told us—something about the gun.

I went out onto the lawn to find out.

"What is it?" I asked him. "No bullets?"

"See for yourself," Bender said quietly. "But keep your voice down. I don't want the mob hearing us."

I knelt down and examined the weapon without touching it. It had a clumsy seam along the ridge of the barrel, where the plastic hadn't quite met in the mold. It was a toy gun, flat black, that somewhat resembled the Smith & Wesson model I'd imagined it to be. It had a little clear plastic nub at the tip of its barrel. It was a water pistol.

I stood there in a daze, still clutching for dear life onto my Glock.

"Put that thing away," Bender whispered harshly.

I did as he said, and snapped my holster shut.

Bender placed his fingers over Taneesha's eyes and closed them. The grass near her head was dark and wet.

"It's OK, kid," Bender told me. "You did the right thing. They might want to rip you apart, but you did the right thing. This could have been any one of us. It could have been me."

"Yeah," I said. "I know."

Bender met my eyes. It would have been crass to say thanks over Taneesha's dead body, so this was as close as he was going to get. But I think we understood each other.

"Dispatch," Bender said into his cellular phone. "Wake up Betsy Cantwell and tell her to get her butt down here, will you?"

Eighteen

1

The next couple of weeks were hell, for me as well as for the city.

The racial tensions that had been bubbling for years in Isthmus City reached a high boil, all as a result of a white police officer having shot and killed a black welfare mother, as if I'd killed her for that reason alone. The numerous front-page stories in the *Isthmus City Sentinel* were all heavily slanted against the police, and public sentiment ran even more strongly against us—against me.

The story made CNN. They were the ones who latched onto my being "gay," which did serve to give me some supporters in Isthmus City's gay community. All the queers in town were calling me up now, asking for dates.

An inquest was scheduled and then postponed for a week. Mayor Beverly Kotzen was assuring the public that I would be found negligent and that any other racists in the department would soon be removed under her new "Clean Sweep" policy. Despite calls from newspaper editorials and television commentators for disciplinary action against me, the police department refused even to consider such action until after the inquest. Still, they "suggested" that I take my vacation now and "try to keep a low profile."

It wasn't easy seeing the whole thing dredged up every day in the papers, on TV, and on the local community-sponsored radio station. There were protests against me on the WSU campus. I was called a racist pig and a murderer.

But the worst thing of all was that the reporters started to *dig*. I knew that it wasn't easy for anyone to learn anything about me—Bender had had a hard-enough time with my background check—but somehow, little by little, they were managing to find things. My official police photo appeared constantly and was also shown on CNN.

This prompted a phone call from the last person in the world I wanted to hear from.

2

"I saw you on the TV," she said. "I don't see what all this fuss is about."

"Ma, I could lose my job. My department's behind me all the way, but the chief just might decide to throw me to the wolves and save the mayor's ass."

"I guess this makes you famous."

"Infamous is more like it," I said. "They're making me out as a criminal when we haven't even had the inquest yet."

"Well, I'm sure you did what was best."

"Listen, Ma, I don't want you talking to any reporters."

"Oh, they're hounding me something awful!" she said, but she sounded like she enjoyed the attention. I could just see her sitting there, twirling her hair.

"Don't tell them anything."

244

"I'm not," she said, but then added, "well, just little things."

"Like what?" Every time I got on the phone with her, I got steaming mad.

"Like they all want to know why we named you Jesse James, so I just tell them it was your father that named you and I had nothing to do with it."

"Great," I said. "Now they'll go looking for my pa."

"I expect he's dead," she said.

"How do you know?" I asked.

"I don't. I'm just supposing. He probably drove himself into a tree somewhere."

"How's Gene Colson, anyway?" I asked.

"Oh, he's dead."

Somehow, this shocked me, even though I knew Gene would be pretty old by now. "What happened?"

"I had him put to sleep. He had this arthritic knee, and I just had to put the poor thing out of its misery."

Arthritis or no, I hated the thought of Ma killing Gene Colson. He was such an innocent, trusting little pissant, so defenseless.

"Ma," I said, "this whole thing's going to blow over real soon. I did everything by the book, and no one's going to fault me for it. I was protecting the other officers on the scene. Someone should have shot her before I did."

"Well, Jesse, I'm proud of you. I never thought I'd live to say it, but I am."

I didn't have any response to that. I didn't know what she expected me to say. I just wanted to get off the phone.

"Jesse, hon?" she said.

"What," I said, impatient.

"I've got a little money saved up. Do you think I could pop up there to Wisconsin and pay you a visit?"

245

"No."

"But Jesse, it's been so long since I've seen you."

"You never wanted to see me," I said. "Not until I made CNN."

"Jesse!" she said, like she was admonishing me for being rude. "I just want to see my baby. You look so handsome in your police uniform, with your hair cut all nice and neat. It isn't true what they said on the TV, is it?"

"What?" I asked.

"They said you're a fag. Why, you just couldn't be—"

"It's true," I said, not even really knowing what was true anymore. But for the purpose of pissing her off, it was true. "And it's all your fault, Ma."

"Jesse!"

"You turned me into a fag," I said. I started grinning, thrilled with the way I'd turned the conversation. "Always touching me the way you did, always fussing over me. Don't pretend you don't know what I'm talking about. You did things to me no mother should ever do to her son."

"Stop it!" she said.

"Do you think after what you did that I'd ever want another woman?"

"That's a lie, Jesse, you know it is!"

"Or maybe I should have just killed myself."

She screamed and then hung up, and the phone gave me back its friendly dial tone.

I sat there alone in my apartment and laughed.

Sometimes the truth hurts, but I was happy to have got it off my chest after all these years.

I hated her, all right. But I hated her for a reason.

3

Every officer who'd been on the scene was called to testify. Berniece James also testified and said that Taneesha had threatened to kill all of them and that she, too, had thought the gun was real, and from up close. A firearm expert was called in who compared the appearance of the water pistol with an actual nine-millimeter, the very Smith & Wesson model it had reminded me of. Harve Bender testified that the gun, as an issue, was a red herring—that every officer on the scene had considered it to be real. He asserted that I'd done everything the way I'd been trained, and that if it *had* been a real gun, I would have saved more lives by doing what I'd done. He also said what I'd thought at the time, that someone else—particularly someone from the tactical unit—probably should have taken her out before I did. To their credit, however, he said that this was one of the hardest calls a police officer had to make, and he wasn't faulting them for their inaction. He testified that he had hoped Taneesha would give herself up, but that she had given no indication that she intended to do so. The entire inquest was very straightforward and businesslike, even though an unruly crowd had gathered outside to await the outcome.

I was exonerated of any wrongdoing. The coroner found that none of the police had done anything improper, and ruled that Taneesha James's death was an unfortunate accident.

This did not sit well with the crowd outside. Some of the courthouse windows got smashed, and a police cruiser was overturned. We made some arrests for disorderly conduct.

Later, on the evening news, I saw Mayor Beverly Kotzen express to a TV reporter her "regret" over the finding of the inquest. She said, "I still can't help but believe that if Officer

Colson had simply given Taneesha James the benefit of the doubt, she would be standing here with us today and her child wouldn't be an orphan."

"Jesus Christ," said Will Gunther, who was over at my place watching with me. "She thinks people really buy this? Last year, they were calling *her* a racist. Now she's all tight with the black community and all the bleeding hearts."

"Oh, well," I said. I didn't have a political slant on this at all. I wasn't happy about what I'd done, but I knew that I would have acted the same whether Taneesha was black, white, or purple.

The news showed the signs and placards held up by the crowd, which said things like KILL ALL RACIST PIGS and HANG JESSE JAMES. They also showed the squad car being tipped over, people being arrested and hauled off, and police scowling at the cameras.

I grabbed the remote and turned the set off.

"It's not over yet," I said.

And I was right.

The next day, the chief issued me a five-day suspension without pay and ordered me to perform a certain amount of community service at Maugham Terrace and also to receive "sensitivity training." Everyone in the department knew it was totally groundless, that the chief was offering me up for the sake of public relations. The suspension made the front page of the *Isthmus City Sentinel* and served to placate many of the department's critics, not the least of whom was the mayor. It also gave Mayor Kotzen a way to save face and patch things up with the police, whose public support she might need to get reelected.

"Officer Colson has been reprimanded," she announced grandly to the TV reporters, "and I'm satisfied now that the police department is taking the matter seriously. I think in the future, the police will think twice before pulling the trigger on an unarmed person."

It was all a hell of a lot of bullshit.

I learned that it was my very own captain, Richard "Buzz" Rollack, who had recommended the suspension to the chief "in the best interests of the department." It was well known that the chief planned to retire soon, and each district captain was running around constantly trying to ingratiate himself with the big boss, who would have a hand in the selection of a successor. My sacrifice was for the greater good of departmental politics and had nothing to do with good police work.

It made me sick to my stomach.

On suspension, I wouldn't know what to do with myself. I loved my job and wouldn't be able to stand having it taken away, especially under such unfair circumstances.

Who would have thought? whispered the badboy in my ear. *You go and do something right for once, and see where it gets you?*

Nineteen

1

I'm lying on my bed back in my old room, back in the trailer home, back in Texas. It smells everywhere like Ma's awful perfume, bubble bath, potpourri. I'm lying on my bed, and it's as if I've just woken up from a long, long sleep. At first I don't want to move. If I get out of bed, something horrible is going to happen—something I'd rather not know.

Ma starts knocking on the door. "Jesse?" she calls. "Jesse, honey, are you up?"

I try not to make a sound. I don't want her to know that I'm in here. I want her to go away.

"Come on out, dear," she says. "The girls are all here, and they want to see you."

Since Ma hasn't heard a peep out of me, she comes in. I pretend to be asleep, hoping she'll leave me alone. But she comes over to my side and rousts me awake. She's smiling down at me, her auburn hair twirled up into a huge bouffant. She's wearing a bright print shirt and a denim skirt, and she's put too much makeup on her face. Her perfume smell is overpowering, and I begin to cough.

"Come on, Jesse, get up."

I do as she commands, standing up off the bed. I look down at myself and see that I'm wearing a dress.

"Turn around," Ma says. "Let me see."

I spin for her, and the dress twirls up past my knee-length hose. I reach down to straighten my hose, then slip into my high-heeled shoes.

"Good girl," she says. "Now come on, let the girls see you."

In my vanity mirror, I see that my hair has grown long and straight, flowing down over my shoulders. It's parted in the middle and frames my face neatly. I've already got lipstick and eyeliner on.

I follow Ma down the hallway and out into the living room. All the neighbor ladies are sitting around drinking brandy Alexanders. They are already laughing and hooting before Ma and I emerge from the hall.

"Jesse, show the girls how pretty you look in your new dress."

I spin for the neighbor ladies the way I'd done for my ma, and I nearly lose my balance in the high heels, but somehow I manage not to topple over.

"Take it off," one of the neighbor ladies shouts, laughing hysterically. All the neighbor ladies start joining in, shouting, "Take it off! Take it off!"

I'm nervous about it, but Ma nods in encouragement.

So I start by slipping out of the shoes, kicking them into the air, and the neighbor ladies catch them, cackling like birds. Then I slowly slide off my pantyhose and twirl them in the air before letting go.

"More!" shout the neighbor ladies.

I reach behind me and unzip the back of my dress. Turning around and giving them my backside, I slip the top of the dress off my shoulders, then wiggle out of it while I push it down over my wide hips. Gracefully, I step out of the dress and let it fall in a heap on the floor.

"Take it all off!" the neighbor ladies scream.

I turn to face them. I pull down my panties. For some reason, I'm surprised not to find a cock down there but a womanly bush and pussy. When I unclasp my bra and let it fall off in front over my shoulders, I'm also surprised to see that my breasts are full and round like a woman's.

Ma gets down on the floor and lifts up her denim skirt. She's naked underneath. She spreads her legs and looks up at me.

"Come on, Jesse," she says, beckoning me with a finger. "You're a big girl now—a big, pretty girl. Say it."

"I'm a pretty girl," I say.

"Don't you want a taste?"

Ma starts fingering her pussy, spreading it open for me.

The neighbor ladies push me onto the floor and press my face into Ma's crotch.

I press my glossy red lips against her rosy opening, but as my tongue goes in, a long metal gun barrel emerges from Ma's pussy and plunges down my throat.

"You're a bad boy," she says, "but you're a good girl, Jesse—a very good girl."

I know that I am.

Then the gun goes off and I wake up in a cold sweat.

2

It was about 4:30 in the morning, but the dream freaked me out so much I couldn't get back to sleep. I was relieved upon waking to find that I was still a man, I was all there and completely intact, and my ma was nowhere to be seen.

My sheets were drenched with sweat, even though I had the air conditioner on full blast. My eyes were wide open and staring at the ceiling. My cock was shriveled up and itchy. My mouth was dry; I needed a drink of water.

I'd seen a horror movie once called *Fear No Evil,* in which the son of the devil proved to be a teenager at some suburban high school, à la *Carrie*. During the big climax, the son of the devil gets his revenge on a tough punk who had been tormenting him: the punk rips open the front of his shirt to find that he's suddenly got this enormous pair of woman's breasts, and lets loose a bloodcurdling scream.

I would have screamed like that, too, if I'd woken up and found I had tits and a pussy.

I knew where the dream had come from, all right—all this thinking about poor Tommy Hess. But I couldn't figure out what my ma had to do with it. She must have appeared simply because she was the *villain*. She'd also been in that other, similar dream I'd had. She'd been the creature that had crawled out of the chimney to kill me. My mind must have reached out and cast her as the heavy because it wanted to offer me a genuine nightmare. It couldn't have made a better choice.

I got up and padded across the carpet, to the kitchen, like a sleepwalker.

I let the tap run for a while to get the water good and cold. I grabbed a glass and opened the freezer so I could get some ice.

And there again, plain as day, was the biker's severed finger, sitting in front of the ice cube trays, fleshy and blue and gathering frost.

Before, I'd thought I'd imagined the whole thing, that it had been a fishstick all along—and that I was done with it. But now I knew it to be true. The finger really did exist, and it had ended up in my freezer, though I couldn't figure out how.

Unless Will had something to do with it.

3

When I woke up later that morning—11:48 by my alarm clock—I felt anxious. But it wasn't the clock that had woken me up; it was the telephone, and it was still ringing.

I picked it up. "Yeah?"

"Jesse?" It was Will. Son of a gun.

"Hi," I said.

"Did I wake you?"

"No, I was up," I lied.

"Hungry?" he said.

"Starved."

"You want to have lunch?"

"Sure." I tried not to sound too groggy. "Where at?"

"I don't care. Your choice."

"How about the union?" I said. I reached over and peered through the venetian blinds. The sun was shining, the sky clear. "It's a nice day. We could eat out on the union terrace."

"All right," he said. "Just give me time to get ready."

"I'll meet you there, say, in an hour?"

"OK," he said, and we said good-bye and hung up.

That was easy.

4

I put my Glock in my fanny-pack (which no one but a sissy would wear on their fanny) before heading out the door. Lots of us carried our guns off duty, and I'd carried mine before. When they suspended you for five days, they didn't ask you to turn in your piece or your badge—that was TV stuff. I was still a cop, suspension or no—I'd be back on the street in no time—and my concealed-weapons license was still valid, still sitting there in my wallet along with my driver's license and fishing license. In fact, I planned on doing some fishing out on Lake Winoma during my days off to relax.

But first, I was up for some hunting.

5

"Are you going to be all right?" Will asked.

"Yes."

"I wish I'd fired instead of you," he said, looking off toward the lake. "Kurtz feels the same."

"Aw, that's sweet, you guys."

Over lunch, we'd talked about my suspension, and he'd told me again how sorry he was—that I'd been screwed over by Buzz Rollack, by the chief, by Mayor Kotzen. I didn't eat much; I'd kind of lost my appetite, and I wasn't much interested in what Will had to say anymore.

He was sitting there with his shirt off, all blond and tan and tightly muscled. He was pumped up and looked like he'd just been to the gym. He didn't have an ounce of fat on him, and the veins on his arms were bulging out. His nipples were big, brown, and hard. He was wearing dark sunglasses, so I couldn't make out his elfish eyes. He had his fanny-pack with him, too, and he wore it in front—provocatively, at his crotch, like me.

I was wearing a pair of mirrored glacier glasses and had succeeded so far in not being recognized by campus radicals as Jesse James Colson, racist killer.

The terrace was crowded, as it always was on a summer afternoon. It could hold over two thousand people, and nearly every table was taken. Most were college students, but some were older, gray-haired alumni—aging men also with their shirts off, and typically paunchy, with fuzzy white chest hair à la Simon Scales, and downy tufts on their shoulders. I hoped I would never look like that.

"Any one of us should have done it," Will went on. I was only half paying attention. "I guess I was too scared."

"I just didn't want Bender to get shot," I said—my usual line. It had worked at the inquest.

But it wasn't exactly true any longer. I had a feeling Bender was going to nail me. If he wasn't onto me already, he would be soon. I had to frame Simon, somehow, before Bender uncovered the truth. I was sure Simon was Alexis: that phrase in his ad about craving monster dicks was far too telling, and he was kinky enough—I wouldn't put anything past him. Bender would get onto him, in time, and maybe Simon would take the rap.

But on the other hand, Simon might lead Bender right to me. Simon could figure out I was the killer from the shabby condition in which he'd found me, and the rough coincidence of the two events. I probably had to get to Simon first and do something about him before Bender scared him into giving up his secrets.

But if Taneesha had had a real gun and I'd let her kill Bender in the first place, I'd be safe now. None of the other detectives cared much about the Chimney Sweeper. No one else had Bender's special something. I wondered now why I'd saved him. Did I want to get caught? Did I have a death wish?

"Come on," I said, jerking my head to the side and standing up. "Let's go for a walk."

Will looked up and smiled like an eager puppy. I imagined that behind those dark glasses, his eyes adored me. He stood up and stretched. Sweat dripped down his naked torso in rivulets that merged at his navel.

"I brought my rubbers," he said, and patted his fanny pack.

My cock grew in my shorts, pressing firmly against the weight that hung at my crotch.

Will and I headed off—he ahead and me behind—past the end of the terrace and down the path, into the thick forest full of greenery and shadows. Will's jeans shorts were tight, and he took long strides that made his butt swing. I wondered if I looked like that when I walked. I sure hoped not.

We weren't the only ones on the path. We were dogged constantly by joggers, bicyclists, and people coming the other way. But of course there were other paths, and more paths off those. The arboretum covered I don't know how many acres, and it was easy enough to get lost. Will and I weren't the first people who'd ever vanished into the deeper realms of the forest for an afternoon fuck. But you wouldn't catch me dead there at night. The Brothers Grimm warned us away from forests, and even a place like Isthmus City had its crazies that you wouldn't want to meet up with in the dark.

"Will," I said, as we took our first fork off the main path. "Do you remember that Z.Z. Ryder, the one in the accident?"

"The finger incident?" he said.

"Yeah."

"What about it?"

"Did you ever wonder what happened to it?"

"Someone took it, didn't they?"

The sun shone down in hazy streams through the canopy of leaves and branches overhead. Our shoes squashed undergrowth underfoot. I saw mushrooms and old weathered stumps and dried brown leaves left over from last fall. Birds chirped. In the distance, students' voices faded along the main path. Ahead of me, Will ducked below some low-hanging branches. I was sure he would find a suitable, secluded spot.

"You sure you didn't take it?" I asked.

Will stopped and looked over his shoulder. "Why would I want to do that?"

"Go on," I said, nudging him forward. "I don't know, maybe you wanted a souvenir."

"Oh, yeah," Will said. "I guess I did take it. I put it in my refrigerator along with my severed head collection."

Will turned off onto another, narrower path. I could no longer hear any human voices but our own. The shafts of sunlight and blotches of shadow played across his naked back.

"Why not the freezer?" I asked.

"That would be better," he admitted. "Don't want it to go bad, do we?"

"That's right." I was having trouble reading him. I couldn't tell if he was stringing me along, or if he truly knew nothing about the finger.

"Just a little further," Will said. "I know just the spot."

"You didn't put it in *my* freezer, did you?" I asked.

"I don't know what you're talking about."

"The finger," I said. "It's right there in my freezer, and I didn't put it there."

"Don't try to scare me," he said with an uneasy laugh.

"I thought I'd gotten rid of it, but that was only a fish-stick. The finger came back."

"Somebody gave you the finger?" he said, trying to be funny.

"You're the only other person who's been in my apartment."

"What about your landlord? Maybe he wants to scare you off." Will's tone was light, like he wasn't taking me seriously.

"No, Will," I said, dead serious. "You were at the accident scene. My landlord wasn't. You copped the finger and put it in my freezer."

"You sound really pissed," Will said. Then, in a louder voice, like he was announcing us to the forest: "Well, here we are!"

He spread his arms and then turned around to welcome me. We were in a small clearing that was mostly shaded by trees but was less densely overgrown than what we'd been walking through.

"Maybe I'm wrong," I said. "Maybe you didn't do it."

"Of course I didn't," he said. He sounded very convincing. "Come here, you goofball."

"You don't believe me." I knew then that Will was innocent, that he hadn't had anything to do with the finger. My mind had been playing tricks on me. I must have taken the finger myself and blanked it out of my mind, and then I 'd convinced myself that Will had done it. And for this, I was going to kill him? What was going on here?

Will frowned. "What's the matter?"

"I . . . I don't know. I'm all mixed up. There really is a finger in my freezer."

"What?" He still didn't believe me. His smile was very queer, in the old-fashioned sense of the word, the way Alice in Wonderland says that things are *curious*.

"I'm sorry," I said. "I guess I was wrong. I don't think you had anything to do with it."

"The biker's finger?" Will said, like he was just then catching on. "It's really in your freezer? You're not shitting me?"

"Forget it," I said. "Forget I ever said anything."

"You took it?"

"*I didn't take it!*" I snapped.

"How did it get there?"

"Someone must have put it there. You're not going to tell anybody, are you?"

"Of course not." Now Will was humoring me.

He stepped back, waving me closer with his hands. He removed his fanny-pack and set it on the ground. My eyes zeroed in on the bulge in his shorts. He was already hard. He went deeper into the clearing, further into shadow, luring me toward him, promising himself to me. He was mine for the taking. He didn't care if I had a finger in my freezer; all he wanted was my cock.

I felt my fanny-pack to make sure everything was still there.

"Remember the last time?" Will said. "When you tied me to the tree?"

"Yeah?" I said.

"That was so hot," he said.

Will unbuttoned the top of his fly, just below his belly button. He was a fucking tease like Miss Jensen.

"I remember last time," I said.

He undid another button, while I just stood there.

The day was coming back to me. We'd spent the whole day together, and we'd gone dancing at Glitz that night. But we'd really gone because I'd wanted to talk to Simon. That was when Simon had first told me about this supposed woman named Alexis and about her transvestite slave, Vanessa.

But it was *Will* who had first mentioned the duo, before I'd tied him up, when we were sitting out on the terrace—though he'd claimed not to know their names. In fact, he'd been the one who'd suggested that Simon might know them. And that was when I'd learned that he'd lied to me before, that he had actually been to Glitz several times in the past. And from Bender's investigation, I knew that he'd been unable to turn up anyone besides Simon and Will who had ever seen Alexis and Vanessa.

"Take me," Will said, pulling down his shorts and standing there in his Calvin Kleins.

I unzipped my fanny-pack and pulled out my Glock.

"Jesse?" he said, caught unawares.

I pulled back the action.

"You fucker," I said. "There is no Alexis, is there?"

"I . . . I d-don't know w-what you're t-talking about," he stammered. "Honest."

But he didn't sound like before, when he'd denied knowledge of the finger. He was lying.

"Put your hands up where I can see them," I said in my best tough-cop voice, though I knew he couldn't have a gun hidden in his milky-white briefs. All he had in there was a hard-on that was fast going soft.

"Jesse, d-don't," he said. "Please."

"You knew about it all along, didn't you?"

"Don't shoot."

I pointed the gun at him.

"You and Simon were in on it together," I said. "Unless you're Alexis."

Will's abdominal muscles were quivering with fright.

"I'm Alexis," came a voice, but it wasn't Will's. It came from behind me.

I felt a gun press against my back.

"Drop the gun, Jesse," he said softly. I'd know that mincing voice anywhere; it was Simon Scales. "I said, drop it."

I held on to my gun.

"Don't be an idiot," said Simon. "I'll kill you right here."

I let my Glock fall from my hand. Will darted up and grabbed it, then trained it on me and took a few paces back.

I'd been led into a trap.

"You keep covering him, Willie," said Simon. "If he makes a move, shoot."

"OK," Will said. He was still trembling, but his aim was fairly true, and he stood at close range. There was nothing I could do.

"Now, Jesse, put your hands on top of your head."

"Simon says," I said, and did as I was told.

"Shut up!"

Simon locked a handcuff onto my wrist and brought the arm down in back. Then he grabbed my other wrist, pulled it behind me, and locked it into the other cuff.

"Move," he said, shoving me harshly.

I stumbled but didn't fall.

"Put your clothes on, Willie," Simon said.

"Yes, sir."

"Now walk," Simon commanded. "My car's at the other end of the arboretum. And don't try anything funny."

I had to suppress a laugh. Simon sounded like Truman Capote trying to be John Wayne.

"Now we've got him," Simon said to Will, who was buttoning up his shorts. "We've nabbed ourselves the Chimney Sweeper."

Somehow I had the feeling they weren't taking me to the police; they had something else in store.

I thought about poor Tommy Hess and wondered why he'd gotten me into this mess.

Twenty

1

Simon had parked his car on a service road deep within the arboretum. I hoped we might run into some couple fucking in the bushes so I could try to get help, but we saw nobody.

They put me in the trunk of the car on top of a rough, scratchy blanket and squeezed me into a fetal position up against the spare, my hands still cuffed behind my back. They stuffed a hard rubber ball into my mouth and sealed it with a long strip of duct tape that they strapped all the way around the back of my head. Then they slammed the trunk lid shut, plunging me into pitch blackness, and immediately I started to cook. The sweat came dripping out of me. The air was hot and close, and I felt almost like I couldn't breathe. I tried to get as much air as I could, but with my mouth closed off and my nose partly stuffed up, it was hard. I thought I was going to pass out, but the jarring of the car as we rode along kept me alert and frightened.

2

When they opened the trunk, I gasped for air, breathing in deeply through my nose. I'd thought they might simply leave me in there to suffocate.

But they didn't want to kill me. I knew that already.

"Come on, Jess," said Simon. "Up and at 'em."

Together they lifted me out and onto my feet. I was un-steady; my right calf muscle had a cramp, and my left foot was asleep. But they held me up and led me along, through the door and into Simon's home.

3

They sat me down on the living room sofa. Will sat across from me, still shirtless and guarding me with my own pis-tol. I wondered if he had a gun in his fanny-pack, too. The fright he'd shown when I'd pulled the gun on him must have been real, because Simon had taken his own sweet time before springing up behind me. Will knew that I could have killed him if I'd acted more quickly, and now I wished I had. Then maybe I would have heard Simon in the trees and had a chance at him as well. Instead, I was in the shit.

I made an animallike growl from behind my gag. Their makeshift contraption was very effective; my jaw was sore from having to keep the ball in my mouth, and my mouth was full of saliva.

Simon came back into the living room with a gas mask in one hand and a pressurized cylinder of some kind in the other.

"Here you go," he said, and slipped the mask over my head. He strapped it tight enough that I felt an intense pressure within my head. The lenses on the gas mask had been blacked out so that I couldn't see. Simon attached something to one of the valves in front, and then I heard the hiss of gas escaping from the cylinder.

I struggled and tried to scream, but Simon held me firmly against the couch, and my noises were barely audible. The gas entering the mask had a noxious odor. I began to feel light-headed and sick to my stomach. My heart beat ever faster, and I was overcome with a sense of dread.

Simon started counting aloud, backward from one hundred. "Ninety-nine, ninety-eight, ninety-seven . . ."

I never knew how far he got.

4

The bricks are on all sides of me, squeezing against my bones. I can hardly move a muscle.

I'm trapped, and I smell soot all around—ancient soot from a thousand fires. I've been buried alive, stuffed up a chimney, and I can't get out.

I scream, but no one can hear me. I yell for somebody, anybody, to please help me.

There's a black cat in here with me. It's trapped, too, and it's starving. It's eating my flesh, bit by bit, and it meows like an angry tom—a haunting, horrible moan. The creature is lost, afraid, abandoned.

The walls squeeze tighter and tighter. I'm being crushed. The cat tears at me, frenzied with hunger.

5

When I came to, I was all alone in the dark, hanging by my wrists. I still had the gas mask on. I could feel the grip of the straps around my head and smell the latex of the thing. But the valves were open and I was breathing real air. The gag was still in place. I heard no one else in the room with me.

I could still move my fingers, though they tingled a little, and although my shoulders were sore, I realized that not all of my weight was hanging on my arms. My bare back was up against a wooden post, and I was secured to it by layers of rope just under my pectorals, around my stomach, and at the top of my thighs. My feet were spread uncomfortably, and I could feel the kiss of steel around my ankles—probably rigid leg irons that were also somehow fixed to the post, for I couldn't move my legs. There was also a length of wood or something fixed between my knees. I was naked except for my briefs.

I knew where I was—in Simon Scales's basement play-room/dungeon. We had spent a lot of time down here when I was his boy—although I had never gone through this gas mask routine. Simon had a keen interest in bondage and domination games—only I had thought it was just for fun. We had never done anything that I hadn't consented to—although I had felt obligated to do anything he wanted, since otherwise I would have been thrown back out on the street. Now I knew that he had more sinister motives.

I tried yanking my wrists free, but with no luck. The ropes around my stomach were especially taut, forcing me to keep my gut sucked in and my chest out. My briefs were damp from the sweat that dripped down my torso. I was fixed well, with no means of escape. Simon and Will could do whatever they liked with me.

I was wrong about there being no one in the room with me; I could hear at least one person breathing. One of them—perhaps both—were sitting around watching me.

I moaned feebly through the gag. I wanted them to take it out. My jaw felt like it was going to fall off.

But they just let me hang there.

I could feel them staring.

6

It was a long time before I heard the scoot of a chair as someone got up.

"I think he's had enough," said Simon. He came over and stood right in front of me. He touched my chest lightly and then squeezed my pectorals hard. "You like these, don't you, Jesse? You like your manly tits."

I tried to pull away from him, but he kept squeezing them and then pinched my nipples.

He reached around in back of the gas mask and undid the straps. Once he pulled it off my head, I realized the room was not dark at all but illuminated by a single lightbulb dangling down from the ceiling. My eyes squinted against the harsh light until they finally adjusted, and I saw that Will was sitting in a chair, covering me with the gun. His mouth was firmly set; he still looked scared, though he must have been exhilarated as well, or he wouldn't have been participating in all of this.

Simon smiled at me. His long gray hair was blow-dried back from his forehead. His pudgy, cherubic face had taken on a vile aspect. His eyes drilled into mine, suggesting things yet to come, things yet to be done to me—things, perhaps, that had been done to Tommy Hess.

"And you thought Will was your friend," Simon said, like I was totally pathetic, a stupid piece of scum. "It was my idea all along that you should become a cop. I've been shaping your destiny since the day you called me."

I stood there huffing and puffing through my nose like the Big Bad Wolf. Only no one was afraid of me anymore. Two of the three little pigs had me in their power. The third I had already killed, and these two were looking for revenge.

"Will was my boy before you," Simon said. "And before Tommy Hess. But you've probably already figured that out."

Simon slapped me hard across the face with vicious force, knocking my head to the side and sending a screaming pain through my jaw. He grabbed me by the hair and set my head straight again.

"Now you're beat," Simon said. "Now I've got you."

He reached behind my head, unfixed the end of the duct tape, and began to pull. It felt like it was taking a layer of skin with it. When he got around to the back of my head, the tape took some of the hair off the nape of my neck. I screamed in pain but still couldn't get the ball out of my mouth. Simon reached in and grabbed it. Drool dribbled down my chin. I began breathing more easily and worked my jaw back and forth to loosen it up.

"There," Simon said, "that's better, isn't it?"

"Motherfucker," I said.

He slapped me again, stinging my newly raw cheeks.

"We'll have none of that," Simon said. "But you can scream all you want. You know as well as I that this room is soundproofed."

He had added to the room since the last time I'd been there. Leather paddles, riding crops, and whips hung from the walls. Behind Will stood a set of wooden stocks like the Puritans had used. Chains, clamps, and other metal implements were laid out on a small table. Along the far wall was a black leather-padded stretching rack. And in the far corner stood a tall steel cage only about three feet wide—a one-person jail cell complete with dog dish and a blanket to curl up on.

"Welcome to your new home," Simon said. "I hope you like it."

The door to Simon's dungeon was concealed behind a sliding bookshelf. If Simon and Will chose to keep me in here forever, no one but they would know where to find me.

"Let's leave him alone for a while," Simon said, turning away from me and opening the door, "so he can contemplate his new existence."

He ushered Will out and then followed, locking the door behind him. I heard him move the bookcase back into place.

7

My only hope was to convince Will to let me go. But I realized that would take some doing. Not only did he know that I was the Chimney Sweeper, but he was also mixed up in this whole Tommy Hess business—apparently up to his eyeballs. Will may have come too far to turn back now, and I was sure that Simon would never let Will come and see me on his own. Will was just as much Simon's slave. Simon must have had something on him, maybe even old photos of Will in a similar position to what I was in now—something with which Simon could blackmail Will if he crossed over the line. I felt sorry for Will, because I knew that at heart—

unlike Simon, unlike me—he was a good person. He had proved that on many occasions.

But if I tried too hard to persuade him, he might think I was tricking him. Why should he ever trust me, when he knew the things that I'd done?

The circulation did finally leave my hands, to the point where I couldn't move them at all. Now my arms were tingling and felt like they might cramp up. The ropes pulling against my chest, stomach, and thighs were chafing my skin from my continued struggling. My mouth was parched.

Finally, they came back in, Will ahead of Simon.

"I need a drink of water," I said.

"Will, go fetch it," Simon said, like Will was his dog.

I hated Simon. I wanted him to die.

Simon was carrying an old army duffel bag, and I wondered what was inside. Women's clothes? Torture implements? Branding irons?

Simon had changed into tall black boots, blue jeans, a leather vest, and a leather motorcycle cap. The vest spread across his vast belly, framing his downy white chest hair.

"What are you going to do with me?" I asked. He was standing far enough away, I knew he wasn't going to slap me for speaking.

"Whatever I like," he said.

"You'll be caught," I said. "You'll go to jail."

"So will you. For the rest of your life."

"I'd prefer that to this."

"You would, would you? And all that publicity? The famous Chimney Sweeper, cold-blooded killer of a harmless transsexual?"

"He wasn't one before you got your hands on him."

"Oh, but he wanted to be," said Simon, like it was all perfectly OK and he had never done anything wrong. "Tommy

answered my ad. There never was any Alexis. I instructed
Will to invent that little lie to throw you and Bender off
track. I never dressed up in a bustier, in case you were wondering. And we never called Tommy 'Vanessa,' either. I
screened him very carefully. He thought I would be a
woman, but once he met me, he realized it didn't matter.
What mattered was that I would change him, that he would
submit to me, that I would control his life. That was what
he wanted. He'd had castration fantasies from the time he
was eight. We hadn't quite got that far by the time you
killed him."

"How do you know I killed him?"

"You don't deny it, do you?"

I said nothing.

"Because we were there," Simon said. "Will and I both.
We witnessed the whole thing."

"That's not possible," I said. "I didn't see anybody."

"There, you admit it. Now it wouldn't matter if we were
there or not, because you've confessed. But we were there.
And we took your gun."

Simon reached into the duffel and pulled out a Ziploc
bag. Inside the bag was a .38 caliber revolver like the one I'd
stolen from the farmer in Minnesota and used to kill Tommy
Hess. I had no doubt it was the same gun.

"I'm sure a skilled policeman could lift a few of your
prints off this. It's been sealed up in here since that night."

"My prints aren't in their file," I said.

"But if they suspected you, they would take comparison
prints, wouldn't they?"

"Probably."

"Especially if someone were to give them this gun."

"They'd ask you where you got it. If you tell them the

truth, you'll be charged as an accessory, or at least for obstructing justice."

"Are you willing to take that risk?" Simon asked, dangling the bag in the air. "Besides, haven't you ever heard of a plea bargain? They might go easy on me, as long as I'm helping them catch you. It'll be a difficult case to prosecute, and they'll need all the help they can get."

Simon was right, but that didn't entirely convince me that he would be willing to turn the gun over to Harve Bender. My predicament was becoming enormously complicated.

"I've got some more goodies in here," Simon said. Out of the duffel he lifted the jeans and sweatshirt I'd worn that first night, which were spattered all over with blood. "If they need any further proof, they'd be able to type Tommy's blood and yours off of these. They could even check on his and your DNA, if it came to that."

"You told me you'd thrown them away," I said.

"I lied," he said. "I've known who you are from day one, as they say."

"Why didn't you turn me in?"

"Because I was already seeing what I could do with you."

Will returned with a glass of ice water and started to hand it to Simon, but Simon said, "Go ahead," and shooed Will over toward me.

Will's eyes met mine as he came closer. I couldn't read him; he still looked frightened, perhaps even apologetic. We had been lovers. We had had a lot of fun together. Our lives had been looking up. Will raised the glass to my lips and let me drink. The ice cubes felt good against my raw lips. The water was nice and cold. Some of it spilled down my chin, onto my chest. He allowed me to drink the entire glass.

"Thanks," I said.

Will said nothing but went back to sit alongside Simon.

"Will is a great little helper, don't you think?" said Simon.

"Are you going to keep him here like me?"

"No," Simon said. "He's free to come and go."

"You're not afraid that he's going to tell somebody?"

Simon shook his head. "I don't have to worry about a thing. Will knows what would happen to him. He's in this as deep as you or I. He helped me with Tommy Hess, and now he's going to help me with you. I have to work, and so does he, but we don't want to leave you alone for very long at any one time."

"If I was Will, I'd be worried," I said.

Will's glance darted up at me.

"I wouldn't put anything past you, Simon," I said. "If you thought Will was going to talk, you'd probably kill him."

"No," Simon said. "I'm not like you."

"You don't think so?"

"If I were, I could have killed him long ago, couldn't I? Will has never had a thing to fear from me."

Will's stare was blank; I couldn't read his thoughts on this. But I was hoping maybe he was getting the idea.

"I think it's time we let you down," said Simon. "You must be beat by now. I don't think you'll be able to put up much of a struggle."

He was right; when he cut my wrists down from the ceiling, my arms fell in front of me, practically useless. But just to be safe, he slapped the handcuffs back on me before untying the rope. Will helped him untie the rest of the knots and kept me standing while Simon placed legcuffs on my ankles and let me out of the rigid irons.

Then Simon unlocked the door of the cage, and Will led

me inside. They left the hand- and legcuffs on me. Simon slammed the steel door shut and locked me in.

"We'll come back in a bit with your supper," Simon said. "You might as well make yourself comfortable."

I sat down on my blanket and stared at my empty dog dish and rubbed my aching muscles as the blood began re-circulating through my limbs, and thought, *First chance I get, Simon is a dead man.*

8

I was expecting Alpo, but they brought me fried chicken from KFC—something I could eat with my hands. They filled my dog dish with cold water, but they wouldn't let me pick it up to drink it. I had to lean down and lap it up, which was much more difficult than I thought it would be. When I was done, Will took the box of bones away.

"You can have my coleslaw," I told him.

Will didn't respond.

Simon yanked on the chain dangling from the lightbulb, and the dungeon went dark except for the light coming through the open doorway.

"Good night," Simon said, and they left. I heard the key turn in the lock. It couldn't have been very late; Simon was probably going out to Glitz for the rest of the evening. Will had the same day-off rotation as I, so I knew that he had to go to work at eleven.

I tried the bars, but they were solid and welded to the steel floor of the cage. The door of the cage was solidly shut and wouldn't budge. I could get my hands through the bars, but nothing outside was within reach.

I curled up on my blanket and tried to go to sleep, but the

blanket was scratchy—probably the same one they had used in the car trunk—and I had too many thoughts racing through my mind.

Will had betrayed me, but somehow I didn't feel like killing him. Simon was my target. I lay there and tried to come up with a way to get him. But nothing came to mind. They really had me; I really was beat.

Eventually, I managed to sleep, but only with my cuffed hands plunged deep into my briefs, cupping my balls.

9

I woke up long before Simon did, or so I imagined. I figured he'd want to look in on me first thing, and I also knew that after a long night at Glitz, he tended to sleep until at least noon. And although the dungeon was pitch-black, I had a sense of how long I'd slept and felt that it couldn't be any later than ten o'clock. But I knew that the longer they kept me in here, the more my sense of time would diminish, until I could no longer track the hours, the days, the months, the years . . .

Being awake did me no good at all. The closest thing I could get to a plan of action was to hope that Simon would get close enough and be off his guard so that I could reach through the bars and strangle him. But the idea of stretching my hands around that fat neck was daunting. I'd never strangled anyone, and I wondered if I could even manage it. And once he was dead, what would I do? What if he didn't have the key on him? My only hope would be that Will would come in due course, be thankful Simon was dead, and let me out. But if I failed to properly strangle Simon, then Simon would exact some kind of severe punishment, or maybe he would decide I wasn't worth the effort and simply kill me.

I gave up thinking about it and, since I had nothing else to do, curled up there on the floor of my cell, pulled down my briefs, and jacked off.

10

Simon and Will came in together sometime that afternoon. Simon yanked on the light, and my eyes blinked several times until they got used to it again.

"Good morning, starshine," Simon said.

Will wouldn't even look at me. He was holding a gun.

I wondered if the handcuffs would allow my hands enough room to encompass the girth of Simon's neck—but decided it would be impossible.

"Or should I start calling you Jessica?" Simon said, and began giggling.

"Don't touch me, motherfucker," I said, standing up in my cell and shaking the bars.

"Oh, will you look at her?" Simon said, and glanced at Will like they were sharing in the joke. "What a spitfire she is! It'll take a lot of hormone injections to change that. Maybe I should fly Doctor Klaus up here and get the ball rolling—or *balls,* I should say."

"I'll kill you," I said. "God help me, I'll kill you."

"God won't help you." Simon dismissed the thought with a swishy, limp-wristed gesture. "Anyway, we don't need the good doctor just yet. I've got something else up my sleeve."

I didn't care that Will was covering me with an automatic pistol. I would take my chances and hope that Will didn't shoot me. I didn't see any reason why he would.

"Put him on the rack," Simon said to Will. Simon took the gun from Will's hand and held it himself while Will came forward with the key and unlocked the cage.

Maybe Simon realized I wanted to make book on my promise—or maybe he didn't trust Will any longer to have the gun while his back was turned.

I didn't offer Will a struggle. I had no doubt Simon would shoot me if I tried anything. I let Will take me to the rack. I sat down on the leather tabletop. Will grabbed my feet and turned me onto it so that I was lying down. He fixed the leather straps around my ankles before removing my legcuffs. He pulled my arms back over my head and fixed one strap around my wrist before unlocking that wrist from the handcuffs. He then pulled my other arm to the side and buckled the last strap around my other wrist, then removed the handcuffs. The straps securing my limbs were attached to chains, which were spooled onto hand-crank winches at either end of the table. As it was now, the chains were fairly loose, but I couldn't move my arms or legs very far.

"Tommy Hess was different from you," Simon said, still in control of the gun as Will checked to make sure each of the straps was secure. "He practically begged me to turn him into a girl. We were only halfway there when you interfered. He was scheduled to see Doctor Klaus again soon to have his dick turned into a pussy. That's what they do, you know. They take off your dick, turn it inside out, then put it back inside you. Then, *voilà!*—you're a girl. Tommy was all set, but he wanted to have his cock sucked one last time, and that's where you came in."

Simon was freaking me out. I couldn't take the thought of anyone turning my cock into a pussy.

Silently, from behind me, Will reached down and stuffed

the rubber ball back in my mouth, then strapped it in with duct tape as before, all the way around my head.

I screamed into the gag.

"Doctor Klaus had already been giving Tommy massive estrogen injections," Simon said. "And he'd given Tommy a nice set of fake breasts. Tommy was very proud of those. He was starting to feel like a real woman. I admit he looked like something of an Amazon, but at least he was happy."

Will began cranking the winches, tightening the chains.

"But I was already getting bored with it," Simon said. "It was fun at first, but there wasn't much challenge to it. This was what Tommy *wanted*. And I got to thinking—once he was a woman, then what? What fun would that be? I was already trying to line up somebody to take him off my hands. I correspond with a variety of like-minded people, and I thought Tommy might like to have a true mistress like he'd wanted from the beginning. He craved the humiliation of being turned into a girl, but after that, he wanted more humiliation, and what better than to be the girl slave of a real mistress?"

The chains grew taut, and so did my muscles. Some of my joints popped the way they would under the hands of a chiropractor. I was completely stretched out, immobilized.

"But the whole experience with Tommy had turned me on to a new idea. Why not take a man—a *real* man, someone macho who wallowed in his own masculinity—and turn him into a girl *against his will?* I even thought that I might find someone that night, when we sent Tommy out and followed him. I suggested he go cruise the bus station, since that's where all the rough trade hangs out. Most of my boys have come to me through that phone number I put in the john. Greyhound keeps painting over it, and I keep putting it back. Anyway, we were parked in a car across the street from where Tommy pulled up in front of you. Once he took you into the lot, I was already thinking that I might try to snatch you.

"Because that's what it was supposed to be—a snatching. I was going to kidnap some piece of trade, take him home, and keep him. Gradually, I'd tame him and turn him into a girl. No one would miss him. No one misses someone like that—someone like you.

"But then you took out that gun and shot Tommy. We didn't know what to do, but we didn't want to call the cops. Will was just about to start at the police academy, and we didn't want to jeopardize that by his getting mixed up in all this. We hadn't done anything illegal, since Tommy had consented to everything. But we knew Will's chance at becoming a cop would be lost.

"I wanted to snatch you right then. It would be the perfect thing—you would be on the run from the law and needing some protection. But you stole Tommy's car and sped away. Will and I got out to see if Tommy was still alive, and it was then that we took the gun. Then we went looking for you but couldn't find you. I was very surprised when you called me the next morning, and I came out to the truck stop and saw that it was you. It must have been fate."

Simon came over and slapped my stomach hard.

"Mmm," he said. "Nice and tight. How do you think you'll look with all this chest hair gone, with your legs shaved each morning, with nice big tits and a nice, wide-open pussy?"

I bucked my hips off the table, tried to make any possible movement to get away from Simon's touch.

"I think Tommy was always a girl, inside. You—you'll always be a man. Think of it—all the torture Tommy went through his whole life, being a girl trapped in a man's body.

And now you, a big, strong man—a murderer, a cop—
you're going to be trapped in a pretty girl's body, aren't you?
What do you think of that?

"I held off on doing this," Simon said. "I could have done
it before, but you were just so pathetic. I decided to make
you into a self-reliant, respectable member of society. I
thought you should become a cop, like Will. You'd had a
hard life, and I wanted you to have a taste of the real world
before I took it away, because that would make the torture
all the more sweet. Now I think you've seen enough of the
world. Maybe you'd even like to escape into mine. When
I'm finished with you, you'll be like my little Eliza Doolit-
tle. I'm going to teach you how to walk, how to talk, how to
act like a regular lady, and then you'll become my wife, and
we'll attend parties together at Tommy Thompson's."

I wished I could bust my chains and wrap them around
Simon's sick throat.

"And don't worry about Doctor Klaus," Simon added.
"He'll do anything I pay him to do. He'll be more than
happy to. But there's one thing we can do without the good
doctor."

Simon opened up a box and grabbed a chrome-plated tool
that looked something like a giant pair of pliers, with large
prongs on one end and two large handgrips. Then he held a
tiny round rubber band in front of my face.

"See how small this is?" he asked. He held up the plierlike
thing. "This is called an Elastrator. Do you know what that
is?"

I shook my head.

"My friends out west turned me on to it. It's used to cas-
trate bulls nonsurgically. You simply place the high-tension
rubber band on these prongs, expand it, stretch it around the
testicles, and then let it go. The rubber band cuts off the

blood flow. The testicles become purple, then black. Eventually, they fall right off, and there's no blood. It's really quite ingenious. I never had the chance to try it on Tommy."

I began whimpering—crying like a baby and pleading with my eyes. I looked to Will, but Will stood there, impassive.

"I think we're all set," Simon said. "Here."

He handed the gun to Will and fixed a rubber band into the mouth of the Elastrator.

Come on, Will, I thought. *Shoot him!*

Will's hand was trembling, the gun quaking. Simon had his back to him.

Do it! KILL HIM!

I watched as Simon pulled my cock and balls out of my briefs, then slipped the contraption around my balls. He then slowly squeezed the handgrips and allowed the rubber band to squeeze my scrotum. I began to feel sick to my stomach. It squeezed tighter and tighter and more painfully, until finally the rubber band was free of the Elastrator. The pain was great, but the constriction around my balls was starting to produce an erection.

"See, look at you," Simon said. "You like it."

Suddenly, the gun rang out, and I was splattered with Simon's blood. Simon fell against the table and slid down onto the floor.

Will stood there shaking like a leaf. A wisp of smoke wafted out of the gun barrel. He let the gun fall to the floor.

"We've got to get you out of here," Will said. He first went for the gag, abruptly ripping the duct tape off my face, then plucked the ball from my mouth.

"Get it off me!" I screamed. *"GET THAT FUCKING THING OFF ME!"*

Simon rose to his knees. He had the gun in his hand.

"Will!" I said.

Before he could turn, Simon fired.

Will looked at me in shock, and a trickle of blood dribbled out his mouth and down his chin. "I'm sorry, Jesse," he gasped. He reached out to touch my face and then fell back onto Simon. They both collapsed on the floor.

"Simon?" I said, but there was no reply. *"Simon? If you can get up, for Christ's sake, get this thing off me!"*

But I heard no movement below the table. They were both dead.

I screamed and kept on screaming until—hours later—I passed out from exhaustion.

Twenty-one

1

"Jesse! Jesse! Wake up!"

Someone slapped me back into consciousness, and I thought it must be Simon. My eyes blinked open.

It was Harve Bender.

"In here!" Bender yelled over his shoulder. Several police officers came running into the dungeon, assaying the crime scene. They were North District cops that I didn't know very well.

"Jesus Christ," one of them said.

The air had a foul odor.

"Jesse! What happened?" Bender said.

"Take the . . ." I said feebly, my words slurring together. My throat was dry and raspy. I wondered how long I'd been out. I couldn't feel anything down in my balls. "Please, Harve. The thing . . . down there . . . cut it off . . . please, cut it off."

"Oh, my God," he said, looking at my crotch.

"Are they still there?" I said. I had no strength to lift my head up and see what had happened to my balls.

"They're purple," Bender said. "We'd better get that thing off."

"They're still there?" I asked again.

"They're still there, Jesse."

Bender went looking around the room and found a pair of hawk-nosed clippers of some kind. He poked the thing down around my balls and squeezed the handles. I saw the rubber band go flying off into a corner of the room.

A searing pain shot through my balls as the blood began flowing back into them.

"Ow! Fuck!" I gritted my teeth and breathed rapidly. Bender touched my balls lightly—not in a sexual way, but massaging them tenderly, helping the blood come back. The pain was receding; they began to tingle and feel somewhat better. My cock was shriveled up, and it felt sore, too.

"Jesse, what happened?" Bender repeated.

"I'll tell you as soon as you get me out of this thing," I said.

"Right."

One of the officers helped him unstrap my wrists. My hands went flying down to knead my aching balls. Then they unstrapped my feet, and I brought up my knees into a fetal position, continuing to lie there tending to myself.

"We'd better get you to a doctor," Bender said.

I nodded and tried to lick my lips, but I had no spittle.

"Did you see what happened?"

"Will shot Simon," I said. "He was trying to save me. Simon must not have been dead. He grabbed the gun and shot Will. What time is it?"

"Twenty oh five," Bender said.

"Christ," I said. I'd probably been on the rack for eight hours. I wondered how long it would have taken my balls to turn black. "How did you find me?"

"Will left me a note," Bender said. "Right there on my desk, in an interdepartmental envelope. He said Simon had kidnapped you, that we would find you here. Will confessed to being the Chimney Sweeper, and he said that Mr. Scales was our elusive Alexis."

"He confessed?" I tried to sit up.

"Now, now." Bender pushed me back down. "You don't want to look. We're going to get you an ambulance. You just sit tight."

"Are they both dead?"

"I'm afraid so. I'm sorry we didn't get here sooner. I got his note at sixteen hundred, but it took a while to obtain the search warrant. He said we'd find the gun he had used to kill Tommy Hess. He drew me a map, showed me how to find this room. Christ, it looks like a goddamned dungeon."

"It is," I said, still rubbing myself. "That's exactly what it is."

2

They took me to the emergency room, where I was examined carefully—but in the end, they said I would be OK, that I wouldn't lose my balls.

While I was recovering on the paper-covered bed, Bender came in to take my statement.

I told him basically what had happened to me, trying to stick within the realms of Will's "confession." I told him how Will had lured me into the arboretum, into Simon's trap. I told him about being abducted at gunpoint, trussed up, and thrown in the trunk of the car. I told him about the gassing, the stringing up on the post, the all-night imprisonment in the jail cell. I told him that Simon had planned to turn me into another Tommy Hess. I told him what the tiny rubber band was supposed to do to my balls.

"This is sick," Bender said, taking it all down. "Really sick."

I told him I agreed.

"Why you?" he asked.

I shrugged my shoulders, told him I didn't know—other than that Simon had known me before. I conjectured that Simon might have suspected that I knew he was Alexis and had wanted to keep me quiet. I also passed along for good measure the bit about Simon's wanting to turn a macho cop into a pretty girl.

"Scales couldn't have gotten away with it," Bender said. "I was already onto him."

But he didn't elaborate, and I didn't ask him to.

"You know, it's strange," Bender said. "I did Will's background check, too. He had a history similar to yours, which was part of the reason I had no reservations about hiring you."

I swallowed hard. Bender was making me nervous.

"I guess he was just a bad egg," he said.

"I guess so," I said, relieved that this was his sole conclusion. "I never knew Will had been with Simon."

"We've recovered the gun," Bender said, "and some bloody clothing that probably would have fit Will. We're going to search Will's apartment and see if we can turn up anything else. But somehow, I don't think we're going to find anything."

I wondered what he meant by that. Was he still playing games with me? Did he suspect me? Had Will's "confession" been limited to what Bender had told me, or did it go on and say something else—something about me? Or maybe

Bender simply saw through the whole charade. He was a tough one.

"I guess this is good enough for now," he said. "I've got my hands full with everything else. But I might want you to come down in a couple days and give me a more complete statement, is that all right?"

"Sure," I said.

"I hope you're feeling better," he said.

I nodded, smiling vaguely. "Thanks for saving me."

"Tit for tat," Bender said, and left.

I was relieved that he was gone.

Soon after, the ER doctor prescribed me some Tylenol-3 and sent me on my merry way.

I went home, locked my door, popped a few of the wonderful pills in my mouth, and sacked out.

3

The *Isthmus City Sentinel* the next day carried the basics of the official story:

'CHIMNEY SWEEPER' SLAIN
IN BIZARRE DOUBLE MURDER

A photo of Will Gunther identified him as the mysterious Chimney Sweeper. Alongside it was a photo of Simon Scales in dark sunglasses, with a wicked grin spread across his face. His caption read: "Simon Scales, Gunther's accessory, died in a shootout in his own S&M dungeon. Scales fired the shot that killed the Chimney Sweeper before succumbing to his own wounds. The two had abducted an Isthmus City policeman, who barely escaped with his life."

The main story on page 1 referred the reader to an inner page, where my photo ran. "Jesse James Colson," the caption read, "controversial Isthmus City policeman, was imprisoned in Simon Scales's dungeon while on departmental suspension. Was he to be their next victim?"

The story recounted much of what Harve Bender had learned from me—although, thankfully, readers were spared details of my impending castration. As Will Gunther's lover, I was portrayed as the victim of an "obsession" of Will and Simon's. Bender theorized that all the recent publicity around the Taneesha James incident had driven Will and Simon to act. Much of Tommy Hess's story made it in, as well, and Bender added that "if Officer Gunther hadn't confessed, Officer Colson might have met the same fate, and we might never have known about it. They could have kept him in that dungeon for as long as they liked, until they were through with him. Then Officer Colson probably would have turned up stuffed in a chimney somewhere, is my guess."

The newspaper asked Bender if he was aware of any other Chimney Sweeper murders, and he said, "Not to my knowledge. But once killers like this get started, they often find it hard to stop."

4

Lydia Kurtz and Jodi Sommers had me over for a private wake of sorts after Will's funeral. We had all attended the funeral—including Bender—and felt it was fitting, seeing that even though Will was the Chimney Sweeper, he had saved me from a fate worse than death. None of us attended Simon Scales's service, though some of his ex-boys did come in from out of town.

"Here," Kurtz said, and handed me a business card that read: DR. JOAN CARTWRIGHT—COMMUNITY PSYCHIATRIC SER-VICES. "Don't be insulted. We thought you might want some counseling."

"I'm not," I said. "Is she a lesbian?"

"Yes. Why?" Kurtz said defensively.

"Good," I said. "Then I can trust her."

Since Kurtz and Sommers had turned out to be the only friends I had, I was beginning to believe that lesbians were the most trustworthy of people. At least, I didn't have to worry that they wanted to suck my dick. If my ma had been a lesbian, maybe none of this would ever have happened.

I even thought that I might give Dr. Cartwright a call. Maybe I could even tell her about Ma and get if all off my chest at last.

"Thanks," I said, and put the card in my wallet.

Kurtz and Sommers served me up steak and potatoes, and we all sat around the TV set and watched *Raymond Burr's Mysterious Disappearances,* which ran a follow-up piece on the Chimney Sweeper case. Once the segment was over, we switched to a Milwaukee Brewers–Baltimore Orioles game and broke out a case of Leinenkugel.

The Brewers lost, and I won ten bucks off of Kurtz.

5

A few days later, I heard a knock at my door, and I thought, *This is it. It's my ma.* After all the publicity, she was bound to turn up on my doorstep sooner or later.

I looked through the peephole, but it wasn't my ma.

It was Harve Bender. He was dressed in a suit jacket and

holding up a bottle of Jack Daniel's that was grossly distorted through the fish-eye lens.

I unfastened the chain lock and opened the door. I looked out in the hall; Bender was alone.

"Hi, Jesse," he said.

"Hi," I said. "Come on in."

"How you doing?"

"Pretty good."

"You got glasses?" he asked.

"Sure. Have a seat."

Bender parked himself on my couch while I went into the kitchen and got two rock glasses.

This is it. He's going to make his move on you.

"Want ice?" I asked.

"Not for me, thanks," he said. Then he suddenly appeared in the kitchen. "Actually, why don't we sit down here?" He pulled out a seat for himself at the kitchen table.

"OK," I said. I wanted ice, myself, but didn't want to open the freezer in front of him. The finger might be in there.

Bender poured us both generous amounts of whiskey. He took a gulp from his and winced.

"So what's up?" I asked, sitting down across from him. The fluorescent light in the kitchen gave Bender heavy purple bags under his eyes; he looked like he hadn't got much sleep of late.

"This whole case has got me confused," Bender admitted. "There's things about it that just don't gel."

"That's a line from *Psycho*," I said.

"Oh, right," Bender said. "Arbogast. The private dick. Martin Balsam."

"Yeah. He comes back to the Bates Motel to confront Anthony Perkins, and he says, 'If it doesn't gel, it isn't aspic— and this ain't gelling.' "

"Well, Norman, this ain't gelling." Bender smiled a sly smile and downed another gulp of whiskey.

I laughed nervously. "You don't think I've got my ma stuffed in my back bedroom," I joked, and drank some of my Jack Daniel's.

"Nope," he said. "And you haven't got a chimney."

My eyes darted up to meet his.

"You're the Chimney Sweeper," he said, "not Will. Want a cigarette?"

He proffered a Pall Mall, and I took it without answering. Bender lit it for me with a match, then lit his own before shaking the match out. I grabbed an extra ashtray I kept in the cupboard and set it down before us on the table.

"Don't you want to protest?" Bender asked, blowing out a cloud of smoke.

"I want to hear what you have to say," I said, trying to stay cool. The Pall Mall's smoke was harsh in my lungs; this was Bender's "real man's cigarette."

"That gun we found is the right gun, all right," Bender said. "The slugs from Tommy Hess's skull match up perfectly."

"So?"

"In Will's confession, he told me the date of the murder. It roughly matches up with when you first came to Isthmus City, according to my background files."

"That doesn't mean anything. You probably got that information from Simon Scales."

"You don't deny it, do you?"

"I don't know," I said. "I don't know what date you're talking about."

He told me, and I admitted that sounded like about the time I came to town.

"And before that, you'd been in Minneapolis, and before that, Denver, is that right?"

"Yes."

"They've got an unsolved murder up in Minneapolis from the night before Tommy Hess was killed. Some Nazi skinhead named Jeff Abbott. Name ring a bell?"

"No," I said.

"He was shot once in the head. The killer stole his Doc Martens. The slug from Jeff Abbott matches the same gun that was used to kill Tommy Hess, and what's more, the gun itself was stolen a few weeks before, from a farmhouse in rural Minnesota. The farmer was killed, too, with a single shot from his own gun. That slug matches up, too."

"So?"

"I don't know where Will Gunther was on the night Tommy Hess was killed, but I know where he was for those other murders. Simon Scales's business files show that Will was working for him as a bartender at Glitz on those nights, right here in Isthmus City. He couldn't have been in Minnesota."

"That doesn't mean he didn't kill Tommy Hess," I said. "Two different people could have used the same gun."

"That's true," Bender said, refilling his glass with whiskey. "But I went up to Minneapolis and showed around a photo line-up to some of Jeff Abbott's friends, with Will's and your official police photos among them. Even with the uniform, they all picked you out as the one who'd been hanging around with the unfortunate Mr. Abbott in the week before his death."

"That doesn't mean a thing," I said. My glass was empty now, too. Bender offered me more. I nodded my head, and he filled it back up.

"Nobody saw you with the farmer," he said. "But if you were the one in possession of the gun, I'd be willing to bet you killed him, too."

"Sounds pretty far-fetched."

"Not at all," Bender said. "Not at all."

"Why would I want to kill some stupid farmer?"

"For the gun. Maybe you were simply burglarizing his place and he surprised you, so you fired. I don't know. It's not my case."

"Then why do you care?"

"I'm just looking for the truth," Bender said, and stared me down. I tried to read the look in his eyes, but he maintained a good poker face. Both he and I knew that it wasn't a bluff.

"Does it gel for you this way?" I asked.

"Maybe," he said. "I think you killed Tom Latimer, too. I think you pushed him off that roof."

"That's a lie," I said. "The inquest cleared me."

"That doesn't mean you didn't do it. They didn't have any witnesses. It was your word against a lot of inconclusive evidence. They never could have convicted you, so they just let it go. Or they actually believed you, I don't know which. But I know what I think."

"I didn't kill any of those people," I said.

"I think you protest too much," Bender said. "I've got a Badger Security guard who can place you at the bus station the night of Tommy Hess's murder. I showed him your photo. He remembers you clear as a bell."

"What else?"

"A prostitute who says you drew a gun on her and threatened to kill her. She could tell me which direction you came from and which way you went. You were heading back toward the bus station, probably just before you shot Mr. Hess—or should I say 'Miss'?"

Bender's laugh disconcerted me. He rubbed his weary eyes with his thumb and forefinger and lit another cigarette.

"That's not all," he went on. "Jeff Abbott's skinhead

friends told me he used to hang out in Isthmus City. He'd told them about an abandoned house where he'd often spent the night. He also told them the bus station was a good place to cruise if they wanted to bash some faggots. They had their suspicions about you, by the way. They thought you were one. They remembered your name was Jesse. One of them saw you recently on Raymond Burr's show."

I'd stopped protesting.

"And one more thing," Bender went on. "Some truck driver who saw a story in his local paper that had Will's photo and yours, as Chimney Sweeper and potential victim. He thought the paper had got the photos mixed up, because he recognized you as the guy he picked up the morning after Tommy Hess's murder, and your clothes were all bloody."

"That asshole," I said. "He raped me."

"So he did pick you up," Bender said, and nodded. "He gave me this."

Bender pulled a thick paperback book out of an inner pocket of his jacket. It was my tattered old copy of *The Stand* by Stephen King, and it was speckled with old brown stains.

"I bet if I checked out this blood, it would match up with Tommy Hess's. We could run a DNA check, too."

"So?" I said. "Who says that's my book?"

"Right in here," Bender said, and opened it up.

My signature was right there on the inside front cover: *Jesse James Colson*. I forgot I'd done that.

"Now I want to hear it from you," Bender said. "The whole, unadulterated truth."

"What are you going to do to me?" I asked.

"That depends on what you tell me."

I took a deep breath.

"Want another cigarette?" Bender asked.

296

Twenty-two

1

"Tom Latimer was a son of a bitch," I began.

Bender sat in rapt attention. He was fascinated by me, I could tell. He'd nabbed the biggest fish of his career. All points in his life had led to this moment. Singlehandedly, without help from the FBI, Bender was going to capture the notorious Chimney Sweeper, who'd turned out to be something of a serial killer.

"I ended up in Denver after running away from home, because that's when my money ran out. I began hustling on the streets. Usually, it was older guys driving around in their cars. They'd stop for you, you'd get in, and you'd do what they wanted. They usually wanted to suck my dick, but sometimes I had to suck theirs. They'd park somewhere, and we'd do it right there in the car. They'd give you a little cash—enough so you could get by, but just barely—not enough that their wives would notice it was missing.

"Then one day this old guy pulls up in a beat-up pickup truck. It's got the name of his business painted on the door: TOM LATIMER—CHIMNEY SWEEPING. All his tools are clattering around in the back of the truck. He tells me to get in.

Instead of parking somewhere, he takes me back to his place—some rundown old house that he ran his business from. He paid me for sex, but afterward he made me an offer. He said he'd give me a job if I'd be his boy."

"His boy," Bender repeated.

"Slave, really," I said. "Though I didn't understand that at the time. Oh, he didn't have a dungeon or anything like Simon. But I was still his slave. He got to do whatever he wanted with me, whenever he wanted. He was this greasy guy, hardly ever took a bath, and he was always sooty from work. I got that way, too, after working for him a while. He paid me a small allowance, and he didn't keep me on a chain, but I didn't have anywhere else to go, so I just kept on.

"I fell off a roof once, but I walked away from it. He said I had 'young bones,' and that's what saved me. He helped me get my GED, but that's about the only good that came of it. The longer I stayed, the more I hated him.

"Then, that one day, we were up on the roof together. It was a high, peaked roof—a long drop down to the bottom. I took one look at him and started thinking about his old, old bones. I checked to see if anyone could see us, but there was no one around. His eyes lit up in that moment. I think he knew what was coming. I didn't push him very hard. He slipped right off and went skidding down the shingles head-first, then disappeared over the edge. I heard a loud *thump*, and that was it. That was the end of old Tom."

"Why did you run away from home?" Bender asked, like he didn't even care about Tom Latimer.

"On account of my ma," I said.

"You didn't like her?" he asked.

So I started giving him the whole history. How my pa had run out on us when I was a baby. How my ma wished I'd been a girl. How she'd spanked me in front of the neighbor ladies. How she took a keener interest in me when I started developing into a young man. How she retailored all my clothes to emphasize my chest, my ass, my crotch. How she used to touch me whenever she could, and how I used to flinch away from her.

I didn't tell him about Miss Jensen. I wanted to keep that one thing a secret. And I didn't want him to think I'd killed her, because I hadn't.

But I told him about Opal Femrite and how she'd made a cast of my cock so she could make a candle out of it. Bender laughed at this, but it was important for me to tell him before what happened next.

"One Friday night I came home after being out with some friends from the gymnastics team," I said. "I thought Ma would be out on a date and didn't expect to find her home. But there was a crack of light under her door, and Gene Colson was scratching at it, begging to be let into her bedroom."

Bender asked who Gene Colson was, and I told him.

"Anyway," I went on, "I opened up the door to say good night, but Ma didn't even hear me. She was lying there on her bed, naked, and she was fucking herself with one of Opal Femrite's candle dicks."

"And it was yours," Bender said. He caught on fast.

"It was mine. She'd been drinking all night. She had a bottle of brandy on the shelf by her bed. I tried closing the door, thinking I'd just slink on out, but she saw me and told me to come in."

"Jesus," Bender said.

"She started taunting me. 'Come on over to your mama,' she said. 'Show me you're not a faggot.' I just stood there. I didn't want to touch her. 'Come here,' she said. 'Come lick your mama's pussy.' "

Bender poured himself another glass of whiskey. "Go on," he said. "What happened?"

"Are you sure you want to hear this?"

"I told you, Jesse, I want the whole truth."

"I don't know what came over me. I guess since she was my ma, I felt I couldn't say no. I shut the door and kept Gene out. I didn't want him jumping on top of us. She told me to take off my clothes. She wanted to see if my dick matched the candle she'd just taken out of her pussy. That's when I started to hate her. I stared at that candle, dripping with her juice, and I thought things couldn't get any worse than this. She'd already been fucking herself with my dick. I figured, if this is what she wants, this is what she's going to get.

"So I took off my clothes. She made me pose in front of her, show her every inch of me. She kept taunting me, saying that I looked like a faggot to her, that she bet I couldn't even get it up for her."

"Could you?" Bender wanted to know.

"No," I said. "Not really. But I didn't want her to think I was a faggot, so I started thinking about this English teacher I used to know."

"Man or woman?"

"Woman."

"What was her name?"

"I don't remember."

Bender seemed to believe me.

"I'd had sex once with this teacher, and I still fantasized about her all the time. So I started pretending Ma was my teacher. They were about the same age, and they almost looked the same. Anyway, this teacher was the only other woman I'd seen naked like that. It wasn't hard to pretend. So I got onto the bed with Ma."

"Like a dutiful son," Bender said.

"That's right," I said. "And then I slipped it into her. I did it rough like I had with my teacher. You'd call it rape, only it was what she wanted. She begged me for it. I just closed my eyes and pretended she was my teacher. Later, she just passed out.

"I was disgusted. I felt like killing her, but I couldn't bring myself to do it. I thought about killing myself, then, because I didn't think I could live with myself after that. But instead, I decided just to run away. I had a couple months left to go in school, and I would have graduated no problem, but I just had to get away from her. I went to my room and packed a few things, and then I went out the door. I remember little Gene Colson crying after me like he wanted me to take him with me. But I told him he had to stay with her."

"And you made it as far as Denver," Bender said, and poured more whiskey into my glass. "You were with Tom Latimer how long?"

"About a year."

"What happened after you killed him?"

"Well," I said, "after the inquest, some relatives of his showed up and sold off the business—not that I'd planned on sticking with it, but now I didn't have anywhere to stay. I decided to get the hell out of Denver. I had a little money saved from my allowance, and it bought me a bus ticket as far as Minneapolis."

"But you didn't make it to Minneapolis," Bender said. "The farmer lived about sixty miles southwest of there."

"I was kicked off the bus for smoking," I said.

"Jesus." Bender shook his head, sympathetic.

"The driver kept warning me. He said if I kept smoking, he'd leave me by the side of the highway. I thought he was kidding, but he wasn't. And then I was stuck. I had no money left. I tried hitching a ride along the highway for a few hours. Then I saw this farmhouse in the distance. I guess you know what happened from there."

"I want you to tell me," he said. "Exactly."

"There weren't any lights on, and I thought I could break in and maybe find some money. I got in through a window and started rummaging around, but all I found was this revolver in a desk drawer. I stuffed it in my pants and kept looking around. Then I heard someone cocking a shotgun behind me. The room was dark. There was this man standing there in the shadows, wearing a nightshirt and aiming this shotgun right at my head. He said, 'Hand over that gun, mister,' and I thought for a split second what would happen to me if I turned it over. I'd get arrested, and that would be the end of it.

"So I took my chances, and I whipped out the gun. Lucky for me, it was loaded and he hesitated. I was at pretty close range, and I pulled the trigger and got him right in the heart. He fell down. No one else came running, and the house was all quiet, so I figured we were alone. I took his shotgun, thinking I'd take it with me, too. But once I got outside, I realized that you can't conceal a shotgun, so I hid it behind the barn and went on my way. I figured if I ever came back to this farmhouse, I'd know where to find it. I didn't know where I was going to go or what I was going to do. I went back into the house and dug up a wad of money from a pair of jeans lying on the floor of the farmer's bedroom. Then I went back to the highway with the revolver stuffed down my pants and covered up by my sweatshirt. I hitched a ride that took me all the way to Minneapolis."

"Where you met Jeff Abbott," Bender prompted. He wanted me to stick to the nitty-gritty.

"I never liked him," I admitted. "He was this Nazi punk,

hung out with this gang of like-minded types, all with their heads shaved, wearing green bomber jackets and the same style of boot. He bragged to me about all the queers he'd kicked the shit out of. He'd been in Isthmus City, too, where he said he'd spray-painted swastikas on some synagogues."

Bender lifted an eyebrow. "We had a series of desecrations a few years ago. Never found who did it."

"Jeff also said he'd paint-bombed the gay liberation statue over in the park, and he said he was arrested for that. He was proud of it."

"And you hung out with this shithead for a whole week?"

"Oh, he liked me. He thought I was great. Wanted to recruit me into their group. He even tried to shave my head once, when I wasn't looking. In some strange way, I think he had a thing for me. I crashed at his place, but he hardly let me sleep. He kept jawing at me all the time, bragging about all the shit he'd done. He'd say 'Skins rule!' all the time. He and his gang spray-painted it wherever they could in downtown Minneapolis, along with swastikas and other shit. He was impressed with my gun, but I wouldn't tell him where I'd got it."

"Why did you kill him?" Bender asked.

"I don't know," I said, which was true. "I just woke up one morning, and he was still asleep. No one else was around. Sometimes other people crashed at his pad, but not this time. I was wearing this threadbare pair of high-top sneakers. The soles were falling off. I woke up staring at his Doc Martens, which he always kept spit-shined and beautiful. They were in great shape, and suddenly I wanted them."

"Why didn't you just grab them and run?"

"Because they were still on his feet," I said. "He slept in them. I never saw him take them off, except to put them back on and retie them. So I popped him in the head. I took his boots and scrounged the last of his money, and then I bought a ticket to Isthmus City. All he ever talked about was how there were all these queers in Isthmus City, so I figured it was the place to go. I knew how to scam off of queers. I'd hustled and done other shit. I knew I couldn't hang around Minneapolis."

"So you came into Isthmus City," Bender said. He looked dog tired, but he was still hanging on my every word. I was giving him just what he wanted. "Tell me what happened from when you got off the bus."

So I told him the rest of the story, in all its gory detail.

2

When I was finished, Bender put the cap back on the bottle of Jack Daniel's.

"I think we've both had enough," he said. The sky outside my kitchen window was beginning to lighten; dawn was approaching. Birds began to twitter in the trees. A street sweeper drove by outside, its rotating brooms whisking along the asphalt.

"You going to arrest me now?" I asked. I had already decided that I would give up freely. I didn't mean Bender any harm, and the only way I could keep from going to jail would be by killing him. Even that was no guarantee, because he might have told one of the other detectives the facts he'd managed to uncover about me.

Bender reached into his suit jacket and pulled out his snub-nosed Smith & Wesson .38 Special. He swung the cylinder free, demonstrating that it was loaded with six fresh slugs, then clamped it back shut. He set it down on the table.

"Go ahead," he said. "Kill me."

I stared down at the gun, expecting the voice in my head to say *Do it!*— but it was oddly silent.

"Go on," he said. "Pick it up."

Bender put the gun in my trembling hands and placed my finger around the trigger.

"Hold it up to my head."

He made me place the barrel at the top of his nose, right between his eyes. But he didn't stare at the gun. He stared straight at me. My eyes were locked on his.

"Cock it," Bender said.

I just sat there.

"Cock it," he repeated. His fingers molded themselves around mine and made me pull the hammer back.

"Now, gently pull the trigger."

He left me to do that by myself, but I couldn't do it. I didn't want to do it. I liked Bender.

"What are you waiting for?" he asked. "This is your big chance. Your secret ends with me. I haven't told another soul. If you kill me now, no one will ever know."

I pulled the gun back from his head, carefully uncocked it while pointing it at the ceiling, and set it down.

"Have you got a death wish or something?" I said.

"Must have," Bender said.

"You're fucked up."

"Whatever you say."

"What do I win?"

"Jesse," Bender said, "I don't see any reason why anyone else has to know, do you?"

I shook my head.

"Will Gunther is the Chimney Sweeper, have you got that?"

"Yeah, sure."

"And that's all anyone's ever going to know."

"What do you want from me?"

"Pardon?" he asked, surprised by my question.

"You want me to suck your dick?"

Bender shook his head sadly, like he was disappointed in me. He grabbed his gun off the table and placed it back in his shoulder holster under his jacket.

"I don't want to take advantage of you," Bender said. "I'm willing to take a chance, You're a good cop, Jesse. You saved my life."

"No, I didn't," I protested. "Taneesha had a toy gun."

"It could have been real. If you hadn't been there, I might be dead."

"If it *had* been real," I said.

"*If* it had been real."

We stared at each other, and for a moment, neither of us spoke. I wondered if I could trust him.

"I'm going to hang on to everything I know about you," he went on. "I've already put some things into a safe-deposit box, and after tonight, I'm going to put away more. I'm not going to tell you what I've done with the key. This isn't so much insurance for me as it is for you. If you ever kill again, I'm going to magically dig up this file and put you away. But I don't think you're going to. You just proved that to me."

"You don't care that I killed all those people?"

"Not really. Tommy Hess is my only case, and as far as I'm concerned, that was solved with Will's confession. The other murders aren't my jurisdiction or my problem. Tom Latimer deserved what he got. The farmer—well, as far as you knew, he was about to kill you, right? That's the law of the jungle: Kill or be killed. And Jeff Abbott? Who needs another Nazi skinhead?"

"What about Tommy Hess?" I asked.

"You were being raped. It's not exactly self-defense, but given what else we know about the case, I'd say it was a mercy killing."

"What about the others?"

"Taneesha James was in the line of duty. And you had nothing to do with Will and Simon—that much was obvious from how I found you."

"Don't remind me."

"I'm really no better than you," Bender said. "I killed people in 'Nam. I was a regular murder machine. And no matter what the circumstances were, I can't ever get that kid out of my mind—that boy I killed, the one who shot Carol Cowles. Where do I get off sending you to prison, when I went and murdered a scared fifteen-year-old boy?"

I wasn't about to argue with him or tell him that it was in the line of duty. If he wanted to wallow in self-pity, so be it, as far as I was concerned.

"So I'm off scot-free?" I said.

"Scot-free," Bender said, yawning and stretching his arms. "How do you like that?"

"I think I've got one more thing to confess," I said. "As long as you're being so charitable."

"Uh-oh," Bender said. "If it's another murder, all bets are off."

"No," I said. "Not another murder."

I opened the freezer and showed him the biker's frozen finger. I held it out to him, and he picked it up with a curious look on his face.

"What the hell is this?"

"A finger," I said.

"I can see it's a finger. Whose is it?"

"A Z.Z. Ryder's."

"A Z.Z. Ryder?" Bender said, smiling.

"It got caught in his spokes. I was supposed to retrieve it from the accident scene. Somehow, it got lost. It ended up in my freezer, but I don't remember putting it there. Though he never admitted it, I think Will must have done it as some kind of practical joke. Maybe Simon put him up to it. He must have taken it from me at the scene and put it in my freezer when he came over that night. He saw later that I'd wrapped it in foil, and he pulled a switcheroo with a fish-stick. When I destroyed that, he put the finger back in the freezer. I haven't ever figured out what to do with it, so it's been sitting there ever since."

By this point, Bender was laughing so hard that he was clutching his side, holding the finger out in front of his face. Tears were steaming down his cheeks.

"Pack it in dry ice and mail it to their clubhouse," he said. "With a note saying it's unclaimed property."

I laughed just to be polite. I didn't think it was that funny.

"Before I go, one more thing," Bender said, and suddenly his face got serious. I thought he was going to pull a Columbo on me and change his mind, slap the cuffs on me, and take me in. But all he said was, "Are you a bowler?"

"I'm not very good."

"Doesn't matter. They handicap you anyway. The police leagues are about to start, and my team's short one player. We bowl every Friday morning, and the season lasts till May. It's a big commitment. How about it?"

"Sure," I said. "Why not?"

Twenty-three

Once my suspension was up, I went back to my job.

Captain Rollack no longer wanted me in South District, and since a vacancy had been created in Central, I was traded to them.

I've taken over Will's old beat, David Three.

Glitz is in my beat, but it's got a new owner and a new name: Bump.

I'm touched by the sacrifice Will made for me, and I think about him often.

Lydia Kurtz and Jodi Sommers are setting me up on dates, trying to find me a new boyfriend. I never have called their psychiatrist friend, because ever since my confession to Harve Bender, I've felt just fine.

I no longer worry about Jesse the badboy. I know he's still a part of me—but not the only part. I've been determined not to let Bender down, and to keep my part of the bargain.

This should be no trouble at all—so long as my ma keeps her sweet distance.

John Peyton Cooke was born in 1967 in Amarillo, Texas, and grew up in Laramie, Wyoming. He is the author of three previous novels: *Torsos* (1994), *Out for Blood* (1991), and *The Lake* (1989). His short fiction has appeared in *Weird Tales* and *Christopher Street*. He lives in New York City.